Also by Jonathan Dee:

The Lover of History

The
Liberty
Campaign

The
Liberty
Campaign

Jonathan Dee

DOUBLEDAY
New York
London
Toronto
Sydney
Auckland

For their editorial wisdom and emotional support, the author wishes to thank Amanda Urban, Deb Futter, Vince Passaro, and, always, Denise Shannon.

PUBLISHED BY DOUBLEDAY
a division of Bantam Doubleday Dell Publishing Group, Inc.
1540 Broadway, New York, NY 10036

DOUBLEDAY and the portrayal of an anchor with a dolphin are trademarks of Doubleday, a division of Bantam Doubleday Dell Publishing Group, Inc.

This novel is a work of fiction. Any references to historical events, to real people, living or dead, or to real locales are intended only to give the fiction a setting in historical reality. Other names, characters, places, and incidents either are the product of the author's imagination or are used fictitiously, and their resemblance, if any, to real-life counterparts is entirely coincidental.

DESIGNED BY ANNE LING

Library of Congress Cataloging-in-Publication Data

Dee, Jonathan.
    The liberty campaign / Jonathan Dee. — 1st ed.
        p.   cm.
    I. Title.
    PS3554.E355L53   1992
    813'.54—dc20   92-33440
                                                            CIP
                                                            AC

ISBN 0-385-42595-3
Copyright © 1993 by Jonathan Dee
All Rights Reserved
Printed in the United States of America
July 1993
10 9 8 7 6 5 4 3 2 1
FIRST EDITION

All things human have two aspects, much as the Silenes of Alcibiades, who had two utterly opposed faces; and thus, what at first sight looked like death, when closely observed was life. . .

—ERASMUS

The
Liberty
Campaign

One

I served my country in France and Germany, as a soldier in the Second World War. This was in 1944, at the conclusion of the European campaign; I was just eighteen when I crossed the ocean for the first time, though I might have done well to consider myself a newborn. I enlisted after my graduation from high school, eager for some of the honor conferred on those older boys I knew who were already absent from the town in which I grew up, Pittsfield, Massachusetts. Eight weeks later I was shipped to a small village in southeastern England that had, in the offhand way of war, been transformed by the Americans into a gigantic bullpen; shortly thereafter I reached Grenoble and then Marseilles with General Truscott's VIth Army Corps, two months after D-Day, one month before my nineteenth birthday, August 15, 1944.

Our division saw some ferocious small-scale fighting, some sporadic displays of human desperation and fright on the part of the last German soldiers. But compared to those who went ashore ahead of us, I have to say, we had a relatively easy time. There's certainly no shame in admitting it. We were the liberators, town after gorgeous town; sometimes the Axis forces had fled even before we arrived, sometimes they hadn't established a presence at all in some of the smaller villages we marched through, but none of that mattered. It was the high noon of the imperium, an age when there was something empowering about being an American—for better or for worse, but it was undeniably real. Our mere presence signified a great deal, to the citizens of rural France and then, gradually, to us. We were celebrated with an abandon we weren't really in a position to understand, and to an intoxicating degree. On more than one occasion a town's prostitutes let it be known that they were offering limited freebies, within reason, of course. Perhaps only someone of my own generation will understand me now when I say that, as a high-school boy of the forties, I sometimes thought I had wandered into one of my own dreams.

In September we reached the German border and linked up with forces under the command of General Patton—whom I saw but once, and at a distance, though no doubt time and the man's reputation have served, in memory, to increase that distance. Our march to the Moselle met virtually no obstruction—Patton had already cleared our way. I am glad to be able to say now that though I carried my weight in the war, I never killed a man. At the time, I was vaguely ashamed to have to say so, and later even, I'm sorry to remember, lied about it—which was prompted, I suppose, by the same shallow understanding of virtue that is one of the reasons governments conscript nineteen-year-olds. I suffered hardship and exhaustion, but I was never really called upon to act bravely. Many I knew were so called upon; some responded, and some didn't.

Patton led us across the Moselle and into the heart of the Reich on March 7, 1945. Again the fighting was desperate, but our forces were overwhelming; the Nazi army seemed at times to evanesce in front of us, as if we were running through the woods toward something we could never reach. And it was only then—for all practical purposes in the war's aftermath, though the armistice had not yet been signed—that I came face to face with some of the horrors of wartime, with the simple, stunning human capacity for monstrousness. Our division (selfishly I thank God for it) was not one of those responsible for liberating the camps, but there was plenty of less-documented terror, a kind of infernal museum on either side of us as we marched wearily on the wide dirt roads. A Nazi officer had executed his entire company, most likely for cowardice, with a machine gun; twenty feet from the pile of corpses was the officer's own body, a suicide. One magnificent linden tree in a town square had four German soldiers hanging from it, three in uniform and one naked. A group of Allied prisoners had been rapidly executed in the panic of retreat and left to decompose; some of the faces and postures still bore the last expression of a plea for mercy and sanity. Starved-looking citizens came out of their houses as we passed. Soldiers and civilians regarded each other with open amazement. Here there were no women; when their absence finally struck us, one private in my company with some high-school German asked where they had all gone. From their splintered doorways the men called back that the women, some raped by their own countrymen in flight—men who assumed

5

that in this hour of their judgment it was simply too late for any crime, or any act of charity for that matter, to affect their sentence—were hiding from us because we wore uniforms. Through this wasteland we simply continued to march, knowing we would reach an end.

I am sixty-five years old now, and for the first time in many years I have been working to remember what I can of those days and months. The wonder of it is that the war was not more formative for me than it actually has proved to be. Surely what I saw were the far reaches of human experience. And yet, as easily as I can still reassemble the puzzle of those moments, I can't escape the feeling that in some essential way I have forgotten it all. Because even writing these images down, I discover, does not really bring back that jolt of awe, that humility. Perhaps in truth I never felt them sufficiently to begin with. Nonetheless, it remains all I know firsthand of earthly suffering. The crucial, missing element here may be that, as an American, I was not fighting *for* something, as others were, but *on behalf* of something, in our recurring role—not always a nefarious one— as the earth's policemen. It is a key distinction—and not, I want to think, for me alone. I saw a great many terrible things, a great many conclusions to extreme tests of belief and courage and weakness and cruelty. But perhaps that's just it. I *saw* them.

Even those who know me best, I think, would consider such introspection to be unlike me; and in fact, out of some ill-defined embarrassment or fear of inquiry, I have kept it to myself. I can date its beginnings exactly—to the Fourth of July, in fact, neatly enough, of last year. That was the day a reporter first appeared on our street. I couldn't identify him as such when I saw him; although I had spoken to many reporters in my life, in connection with my job, all but a few of those conversations took place on the telephone, and the handful of those I had actually met were media analysts and financial writers, newsmen of a very different stripe. Now, of course, my perceptions are changed; I sometimes feel as if I can pick one out in every gathering of strangers, standing behind me in line at the bank or sitting behind sunglasses in the rearview mirror of my car.

He had chosen a day when he was likely to find everyone in the neighborhood at home; but perhaps he was overeager, because he had appeared at eight-thirty in the morning, and, it being a working man's holiday, the street itself was still empty. He didn't look anxious, though—far from it. He stood with his hands clasped behind his back, in a short-sleeved madras shirt, khaki slacks, and Top-Siders—if he meant this to serve as camouflage, he had put it together in a knowledgeable way—staring off across the road, rocking back and forth, on the edge of the Wintons' lawn, just next door to ours.

There was something peculiar about it, though certainly not sinister—in fact, barely interesting; it registered with me in the same way any slight modification in a routine will register, seeing a new billboard through the train window on the way to work, say, or a new man behind the counter at the place where you always get your morning coffee. Just a raised eyebrow, or the mental equivalent, and that's it. I watched the young man (he appeared to be in his early thirties) from behind the picture window in my living room. I was up early for a tennis game, trying to get in a set or two and still be back in time for the town parade. Ellie was asleep upstairs. I was in a white shirt and tennis shorts, still with some empty time to kill before starting the five-minute drive to the local courts. I was going to walk down to the road to get the local paper out of the mailbox, and while the stranger's presence didn't do anything to deter me, he did make me self-conscious enough to put on my socks and sneakers, even though it was a warm morning and the dew was off the lawn.

He heard the screen door snap open and turned to look at me. I smiled, a little self-conscious in my athletic togs, and nodded to him. The lawn looked in good shape as I walked down the slope; the Garrison boy, who lived two blocks over on Monadnoc Street, was taking care of it for us. I believe it was the boy's first paying job, and he was very eager to please. The weekly Belmont *Advocate,* good for almost nothing in the way of news but still able somehow to inspire allegiance in the town's residents, was even skinnier than usual, owing to the holiday. I folded it in half and turned around. Walking back up toward the house I saw that the thin young man in the colorful shirt was cutting across my lawn, apparently needing to ask me something.

I stopped to wait for him, smiling, a little put out that he was wandering uninvited across my yard, but embarrassed, too, by such suburban proprietary feelings toward such a small piece of territory. There are nine houses on our block of Fairly Avenue, all of them visible from my mailbox; the proximity of the homes leads a lot of people to grow low hedges or build low fences, but I've always told myself I'm not the sort of neighbor who goes in for that kind of thing. He was in no hurry. I checked my watch, conspicuously, I thought; still plenty of time. He stopped next to me, put his hands in his pockets, and turned again to gaze out at the street, an oddly intimate posture, as if the neighborhood itself were a venture in which he and I were partners.

"How are you this morning?" he said.

"Just fine, thank you. Yourself?"

"Good, good." He smiled. He didn't seem agitated, but if there was in fact some reason for his cutting me off on my way into my home, he apparently wanted to work up to it. He had wiry hair of a nondescript brown color, and his features, though respectably handsome, seemed a size too small for his face.

Mystified, I said, "You're staying with the Wintons, are you?"

He shook his head slowly, still staring off across the road. "They're the family there?" he said, pointing with his thumb toward the house in whose shade he had been standing with such ease. "No, I live over in Port Jeff, actually. Don't get over near the South Shore too often. That's my car," he said, as if that clarified anything, pointing with his chin this time to a red Toyota parked illegally between the Cantwells' and Fran Phister's driveways.

"So what brings you here today?" I asked.

"Actually," he said, "I'm looking to buy a new house. I've had some business successes recently, and, well, it's time to move up. I've always had an eye on this part of Long Island, ever since I moved out here. Nice, convenient to the city, but far enough away from the shore that it doesn't get insane in the summer, you know what I mean?"

"You're right about that," I said.

"Plus, good schools, and my wife and I have a six-year-old."

"Well, you could do a lot worse than here, that's true," I said. "It's not a bad commute either. You work in the city?"

He shook his head. "But I need to get in every so often, for one reason or another. Like everybody, I guess."

"What do you do, if I can ask?"

"Management consulting," he said.

"Oh, really? For whom?"

"Privately." He seemed not to want to talk about it. Nothing unusual in that.

9

Fran Phister came out of her house, dressed in a blue T-shirt and white pants, and went down to her mailbox to get the paper. She looked at the strange red car parked on the street, then, shielding her eyes with the paper, at the two of us, the unfamiliar young man in his madras, I in my whites, standing in the middle of the grass. After a moment, she waved to me, I waved back, and she retreated into the house.

I was beginning to think it odd that the young man hadn't yet told me his name, or asked mine. He did have all the slick, nearly criminal poise of a man who had made himself rich at his tender age. The sun was up a bit higher, and the day was warming. "You know," I said, "I'm surprised to learn that any of the houses on Fairly are for sale. I'm sure I would have heard about it if they were."

"Oh, they may not be," he said, smiling. "At least not now. But, you know, I'm hopeful that if the right person gets a persuasive enough offer, he or she will be open to making new plans."

I frowned for just a moment at this arrogance, thinking it bad form. "It seems unlikely, I have to tell you," I said.

"Maybe you could tell me a little about some of the people here, give me an idea where to look. I've really just fallen in love with your block."

It seemed a folly, and I didn't have much patience with it, but I felt I couldn't simply walk back into the house and leave him standing there. I looked again at my watch, hoping to prompt him, but he didn't see it, or, just as likely, pretended not to.

"For instance, back there, the Wintons, you said it was?"

I looked at the two-story white house, with its gabled windows and its long front porch. "Well," I said, "Ted Winton's been here for over twenty years, raised his whole family here. I don't think you'd have any luck with him. Besides, wouldn't it be awfully big for you, with just one child?"

"Uh-huh," he said, seeming to have lost interest almost immediately. "Maybe you're right. What about that one?" He pointed in the opposite direction, virtually at random, at a smaller, one-story, white clapboard place that belongs to Bob Locke.

"I just don't think so," I said. "The owner of that place is retired, his wife died there, and I don't imagine you could dynamite him out of that house, whatever you're offering. Listen, I don't mean to be rude, but I have a tennis game—"

"No, no, don't worry, you're being very helpful. Okay, that place is out." He took a few steps forward and pointed to the house at the north end of the block, a very pretty one-story place surrounded by a neat, chest-high hedge, with a huge, spreading maple tree right in the corner of the front yard, shading the kitchen and the patio. "Now, how about the place at the corner there?" he said.

"Probably wouldn't have much luck there either," I said, a little annoyed by now. "He's a retired man, too, been here seven or eight years, I guess. That makes him a relative newcomer, but still."

"Do you know him well?" the young man asked.

"The owner? Not well. To say hello to. Why?"

He was beaming more than ever now, and all at once his expression showed me that he was at great pains to seem at ease. His smile was childlike, the sort of anxious, helpless smile a young boy will offer to conceal excitement or nervousness.

"What's he like?" he said.

"What's he like? He's a nice guy. A Spanish fellow, or Mexican. I told you, I don't know him all that well. Why does it matter?"

11

He backed off a little bit. "I'm just trying to get an idea of whether Mr. Ferdinand would be willing to entertain an offer. He hasn't said anything to you about planning to move or anything, then?"

I stared at him. He looked as if his patience were wearing thin, as if he were straining to be polite, to hold himself back. My own pulse was a bit faster now as well.

"How did you know," I said, "that his name was Ferdinand?"

I heard the sound of a window opening behind me. I looked over my shoulder and saw my wife, Ellie, still in our second-floor bedroom, in her nightgown, arms on the sill, her gray hair down. She started to say something, but was interrupted by an extravagant yawn.

"Just from his mailbox, that's all," the young man said. His voice was suddenly just above a whisper. "Same way I know your name. E. Trowbridge. What does the E. stand for, sir?"

"How come you never asked me about this house?" I said.

"Gene," my wife called tentatively. I raised my hand to signal to her that I'd be with her in a second. The young man was beginning to sense that his time was up.

"When did you say Mr. Ferdinand moved here?" he said.

"It's none of your business—"

"Did he ever say anything to you about where he moved here from? Or did he mention it to anyone else that you know of?"

I stared at him.

"Does he have any particular friends in town? Does he ever say anything about his past?" There was a short pause after each question to see if I would answer. "Has he ever held any job here that you know of? Have you ever heard anyone, a visitor maybe, call him by some other name?"

I was beginning to tremble, in spite of myself. I made my angriest face, thinking for some reason that I was about to get into a fistfight, my first since school days. It was the same bristling, boyish sensation I remembered from the two times I had been mugged in Manhattan; now, feeling my home endangered, and forgetting for the moment the thirty years that lay between us, I caught myself wishing I were a more substantial man.

"Who are you?" I said.

"Gene," Ellie called, a little louder this time. I turned my head. "You'll be late, honey," she said. "It's five of."

"Thanks," I said, "I'm on my way." She disappeared from the window, leaving it open. I turned back to the stranger and took a step away from him.

"What is your name?" I said.

He dipped his head, as if he had only now been caught, and tried to salvage things by looking sheepish. "I'm a reporter, Mr. Trowbridge," he said. "I write for *Newsday*. I know it was dishonest of me to approach you this way, but people can be very protective, they're sometimes very distrustful of reporters—"

"Get off of my property," I said.

"—and we're trying to find out some things about your neighbor, it may well be nothing, we may have the wrong man, but you understand we have to check it out, we have our job to do—"

"I'm going in the house now," I said, feeling my color rising, "to call the police."

He sighed. "Well, nobody wants that," he said. "I don't have any criminal intent here, you must know that. I'm just interested to know if you can remember any conversation at all you might ever have had with your neighbor Mr. Ferdinand—"

I turned and marched back into the house, passing the hallway mirror, which showed me that not just my face but, to a

13

lesser degree, my arms and legs were quite red. I don't know that I had ever seen myself angry in shorts before. I picked up the kitchen phone, held it to my ear, took a few deep breaths, and hung it up again. When I went back out onto the porch, the young man and his car had both vanished, and there was a business card laid on the newel post at the foot of the porch stairs.

His name was Sam Boyd. The card had the *Newsday* logo on it as well. I put it in my pocket, went back into the hallway, and grabbed my racket. Though I was late already, I had to sit in the car for a minute or two, my hands flexing around the wheel, to relax my heart. Then I drove off to play tennis.

Belmont is a small town, and the Fourth of July parade on Belmont Avenue is correspondingly modest. But no one—at least no one who lives here—would be likely to find it paltry or embarrassing; on the contrary, there is something undeniably touching about it, something that brings to the surface a kind of eccentric pride in our own stubborn customs. No one, I am sure, would like it ever to grow any bigger or more ambitious than it is.

My tennis game that morning was unusually vigorous—it was a doubles match, in which Parker Smith and I split sets with Joe Sandberg and a weekend guest of his, a pretty fair player— and afterward I hung around the courts for a while, on the tiny flagstone patio with the uneven white tables, in the shade of the maple trees. The four of us had some iced tea and compli- mented each other in an informal way on our game. We talked a little business; Joe's guest, it turned out, was a partner at Willkie Farr & Gallagher, and ruefully described the atmosphere there on the day of a recent batch of associate layoffs. I wiped my neck with a small white towel, and watched a mixed doubles game being played in a flirtatious manner on the court we had vacated. I relaxed, enjoying the muscular satisfaction of having played well.

The tennis courts in Belmont aren't part of a country club, strictly speaking; they're owned by the town, and we pay a seasonal fee for their use and upkeep. They're well tended, and there is a clubhouse and locker room. But it's not a social center, with its attendant snobberies and obligations, the way a country club is. This may seem like a semantic difference, but it's part of the reason the town feels less traditionally suburban than the more famous bedroom communities in Westchester and Fairfield County, and thus part of the reason Ellie and I decided to move our life here twenty-three years ago, when we'd had enough of Manhattan. Belmont occupies the spiritual as well as the literal ground between built-up, eyesore communities like Patchogue on the one hand and the stupendously petty and expensive social whirl of the Hamptons, Sagaponack, and Sag Harbor on the other. It's a longer commute from here than most people who work in the city are willing to endure, but well worth it.

By the time I got home, it was nearly eleven-thirty; there was a note from Ellie in the kitchen saying she had run into town to buy some food for the parade. So, after showering and changing, I put a couple of folding chairs in the backseat of the car—from my driveway I could see Frannie doing the same—wrote a note at the bottom of Ellie's note telling her to meet me at our usual parade spot on the sidewalk in front of the hardware store, and drove up Fairly, onto Smallwood, and parked in the lot behind Ace Hardware on Belmont Avenue.

Belmont's main drag is about six hundred yards long, and all of the town's businesses flank it, the only exceptions being two or three real estate operations run out of spare wings on people's homes. There is a bank, a dry cleaner, a drugstore and supermarket (both so overpriced, with cheaper alternatives just one town away, that it's only through the gift of others' laziness they stay in business), a few notions shops run by bored wives, a nagging embarrassment of a local art gallery, a liquor store, one nice restaurant, and two sandwich places. A few of the older private homes on the street have survived as well. Some places are paved for sidewalks, other stretches just have a worn dirt path. I'd have to be more of a sociologist than I am to know why a place like this has had such a splendidly arrested economic development, never expanding, never withering, a kind of upper-middle-class tide pool with life forms far more strange and variegated than towns I could name within the very same county.

I checked the lot but didn't see Ellie's Civic there; so I pulled out the two folding chairs, reached into the glove compartment for the sunscreen, and set up on the sidewalk in front of the hardware store. Most of the others were already out—the McClements, the Golds, the Brights, who were getting divorced and looked it, and many others whose names I felt I should have known. Over the years I have come to rely too heavily on Ellie to cover for my gracelessness in neglecting to introduce people or momentarily forgetting the names of neighbors I have met several times before; what sometimes comes off as rudeness on my part is more like a lack of concentration. Up at the top of the road was the fire station, where the marchers, mostly young people, were assembling; they were all in plain sight of us, but I didn't look in their direction, more concerned about spoiling the surprise for them than for myself. I smoothed on some sunscreen, waved to a few people, and checked my watch. I tilted my head back to let my vision rise above the shingled roof of the

Booth Pharmacy across the street, where a few gauzy, motion-less clouds were stretched across the rich, undiluted blue of the country sky. I closed my eyes.

As I reclined there, trying to think of nothing, it came to me that I hadn't seen Ferdinand—his first name was Arthur, or Albert; Ellie would know—anywhere in the familiar crowd on Belmont Avenue. In fact, now that I tried I couldn't remember ever seeing him at this or any of the few yearly communal social functions—but then, my memory when it came to matters like that, I was well aware, was completely unreliable. It would have been just like me not to notice.

There was the soft crunch of a wicker picnic basket drop-ping on the pavement beside me, and I opened my eyes just in time to be kissed on the forehead by my wife. She had her hair back in a ponytail and a camera on a strap around one shoulder; up close, I could see the faint grease of suntan oil on the skin around her sunglasses. "Don't fall asleep," she said. "Look who I found." I turned in my chair and saw Don and Toni Greaves, a couple who have lived in Belmont even longer than Ellie and I have, which is a rarity. It's for that reason, and not for reasons of general compatibility, that we're friends at all. Not that they're not nice people; but we both find Toni in particular, I think, to be a bit dim. Relationships like this, we long ago acknowledged, are one of the small prices you pay when you move from the relative sanctity of a city home to some place with remaining vestiges of the small-town life.

I knew that the Greaveses must have in fact found Ellie and not the other way around; but she wasn't letting on that she was anything less than pleased. Besides, I thought as they set up their own chairs on either side of us, it was a parade, and wouldn't lend itself to much conversation. And I was further mollified when Don offered me a beer from out of their Scotch cooler; Ellie, not entranced by the image of her husband sitting in a chair in the center of town at high noon drinking a beer, no matter what day it was, would never have thought to bring any of our own.

The thin gaps on the sidewalks were filling up with spectators. Up the street at the fire station, at the edge of my vision, colors were coalescing into patterns. Don popped two light beers and handed me a can. We smiled conspiratorially, touched cans—the thin aluminum giving way with even the lightest pressure—and drank.

A police whistle blasted up at the fire station, and the volume of the public conversation diminished.

"Hey," Don said to me. "Aren't you missing a Braves game for this?"

I shook my head. "They're playing at seven-forty," I said. "So they can get in a fireworks show at the stadium after the game."

"Ah, of course," Don said.

I was nearly halfway through the can of beer by the second swallow. It's different if you're at dinner, or in a bar, but when you're outside under a hot sun, there are unique and undeniable pleasures in that good, watery American beer, and of course light beer is the most watery of them all. Strains of music began to bleat up the road, and there was some tentative applause from spectators nearer that end of the line. My mood was growing ever lighter and more receptive.

The first few parades I saw as a member of this community, back in the late sixties, reflected, in their modest, miniature way, the seismic shifting of the eras. The local high school, for instance, still had a junior ROTC program then, and a group of adolescent boys would march in uniform behind that banner. There were cheerleaders, and a Future Entrepreneurs Club, and a local American Legion outpost. It was still a small parade by any standard, but it had more of an element of drill and pomp to it. Of course, those particular groups were falling out of favor then, in particular the Rotsies and cheerleaders and other high-school associations. Teenage social pressure is a fearsome thing. I remember vividly the sight of a coed group of football cheerleaders, several of them crying, as they high-stepped and cartwheeled past a group of long-haired classmates who were performing a crude parody on the sidewalk, jeering them, swearing at them, while the rest of the town looked on, more in confusion than in outrage. No high-school student has principles that will stand up to that kind of ridicule; the pep squad dropped out of the parade, followed by the Rotsies and the Future Entrepreneurs. The whole parade became a far less formal affair.

Still, to a young child—to a child as young as my son Jack was then—to march down the main street while everyone watched was, and remains, an untarnishable kind of de facto heroism, greatly to be coveted. And so, at some point, the ceremonial barrier, flimsy to begin with, came down, and the townspeople began allowing their children to take part in the parade. They were unforeseeably cute, really, and they fit our increasingly ambiguous feelings about the notion of the parade itself and what it was now supposed to celebrate. Over the course of just a few years, the children took over the Fourth of July completely. Some wore patriotic costumes they had made themselves; some wore outfits sewn by their mothers, Abraham Lincoln or the Statue of Liberty most commonly, though it was an unspoken custom from the outset that too detailed or competitive a costume was not in the spirit of the day. Some boys, in emulation of beloved machines, perhaps, pulled smaller, bewildered-looking siblings behind them in red wagons. There were

19

always two or three who got scared and lost their nerve, and stopped dead in the street, waiting for their mothers to swoop down and rescue them, which they always did.

Even when times changed again, the old, comparatively solemn character of the parade never returned. We seemed to realize that we were onto something here. Seen from the point of view of those who had taken a dislike to the parade in the first place, the whole thing was, I'm sure, as hokey and false as ever; but the town, by entrusting these sentiments to their smallest children, had protected itself from dissent. One look at the confused, halting, smiling, arrhythmic procession was enough to put the entire holiday safely out of reach of ambivalence.

The music—there is still a high-school marching band, ever unfashionable but not, I gather, politically suspect—grew louder and more distinct; the applause and restrained shouting spread down the lines, and the front end of the parade was upon us. First in the procession was a flag bearer, the local deli owner, in fact, who was part of a parade unit at Fort Bragg during the Vietnam War. He marched as if toward his death and the life beyond it, incongruously dignified, eyes focused on nothing, his neck as if made of iron. A few gentlemen on the sidewalks, men of my own vintage, stood and saluted, but I think that that sort of behavior in this particular setting is just self-important foolishness, and I've never gone in for it myself.

The band went by, led by two high-stepping girls in tall hats who held a banner at waist level that read "John Dewey Memorial High School Class of 1990—Go Cougars!" The girls glanced surreptitiously at the sidewalks, anticipating the moment when they would avoid the eyes of their parents; they also looked at each other, continually readjusting the height of the banner to keep it level, so that it rocked back and forth as if they were trying to hang a framed picture. The students played, as they most likely knew it, "Be Kind to Your Web-Footed Friends." They were nothing but horns and drums, lots of drums, and I noticed that one boy struggled with a tuba, the hairshirt of the suburban musical world. The band passed before us, their sound thin and not always in time; a music made by still-forming personalities.

Behind them were twelve members of the local Suffolk County police barracks, already in their second small-town parade of the day, smiling as they marched. Their foreheads were sweaty, but they looked otherwise at home as they strode by in an easy parade gait in their dress blues, able to stay in step without concentrating on it. I was finishing my second beer and eating a thick roast beef hero Ellie had reluctantly brought me. I cannot concede to the idea of watching what I eat.

The policemen served as a symbolic as well as a literal barrier between the forward-looking teenagers and the ragtag procession of small children at their heels. When the twenty or thirty youngsters came into view and began their amoebalike movement up the street, the volume and the character of spectator participation changed. Cameras and video recorders began whirring and clicking madly, as if we were all at a press conference. Ellie, who was, technically, on the job—her nature shots and small-town photo essays appeared from time to time in the *Advocate*—was more judicious; she took only half a dozen shots that I noticed. Seven or eight years ago, when she was just beginning to get back into photography more seriously after Jack left home, Ellie once shot an artier roll for her own pleasure at the Fourth of July parade that seemed to look for, and occasionally to find, a kind of Diane Arbus quality, a gruesome cheerfulness and anxiety, in the faces of parents and children. I thought the prints were quite good; in fact, I may have praised them too much, for she then went about mounting an exhibition

21

of them at the gallery on Belmont Avenue. It's not that they weren't accomplished enough to be shown in public; but, of course, these people in the photographs were our neighbors. Ellie faced the same problem as any small-town artist, whose subjects and whose audience are identical. The show was received with befuddlement; needless to say, no one bought any prints. Now she took only a few easy, traditionally kitschy shots for the *Advocate* photo editor every year, for him to use if space and his disposition permitted.

The children were adorable, and, just as every year, in our adoration we were intimidating all but the most gregarious of them. There was a minor crush on both sides of the street as parents with cameras struggled to reach the front of the crowd; the struggle was barely visible, but emotionally, somehow, there was no mistaking it, and the children were the most attuned to it of all. Occasionally one of the mothers or fathers would dart right out into the street, get down on one knee, and snap a picture of their startled offspring before hurrying back off the parade route. Just as every year, two or three of the marchers, average age about six, started crying, but marched resolutely on, toward the end of their ordeal. One boy—Ellie told me later he was the Deckers' grandson, visiting for the holiday weekend—fairly goose-stepped with glee at the head of the children's procession, carrying one of his grandfather's canes as a kind of baton, thrilled to be under the eyes of all these complete strangers, in his glory.

He reminded me a bit, in his fearlessness, of Jack, who was about that age—perhaps six or seven—when the custom of parading the town's children first began. We put him in the procession for two years, once in a Davy Crockett costume (God forgive us, new parents that we were), and he was completely unfazed, strolling with casual engagement past his elders, never

22

saying much about the experience either before or afterward. He was always that way, it seemed—outgoing, effortless, without any of the social fears Ellie and I both remembered circumscribing our own childhoods. When he told us, at age eight, that he wasn't going to march in the parade that year because he was too old for it, we took him at his word. I was secretly relieved; for I had discovered that benign detachment was the key to one's untroubled appreciation of all this mock pageantry. Parenthood's moronic fuss had brought our household too far from, or maybe too close to, the genial heart of the whole ceremony; it was easier to swallow if one limited oneself to a role as spectator rather than as full participant.

About half the kids were either in some sort of costume or in formal clothes such as a jacket with matching shorts and a clip-on tie; the rest looked like they were on their way to, or from, the shore. None of them was bothered by the heat, which was at its apex. One little girl pulled a wagon with a cardboard, double-sided sign standing in it that read "Three Cheers for the Red, White and Blue." The effect of this was undercut in a curious manner by the presence, at her right side, of a smaller boy who pulled behind him an identical red wagon that contained nothing at all. The girl seemed to realize she was being subtly mocked in some real, if unintentional, way, and she scowled at the boy to move him away, but he marched obliviously in time with her, with loud, flat-footed steps.

The children moved at individual speeds toward the intersection at the foot of Belmont Avenue. Many of the parents waved to them, but they almost never waved back, whether out of embarrassment or fear of impropriety I wasn't sure. By the time the few stragglers—one looking for his mother, one enjoying himself so hugely that he was walking in a rough circle so that the wonder of it might not end—drew even with me, I could feel a broad smile across my own face, and I applauded loudly for them, for the childishness of them. Toni alternated between snapping pictures and pointing out one child or another to Ellie, who would look and nod once, knowing them all.

Next in line was a group of eight or ten adults—half of them firemen, half of them stubborn veterans—who marched every year as a kind of community service, since they served as a human buffer between the children's brigade and the fire engine that crept along behind them, the afternoon's appealingly prosaic coup de grace. Indeed, one of the firemen had scooped up a crying child and held her to his chest as he walked, rubbing her back gently, as if he had just saved her from something far worse than the unfathomable willfulness of her parents. The firemen, all volunteers, smiled as they walked. The veterans were paying more attention to the music, moving in time to it even when it faltered, as it did more often now that the band members had reached the foot of the street and could no longer aid their own sense of time by marching. Harry Tracy, part owner with his father of the Belmont barbershop and a decorated Vietnam veteran, looked somber and uneasy with the informality and general high spirits of the parade, as if he were being taunted all over again. Of course, he had that put-upon look every year, and no one was forcing him to march. We all are too reluctant, I suppose, to let go of any kind of strong feeling. Other, older men—our next-door neighbor Ted Winton, who fought in Japan, Michael Baldwin who was a medic in Italy and is now retired from his Manhattan practice as an orthopedic surgeon, Albie Barnes, a funny, dear man, who runs the liquor store and lost the hearing in one ear in Korea—met the occasion with the good cheer that it deserved, though they, too, had retained their military bearing as if it had been bred into them.

A few children who had reached the end of the parade route now ran back up the street, fell in among the grownups, and started off again, to delighted laughter. The band, their obligations met and their faculty advisor absent, launched into a self-taught brass-and-drums arrangement of "Sympathy for the Devil," a song I recognize only because I tried and failed to license it for an ad campaign years ago.

Finally came the town's one fire engine, inching along, its bell clanging like a toy, red, white, and blue streamers hanging from its sharp-looking edges, like a hunting dog tarted up for Westminster. Standing in the back, waving with one hand and with the other holding tightly to a ladder for support, was the town's First Selectwoman, Adele Bond, a person all of us know and like well enough to indulge her once a year in this fantasy that she is a respected public figure and not just a nice, smart woman with a public stipend whom we occasionally run into at the dry cleaner's. She waved at all of us, as we hailed her by name, with an equal, queenly beneficence, never letting on that, unlike a true politician, she knew nearly all of us personally, and liked and trusted us in measures that varied widely.

In another minute or two the engine reached the foot of Belmont Avenue, and parked. Adele climbed down with help from the driver; the red-faced musicians dropped their horns to their sides and undid the top buttons on their uniforms. The whole thing had taken, as it did every year, less than half an hour. The children, overexcited, were playing roughly with one another on the pavement, with no regard for their own or others' good clothes, indeed for the idea of good clothes. All of this still in plain sight of all of us. The adult marchers began wandering casually back up the street; we stood along with the other spectators and started toward them, and this momentary, voluntary separation of the citizenry into the observers and the observed was forgotten.

I showered again when we returned home. Though the sun was no longer high, it was still hot, even with the windows and front door open, so I left my hair wet to stay cool, combed straight back like some dance-hall shark of my youth. While Ellie changed upstairs, I poured myself a soda and sat down in the living room with my overdue library copy of Paul Kennedy's *The Rise and Fall of the Great Powers*. There was not a sound from the street, or from anywhere beyond the trees. The town's children had worn themselves out, and the neighborhood was blissfully still. It was the hour when you turn on the lamp to read by, then turn it off again when you see that it makes no difference yet. The sense of a pause in the day was so graceful, so lovely, in fact, that it was difficult to concentrate; and so I sat quietly with the book in my lap, feeling the slight sting of the day's sun on my cool skin, letting my mind unfocus.

Ellie came downstairs. Just on the edge of my perception, I saw her slow to look at me, smile, and proceed into the kitchen. I heard the faucet come on, then the noise of the garbage disposal as she took care of the detritus of the picnic; the guilt I suddenly felt for not having done this simple chore myself broke the bubble of my reverie, and I snapped the book shut and laid it on the end table.

"Let me do that," I called. I heard the water shut off, and Ellie came and sat on the sofa beside me, drying her thin hands.

"It's done," she said, smiling. "That's the wonderful thing about picnics. Everything just goes straight into the garbage."

"Good point," I said. "Maybe we should start eating all our meals this way. Paper plates, paper napkins, plastic silverware, Dixie cups. Think of all the spare time we'd have."

She raised her eyebrows coyly, as if I'd said something lascivious, and reached out to pat down my wet hair. "How environmentally incorrect of you," she said. "So I've been meaning to ask you all day. Who was that man you were talking to out in the yard this morning?"

Though that episode, so discrete and surprising that it had the character of a dream, has reasserted itself to me two or three times that day, somehow—to my credit, I supposed then —I had managed not to give it much conscious thought. So I would have to ask myself afterward if the explanation I gave myself for my answer to this question was simply rationalizing, or a genuine decision that I had thought out without articulating it even internally, the whole thing simmering beneath the onslaught of the music and the marchers and the beer and the sun.

"It's interesting," I said. "The guy was from over in Port Jefferson. He's a young family man, making some decent money, and he's always coveted this neighborhood, he says. So he planned to knock on doors and make people offers on their houses, on the spot."

"You're joking. Cash?"

"I don't know. Presumably. It wouldn't surprise me."

"Maybe he's a criminal."

"Management consultant, he said. Splitting hairs, maybe—"

"So what did he offer?"

"Sorry?" I said.

"What did he offer for our place?"

"Oh. He didn't make me one, actually. I think he could tell I wasn't really interested. He just asked me about the Wintons' place, and Bob Locke's, and a few others. Why, do you want to move now?"

"No, of course not," she said, reaching out with one finger to straighten a framed photo of hers that hung on the wall beside her. "Curious to know what a stranger would guess a place like this is worth, that's all."

She went back into the kitchen for a moment and returned without the dish towel.

"So who did you tell him was most likely to succumb?" she said.

"Who'd be liable to move away from here on short notice for a lot of money? I didn't tell him much, really. He was a bit of a jerk. Awfully cocky about this whole proposition."

"Well, you were probably smart," she said. "Sounds like he'd make a lousy neighbor."

She started toward the kitchen again.

"So," I said, and her head reappeared around the door frame. "You haven't heard about this guy talking to anyone else in the neighborhood? No one else we know been approached by a stranger, asking about the people that live around here?"

She thought for a moment. "Nope," she said. "I would have remembered that. Looks like you're the chosen one." She widened her eyes sarcastically and smiled.

It's difficult to explain why I didn't tell her the complete truth at the beginning. Clearly, I had no personal stake in the matter, nothing to feel protective about, up to that point. It's not that I had a low opinion of my wife, or didn't think she could be trusted; but rumor is a powerful thing, especially when the seal of the media is attached to it. I know whereof I speak. I didn't know Ferdinand very well—not even well enough to have the foggiest idea what it was he might be suspected or accused of. He may well have been guilty of whatever it was, for all I then knew. But he was a nice man. I have seen in my career the way an intriguing, sinful idea, something that people would be titillated to believe, can take hold of a group of people, can become, if not fact, then even more dangerous than fact. Belmont is a small community. I was not going to be in any way responsible for any sound of suspicion or upheaval. Let him stay innocent, I decided, if only through others' ignorance, for the full term that the law decreed his innocence. If, in fact, this was a matter of breaking the law at all. If this reporter had come to me, he would likely go to others, and so perhaps all this was just empty posturing on my part; whatever would happen would happen. But if it did, I didn't want it to be on my hands. I wanted to be able to say that I had no part in it.

Of course, now, in moments when I am less generous to myself, I admit that I wanted, at least for the time being, to keep this strange kernel of deviation and mystery to myself, keep it for myself, until I decided what to do with it. There is pleasure, and power, in knowing something nobody else knows, not even your own wife of thirty-seven years.

Still full from picnic food, we had just a light dinner. At seven-thirty, I looked pointedly at my watch, wiped my napkin across my mouth, and stood up from the table with an apologetic grin.

"Game time?" Ellie said.

I nodded. "Want to watch it with me?"

"I don't think so, thanks. Call me if Jack comes on."

I said I would. I put away the dishes, went into the TV room, picked up the remote control, and turned on TBS. There were two white-haired men talking in front of a blue-screen image of the field in Atlanta Fulton County Stadium. The players, too small to identify, could be seen warming up. The game was starting a few minutes late to allow for a gala holiday performance, by combined military bands, of the national anthem.

I grew restless, thinking about my conversation with Ellie, and my restlessness did not subside even when the game got under way. Nor did the ads between half-innings, usually of comparable interest to me with the game itself, engage me—they looked familiar and dull. Truth be told, I am not a diehard Braves fan; it is difficult to root for a team in a distant city, even when all their games are carried on my cable system. I decided I could skip the first few innings—John Smoltz, one of their better pitchers, was starting, and would probably last until at least the fifth. I turned the sound down, but left the picture flashing.

I asked Ellie if she felt like going for a little walk around the block with me; she said no, she was still tired from so much sun, and would probably go to bed early. The empty street was cool in the twilight. At the end of the driveway, I started left, hesitated, then turned right, and walked slowly up Fairly Avenue.

I should mention here that in one important respect I hold a kind of title among the men in Belmont—indeed, I find, among the men everywhere I am known. My son, Jack, is a professional baseball player. Age twenty-six, he was at this stage a relief pitcher for the Atlanta Braves, his fifth professional franchise in eight years, if you count his minor league affiliations. This was only his third stretch in the majors over those eight years, and he was hanging on to his spot on the Braves' roster by his fingernails, still, at least by his own reckoning, recovering from surgery on his right shoulder two years earlier. As for my own position, it is the fulfillment of a common dream of American males (once they reach adulthood, that is, and are forced to give up the primary dream of becoming professional athletes themselves) and yet it seems considerably more foolish and unworthy to me now than it ever did before it came true.

By the most conservative standard there are millions of

young boys at any one time who want to play major league ball, and, at any one time, there are only six hundred and fifty who have made it. But Jack, having entered the guild, was at the bottom of his profession, and—except for here at home—the kind of admiration he had been accustomed to since junior high school was withheld from him now. I understood that he was widely loathed in Atlanta, seen as a dismal symbol of the team that was itself a dismal symbol of the city. He was, in the parlance of the game, a mop-up guy, someone used to save the arms of the more valuable pitchers from unnecessary wear when either the Braves or their opponents had opened up an insurmountable lead. He pitched himself into that spot by losing three games and blowing a save in his first five appearances of the season, back in late April. I saw those games on TV, on the cable superstation that beams every inning of every Braves game to millions of indifferent people all over the country. I continued to watch all of Jack's appearances, though I didn't watch every inning of every Braves game. Since he was used only in certain low-pressure situations, it was possible to know when to turn the game on, or off. This fact, and the fact that I didn't care a great deal for the pathetic fortunes of the Braves in general, allowed me, for instance, to watch a game from the beginning and then turn it off and go to bed with the score 2–2 in the ninth.

Jack had one fair season in the majors, when he was twenty-three, and several good years in the minors. Before Atlanta, he was under contract to the organizations of the Seattle Mariners, the Milwaukee Brewers, the San Diego Padres, and the Philadelphia Phillies. Even a casual fan like myself, with nothing like the detailed knowledge of a pro ballplayer or coach, could see how his skills had eroded, particularly since his surgery. When he had that bad run in April, it was painful for me to watch him, not invigorating, as it used to be; it was something for a parent to bear. It hurt to watch him walk from the mound to the dugout, red-faced, confused, his jaw working, while the boos of thousands of hostile strangers rained down on him. Now it was painful to watch him for another reason: because even I could see that his baseball career was ending and yet he could not. Part of me, when he was roughed up by the opposing batters and then removed, was secretly grateful for the thought that something might hasten the twilight of Jack's baseball life; and that secret was my shame and my misery.

At about eight-thirty, the time when I thought I should be returning home to check on the game, I stopped in the road and realized I was lingering in front of Ferdinand's house. I could see over the hedge that a few lights were on; he was not visible in the windows. His old dog, Countess, a gorgeous Hungarian breed called a vizsla with short brown hair the color of baker's chocolate, snoozed on the mat outside his patio door. The dog, with its aristocratic features and friendly mien, was much admired around the neighborhood; it would be no great exaggeration to say she was better known than her owner. It looked like night until you lifted your eyes and saw the colors, the purple and the white and the indigo, still distinguishable in the western reaches of the sky, in the direction of the rest of the nation. This quiet, one-story house had the aspect of any normal suburban home in repose on an early summer evening—that is, it looked that way to me; others, outsiders, apparently were seeing something there that I could not. I frowned, rebuking myself for my curiosity, and walked back home.

Jack didn't pitch that night, his twelfth straight game without an appearance. I turned off the TV just before eleven o'clock and listened to the quiet. A car drove past on Fairly, slowly as if lost, unusual for that time of night. The only light burning in the house was the overhead light in the TV room. I switched it off, waited for the walls and furniture to reassume their shapes as my eyes adjusted to the darkness, and walked upstairs. In just the last few months, the stairs had begun to reveal their malign future intentions toward me—somehow I was always surprised, even after sitting motionless on a couch for several hours, to feel those twinges at the first few steps—and I wondered if I would ever see the day when they would finally defeat me, and I would have to sleep on the first floor as my own father did near the end of his decline, perhaps in the TV room. I slipped quietly into bed beside Ellie, who was sound asleep, and switched on the alarm.

With the mysterious precision of habit I woke and slapped at the switch that next morning one minute before it was set to go off; I swung myself out of bed and walked stiffly, eyes clouded, directly to the toilet and then into the shower. A few minutes later I shut the water off, finally able to open my eyes wide, and leaned back against the wall of the shower stall. I looked down in some ineradicable surprise at my old man's body, skin reddened by the hot water, all the wet black hairs pointing like compass needles toward the floor as if to accentuate my whole physique's inexorable downward pull. I listened to the last few drops ringing off the drain cover.

I put on a dark blue suit and a reddish tie. When I came downstairs, Ellie, who watched the *Today* show with a soap-opera fan's keen eye, had already made a pot of coffee, but I was as usual running too late to have any of it. There were digital clocks all over our house—the bedroom clock, the stove, the VCR in the TV room, the watch on my wrist—and all of them said 7:39. I had taken a 7:51 train to Manhattan five times a week for the last eleven years. All that attention to exact digits —always 7:51, and never just 7:50—had had its effect on me; time's rule seemed more capricious to me in the morning, and if ever those various clocks and watches were out of synchronization, I could become irritable in the extreme. I know that the reason for all those odd-numbered train schedules is to foster in the consumer the quaint idea that railroads are still concerned with punctuality; but even if it's not a sinister plot to change the way we think and feel and measure our lives, it might as well be. I kissed Ellie on the forehead, not waiting for her to move the coffee cup from her lips, told her I'd be home more or less on time, and walked out the door, checking, on the way out, my watch against the clock in the front hall.

The Belmont station of the Long Island Railroad is, for an affluent community, astonishingly seedy. It's an old red barn, the proportions of a cracker box, and to my knowledge hasn't been so much as painted in the twenty years since it opened. Its shabbiness is in sharp contrast to the train line itself, right down to the platform, which, of course, is the LIRR's responsibility, and not the town's, to maintain. The chipped, faded sign on the station house entrance and the streamlined, forward-leaning type on the platform sign stand like opposing flags in the battle for the town's self-image. Inside, at one end of the dusty wood floor are ticket windows, and at the other end is a counter used as a makeshift coffee stand, with stacks of the *New York Times,* the *Post, Newsday,* and of course the *Wall Street Journal,* a silver and black coffee urn with open cartons of milk beside it, doughnuts that the proprietor, Salvatore, buys at Dunkin Donuts on his way in from his home in Patchogue and resells for a dime more than retail, and a cigar box used to make change. Warm in the winter only near the radiator, cool in the summer only directly in front of the two small electric fans, the station's design seems left over from the days when people were more resigned to natural discomforts. I bought a *Times,* a plain doughnut, and two regular coffees from the relentlessly upbeat Salvatore, who I sometimes liked to imagine could buy and sell me several times over, and went to wait on the platform, away from the fetid waiting room. It was seven-fifty.

This was very near the end of my long tenure at the New York advertising agency known as Acker Anderson Kellogg, or AAK. With annual billings of some two hundred and fifteen million dollars, we were, while not one of the industry giants like BBDO or J. Walter Thompson, securely positioned in advertising's version of the map of the heavens. As good an example as any of the stability of the company was my own presence there for the last twenty-seven years, first as a copywriter, then as creative director, and finally, since 1978, as senior vice president, my reward for having helped AAK become one of the respected acronyms on what is now figuratively called Madison Avenue. And now, just over two months before my sixty-fifth birthday, I was facing retirement—my own decision, rather than an agency rule. A large dinner in my honor, to be held at the Park Lane Hotel, was looming on October 1, and perhaps that was a good thing, for it allowed me to be occupied with the various embarrassments of a testimonial evening (writing my speech, principally) rather than with the greater, more ambiguous notion that my life's work, such as it was, was close to its end.

All this was understandably near the front of my mind as I shouldered open the door at the back of the station house that led to the cement platform steps. As a small child I had gone through a period when I was obsessed with the calculability of time, writing out, for example, a calendar for the month of December 1936 every day of which included the number of seconds left until Christmas. I was reverting, at the curtain of old age, to something very like that; I had figured out that I would walk up or down the cement steps one hundred and twelve more times before my retirement from the commuting life. (Much less forbidding than calculating how many times I had climbed or descended the steps since 1967; you'd think the cement would bear the imprint of my shoes. Perhaps that was the sort of task one occupied oneself with after retirement.) There were eleven steps in all; with considerable effort I restrained myself, as the child Gene Trowbridge would not have, from trying to multiply one hundred and twelve by eleven. A morning breeze stammered across the raised platform, each fitful breath of it coming as a relief though the sun was not yet high enough to be seen over the line of trees at the end of the parking lot.

Strung along the platform, wearing lightweight business suits and carrying briefcases, were many of the men I had seen yesterday along Belmont Avenue carrying video cameras, white legs exposed between their baggy shorts and their elastic white socks. There were some women, too—the commuter train was no longer the men's club it used to be, for better and for worse —though not very many, at least not compared to the percentage of women who now worked in offices like my own. In fact, the 7:51—already three minutes late now—was in general the train of an older generation of professionals, since its scheduled arrival time at Penn Station was not until 9:18. Less crowded, less tense in atmosphere than the earlier trains, it was the province of either those who had simply missed their usual trains or those in such positions of corporate seniority that no one kept track of what time they got in to work. These latter had a distinctive air of unconcern, of being outside, at least for the duration of the train ride, of time; reading the paper as thoroughly as if they were sitting in their kitchens, they rarely looked out the window to see where they were, or at their watch, unlike some of the younger commuters who stiffened visibly as the train passed through the outskirts of Queens, checking the time frequently and muttering anxious oaths through their teeth. The older men were, by and large, more confident men, and though I am better, like most everyone, at seeing the surface of others than that of myself, I counted myself one of them.

Belmont is far enough out on the line that there are always plenty of empty seats on the morning train; on this morning, as luck would have it, when the 7:51 pulled in—winking dully in the sunlight, looking dirty and overexerted, suggestive in some way, as I've often thought, of a hangover—one of those double seats that face one another was open. Aren't we all cheered beyond reasonable measure by these little victories, placed divinely in the path of our routines? I sat down and opened my briefcase—not with any intention to work, but only to discourage other passengers from asking to take the seat. The car was filled with the air conditioner's thin roar, like someone blowing on a live microphone. I spread the *Times* across the briefcase to avoid newsprint stains on my fingers and clothes, opened the first cup of coffee, leaned forward so that any spillage would wind up on the already horrid floor, and sailed toward New York City, a happy creature of habit.

When the electric doors of a train spring open in Penn Station, it is as if the train had been holding its breath since the beginning of the line; hundreds of single-minded men and women are exhaled into the building, changing the currents throughout the whole underground complex as they barrel with that quick, forced-march stride toward the open air. Fishing in my jacket pocket for a subway token, I walked through the underground levels of the station, knowing only my own route in the vast maze of tunnels, shiny new sections connecting shabby, water-stained old sections, renovation seemingly without order, as if the purpose were not to spiff up the place but to keep it from collapsing, at various stress points, into the earth. Homeless people—I give in and use the modern appellation, having been weaned away by Ellie from my own generation's expressions, which to my ear are no more pejorative—took up every sheltered corner of the station's passageways, every space behind a covered-up pipe or otherwise safe from the tramping of feet. A few of them rattled coffee cups partially filled with change, their expressions blank, disconnected, as if there were as much chance of success or resolution in this endeavor as in a labor assigned to them in hell. But most were asleep, beneath blankets, in several layers of shirts and jackets; they maintained, as I suppose they had to, physical contact with all of their belongings at all times. They were everywhere one looked, just inches out of one's path. You couldn't help, all else aside, but be astonished by their ability to sleep under what were just about the least conducive circumstances imaginable. Now and then, you'd look into a face the depth of whose unconsciousness was even a bit frightening; it sometimes called to my mind the day I came home to Pittsfield after being discharged from the army and traumatized my mother by not emerging from my bedroom for twenty-eight straight hours. I never dared make such a comparison out loud, though; I saw how it was bad form to be confronted with such a cruel spectacle and be able to see it only in terms of how it reminded one of oneself. It was hard to believe that, at the end of the day, a train ride could appear to take me so far from these human hives of suffering.

I changed to the crosstown shuttle train at Times Square, came up the stairs near the east side of Grand Central, avoiding the giant concourse altogether, passed the newsstands and bathroom-size fast-food outlets, and emerged into midtown. In all my years in the city, the neighborhood most immune to fortune, at least in architectural terms, had been the one surrounding the AAK office on 50th and Third. It seemed to follow a kind of slow-working law of economy and nature; the office buildings, on the avenues, got taller, and the side streets, with their hot-dog restaurants and carpet outlets and stereo distributors, got a bit seedier. In the humid daylight, I walked to the skyscraper that houses AAK—only its second home in its nearly thirty years of life—pushed the express elevator button for the thirty-eighth floor, and felt the familiar elastic sensation in my stomach as I rocketed upward.

Advertising, particularly its creative side, is the province of young people, in their thirties or early forties for the most part; so I had long been entitled to a deference, though sometimes not of the most sincere cast, from the AAK staff. Only recently had it come to seem wholly genuine, even wistful, as my retirement approached, as if they were all escorting me through the passage of days toward the pearly gates. Gayle, the main receptionist—receptionists in large offices seem less and less distinguishable from air traffic controllers, with their featherweight headsets and their computerized workstations—smiled as I passed her in her glassed-in cubicle, keeping that smile out of her officious conversation with whoever was on the other end of the phone. My own secretary, Caroline, snapped guiltily to attention when she saw me, putting down her morning Diet Coke and holding a magazine under her desk. I tried to indicate to her, with a vague gesture and frown as I passed her desk and went into my office, that there was no need to pretend. I wasn't sure she understood. She was a good young woman, personable and with fine skills, and the fact that she saw herself, at least in her working life, as a kind of martyr to boredom annoyed me

39

only very rarely. It made for a happier working environment, it's true, when there was such a thing as a contented career secretary. But no one really yearns for those old days; and even if I did, the spectacle of Caroline's resolute lack of enthusiasm for everything she was asked to do had brought with it a loss of innocence in these matters that was probably good for me.

The fact was, neither Caroline nor I had much work to do that summer. I was already operating in a kind of emeritus capacity. There was no sense in my working on new campaigns, or even pitching new clients, long considered a specialty of mine. I was essentially biding my time until my time was up, with the company's blessing. Every new print ad and boards for every new TV spot would come across my desk for my OK— now considered a formality, where it used to be, for my subordinates, a fearful difficulty. A stack of them was in my office now. Copywriters or fellow executives would come by a few times a day for advice of one sort or another, and in lieu of advice would hear whatever stories they could dredge out of me about the old days. Other than that, my days were half taken up, as often as not, by an expensive lunch with an old colleague, a kind of farewell tour I was conducting. I had one such lunch scheduled that day, with Gary Crawford of Prentiss & Gregg, at Smith & Wollensky at twelve-thirty. I sat at my desk and put my briefcase on the floor. There were no phone messages. I picked up the top board from the stack of fledgling ads.

Words—which in my own professional upbringing were the very blood of advertising—have nearly completed their disappearance from print ads. Insofar as the work of the business's avant garde (if advertising can be said to have an avant garde) points to the future, before too long print ads will contain no type at all, or at least as little as they can get away with. Back in the days of the cavemen—the fifties and early sixties—an ad

40

consisted of a straightforward photo of a washing machine or a cake or a Ford, and, beneath it, sinking like silt to the bottom of the page, literally hundreds of words of copy. You thought nothing of writing four paragraphs' worth of copy about even the most undramatic product, and of expecting that people would read it—something that produces a positively childlike look of disbelief in our younger creative people when I have occasion to mention it. There were certain points you had to hit in that copy, in a certain order, all very pseudoscientifically ordained. The copy, though not always strictly true, was fact-based, meant to sound persuasive and honest and practical. ("The station wagon with the very latest in German-engineered steering," or some such foolishness.) Now, of course, as anyone with a magazine subscription knows, you're lucky to find twenty words on any given page of advertising. It's easy, and common, to ascribe this to—or, indeed, to blame it for—the general decline in interest in the written word, the primacy of the image in modern culture, the debasing of language, and so on. But to me, this is not a matter of cultural literacy, but something more specific, if less ominous. The nature of advertising—how it does what it does, and what the consumer expects it to do—is what has changed.

That first mock-up on my desk provided a good example, and I had the leisure that morning to follow these lofty thoughts to their conclusion. It promoted a well-known line of designer jeans, a client we had recently landed to the tune of about seventeen million a year in billings, to much back-slapping and in-office high-fiving. It was a black-and-white photo, a two-page spread, of one of those supernaturally angular young models in the bedroom of a modest, not quite seedy apartment. She is wearing only a T-shirt and panties. At the picture's extreme right, she is staring, hands on the windowsill, down at the city

41

street below. The light is suggestive of morning. Is she watching someone leave? The bedroom itself—and the photo—is dominated by a rumpled bed, far too large, really, for the room; this, I need hardly say, is redolent of many things, though none of them have to do with the product itself. After staring at the photo for a few seconds, you finally notice, at the extreme left, in the narrow space between the bed and the wall, a pair of jeans—one leg inside-out, rolled into a ball, as if removed and thrown there in haste. You can't really tell what they look like. In the upper left-hand corner of the spread is the company logo —just barely noticeable, like the mark on corporate stationery. No other type at all.

We don't expect ads to educate us anymore—that is a burden of which the creative workers in advertising have been relieved. Perhaps it is only because consumers have become sophisticated enough to distrust such information—it doesn't matter. We expect to be titillated and entertained and pleased. More important, we expect to have to *figure it out,* to have to do some modest imaginative work of our own—finding the logo, finding the jeans themselves. In short, we expect of it what we expect of art, at least popular art; and advertisers are in effect rewarded by consumers strictly on the basis of their ads' aesthetic success. Something in me recoiled when I saw an intentionally unclear ad like the one before me—it went so brazenly against everything I was taught and everything I thought I had figured out for myself. Yet I knew that an ad like that would be enormously profitable to the client. We haven't abandoned our reliance on scientific techniques—test groups, psychological profiles, et cetera—to measure even the most artistic ad's effectiveness. I signed off on it, feeling, as I often did, that a secondary intent of ads like this one was to make me feel outdated and foolish.

I looked over just two or three more mock-ups before I allowed myself to become distracted by my own thoughts. Not bothering to close the door, I spun around in my chair to face the perpendicular windows of my corner office. All around the wide metal shelf beneath the windows were photographs and artifacts—awards from the Ad Council of New York, a Clio award (that ceremony is even televised now, like the Oscars and the Grammys), framed copies of some of my earliest or most successful ads, a wedding picture, a baseball Jack gave to me with which he recorded his first major league save in 1987, some old pipes that I have long since stopped smoking but still like the look of. The view was to the southeast; that is, one large picture window faced downtown and the other across Third Avenue. The former offered a vista that stretched some thirty feet, across the street, to where a fellow high-rise went up nine years ago. In fact, I had an excellent view of *that* corner office, and the man—young-looking, though bald—encased within. The other window showed me a broad section of the concrete-and-dirt landscape from something of an overhead view—fire escapes, water tanks, warped tarpaper, roofs with padlocked doors and one colorful lawn chair. Down in the street, the glinting tops of buses, traffic revealed in its anarchic lanelessness, the dull black dunes of garbage bags. This business of a view in Manhattan, with a few exceptions such as Battery Park City or Central Park South, stood revealed to me, and perhaps to my colleague across the airspace, as a canard. There was little pleasure in it. I was edified by nothing I saw out my window except the weather. Yet I was reliably informed that already there was some jockeying going on for possession of my office the day after I finally gave up the corporate ghost.

I was beginning to understand why it was that old men talked, sometimes without restraint, about the old days, days of their adolescence and young adulthood. It's not at all because the old days were superior, in either a personal or a general way. There is a long period that precedes death, in which you are already not entirely of the world. Nothing makes sense to you anymore because it does not try or even think to relate itself to you in any way. It is as if the earth, without warning, begins turning faster, so that only the strongest can stay with it; already, already, you can feel, and see, yourself being thrown clear of it.

One man who understood about the old days as I knew them was Gary Crawford, an account representative from the manufacturing giant Prentiss & Gregg for the entire time I'd known him, which was more than twenty years. We'd never really taken our friendship out of the professional sphere, mostly because he and his wife live out in Englewood, New Jersey. But we'd had a lot of drunken lunches together and had stayed in touch even after AAK lost the P&G account in 1986.

He arrived at Smith & Wollensky a few minutes late, looking, as usual, distracted and slightly angry about something—to my relief, since I hated it when these last lunches had reverential, last-lunch airs about them. Gary is three years younger than I, with a remarkable, full head of white hair—he wears it a little long, I think, so that others might dwell on its fullness—that rides on the border between dashing and alarming. I was having a Pellegrino, but we decided to order martinis, in a kind of homage to our own pasts. I rarely drank martinis anymore, but scotch, which I drink almost exclusively, is a bad idea, I have found, in the middle of the day.

The headwaiter at Smith & Wollensky was an old friend of ours, and knew I wouldn't be a regular there much longer. He came and took our orders himself, making us a gift of his formality. We were on our second martinis by the time my filet mignon arrived. Gary's doctor, I only then learned, had made him forswear red meat. I wouldn't have ordered it, had I known, and I apologized to him; he dismissed my apology with evident embarrassment, and ate his sole while watching me with an expression like that of a dog watching scraps being thrown into the garbage.

I asked him, out of habit, how his new agency was treating him.

"Oh, you know," he said. "Dismissively. I don't like doing business with people who could be my sons and daughters."

"But they do good work?"

"Good as ever. All the board people at P&G want to see are the hard numbers, and the hard numbers tell the same happy story they've always told, same as when you represented us. Who wouldn't want to see the hard numbers, since they're always the same."

The restaurant hummed with low voices and, beneath it, the steady click of silverware. The waiters stood, when not responding to a request, in precise locations, camouflaged by their surroundings.

"Some little shit in my office," Gary said, "has taken to complaining that I don't spend enough time there, to the goddamn office manager, no less. Because of lunches like this one, and because I dare to go home at five o'clock. I've been working at P&G since this little squid was in grade school. Can you believe it?"

"Yeah, I can believe it. The guy probably wants your job."

"Okay, well, if he just wanted my job I could respect that. But it's worse. He views my job as a goddamn stepping-stone."

"They're cutthroats, these days. Nobody wants to wait for anything."

Gary, seeing from my expression that he was getting too worked up, allowed himself a laugh. "I'll hold him off. I've held off snottier than him."

"Are you thinking about retiring yourself?" I said.

"Yeah. I know what you're saying. But this kind of energy, you know, this kind of jungle mentality, it's all instinct to me now. I can't think any other way. I can't relax about my work. I'll be like this on my last day. Three years is a long time. Actually," he said, leaning forward, "you know something? This may sound odd. The few times I've imagined my death—I mean, I don't obsess about it, but in dreams or whatever—I've always imagined dying at work. Never at home in bed, never on the golf course like you read about. At work. Do you think that's strange?"

I finished chewing my steak and wiped my lips. "Well, yes, Gary," I said. "I'm afraid that is a little strange."

We looked at each other for a moment, our smiles substituting for genial laughter, in the way of an understood joke between two friends. I felt both the strength of our friendship and the strange, circumscribed quality of it. We saw each other regularly but only under certain circumstances. It was similar, in fact, in some respects, to an affair. Yet here was a man with whom, apparently, I could discuss dying, with whom certain confidences, certain similarities, did not need to be articulated. Watching him there, shaking his head, red-faced, joylessly finishing his sole, I was happy, and sad, and getting a little drunk.

Before long we lapsed into stories about our younger years, retelling them, as cronies will do, as if there were an imaginary third person at the table, to whom everything needed to be explained. Such warmth generated by reciting those old stories, overgrown with exaggeration! The time I accidentally spotted Gary at 21 with his secretary (who spurned his advances for years, or so he told me), went back to the phone in the lobby, and had the maître d' bring a house phone to their table to try to fluster him with explicit remarks. The former P&G executive, dead now, who used to reject some of AAK's best work with the remark "It doesn't say Mr. and Mrs. Peoria to me." The day I called him up to demand angrily that we meet at the AAK office that very afternoon—which I knew to be his birthday—only to surprise him by having him sit in on a model audition for a panty-hose ad.

It was nearly three by the time we were ready to part, and our spirits were high. We walked outside and stood on the sidewalk, cursing the heat.

"Do you think they'll fire us for being sloshed at work?" I said.

"No, no, we'll be fine. I'm going to take the freight elevator to the office, though."

We laughed some more, at nothing, really. You'd think that our years would have taught us how to say a fitting goodbye; but I felt unwilling to admit to the finality of anything.

"So," Gary said, "you'll still come into town from time to time."

"Oh, some," I said. "But just for fun from now on."

"Hallelujah," Gary said.

"And you take care of yourself."

"Oh, me," he said. "I'm indestructible. If only by association."

We stared at each other for a few moments; then, emboldened by gin, he held out his arms, and we gave each other an embrace, of the manly, backslapping, faintly silly variety.

Something popped into my head just as he was turning to go. "You know," I said, "I'm sorry I never got to meet your kids."

He looked surprised, then shrugged. "They're a good bunch," he said. "Of course, not as impressive as that boy of yours."

"Genetic fluke," I said.

"You're right. Maybe he's not even really yours."

From a distance of about two feet, we waved to one another —things having gotten awkward by this time, despite our best intentions—and we turned and walked away. Back at the office, I told Caroline as I passed her desk to hold all my calls. She smiled knowingly. I closed the door to my office, hung my jacket over the back of the chair, lay down on the couch and slept for an hour.

For a week or two, I approached the newsstands—in the train station on weekdays, in the drugstore on Belmont Avenue on Saturday and Sunday mornings—with an unnameable feeling made up of equal parts trepidation and excitement; in the forest of print my eye would be drawn to the blue *Newsday* logo and to the headline beneath it, as I wondered if today would bring the story that would enlighten me as to their research about Mr. Ferdinand. After being disappointed—that was the word—by the front page, I would open it up and scan the local news section as quickly and casually as I could, before replacing it and picking up the *Times* I customarily bought. I did see Sam Boyd's byline several times, but it was always affixed to small stories about local elections and the like, nothing flashy, and nothing that seemed as if it could remotely connect, other than in its mundaneness, with the figure of Mr. Ferdinand or with life on our street. Boyd was evidently one of their most junior report- ers, as his youth and his ham-fisted undercover work might have led me to believe. After two weeks of anticipation, my attention began to wane. I would still check the paper every day, but with less hope of success, often remembering to do so only at the last minute; it became something of an annoyance, in fact, in the way of a reluctantly held superstition. I began to wonder if Mr. Boyd's inquiries had come to nothing, or if he had just been plain wrong about whatever he was trying to ferret out. Of course, while that thought made me gladder than ever that I had kept quiet about it, it didn't lessen my own interest as to the nature of the investigation.

One Sunday in the middle of July, on one such routine trip to the drugstore to pick up the Sunday *Times,* the first thing I saw as the door closed behind me, setting off the little electronic bell, was Ferdinand himself. He was a tall man, thin but with a slight drinker's puffiness to his stomach and his face, which was browned and freckled by years of overexposure to the sun. He was stooped over, gazing in apparent confusion at the array of aspirin, aspirin substitutes, headache relievers, cold and flu symptom relievers, antihistamines and expectorants. I felt a touch of sympathy for him right there. Though not a strong man, he was athletic-looking. His thinning hair, still black, accentuated the aristocratic, faintly sad sharpness of his features. He wore a white short-sleeved shirt and lightweight, pleated blue pants. I had the impression that he had a Latin look about him—though that may well have been prefigured by the few times I had heard him talk, when he spoke with an accent that seemed to enhance, rather than impede, the schooled clarity of his English. Whether this accent might have indicated that he was originally from Spain or Mexico or Puerto Rico or Colombia or somewhere else, I had no idea. My sense of these things, like that of most people of my race and generation, I suppose, was undeveloped.

What I expected to happen, there in the town drugstore on a

Sunday morning, I had no notion, but I felt as if this were an opportunity of some sort. I lingered over the display of magazines, in order to time it so that we would be at the cash register at the same moment. We were the only two customers in the store, so there was no question of a line. I walked to the stacks of newspapers, picked up a copy of the *Times,* and flipped through it to make sure all the sections were included, something I don't think I had ever done before but had seen many other people do. I even dared to conduct my customary, unsuccessful check of *Newsday,* in order to pass some more seconds. At last he found what he wanted and started for the counter. I went and stood behind him. At my approach, he nodded and smiled pleasantly, and I did the same.

We did have to wait after all, for Sonia Booth, who ran the pharmacy in a hellish, contentious partnership with her sister Lily, was on the phone behind the pharmaceutical counter.

"No," she said. "No. They will not appreciate it."

I stared at the back of Ferdinand's tanned neck. There was no excuse, really, for my not putting down exact change on the counter and leaving, and I became absurdly concerned that Ferdinand would think of this and wonder what was wrong with me. Beyond him, at the rear wall, were some unpacked cardboard boxes and a back door, which was always kept locked from the inside with a simple chain and bore a testy, hand-lettered sign reading "Employees Only!"

"Do you remember last time?" Sonia said in a loud voice, perhaps unaware there was anyone else in the store. "Am I the only one who remembers last time?"

Ridiculously, desperately, idiotically, I said to Ferdinand, "Headache?"

He turned to face me and smiled politely. "A summer cold,"

he said in his vaguely British inflections. "Or perhaps it's an allergy. It seems to happen this way every year."

Though almost ostentatiously well mannered, he was more forthcoming, even on this simple subject, than I had expected him to be. There was something a little distancing about him, but not forbidding; he was simply someone to whom, for one reason or another, I had never really spoken. Perhaps it was only because he was superficially different from me and from my friends, though it would have been a painful thing to admit to myself.

Sonia finally came forward, with a loud, exasperated sigh. She addressed us, in her usual manner, as Mr. Ferdinand and Mr. Trowbridge, though I only had about ten years on her and he may have had less. He paid for his medicine. While he put the change into his pocket and the receipt into the plastic bag, I paid for the paper with a five-dollar bill even though I had exact change. I followed him out of the store, three or four steps behind.

His car, a tan Mercedes, was parked just outside, and he stood for a moment with his arms crossed on the roof, squinting up at the sky. It was a gorgeous day, over eighty degrees but with a consistent breeze. There were no clouds.

He looked down and saw me watching him.

"Smell the sea?" he said.

Though we are a whole town inland from the South Shore, there are days, when the conditions are right, when you can indeed pick up the smells of the ocean on the wind. I raised my head slightly but could detect nothing. I shook my head.

He laughed. "You're right," he said. "I'm probably imagining it." He opened his car door. "Have a good day, Gene," he said.

I waved. My own car was just twenty feet or so from his. I

got in and drove up the street, only to find myself right behind him at the traffic light. This made the remainder of the trip home a little awkward; I imagined him glancing in his rearview mirror, thinking I was following him. I could hardly do otherwise, though, since we lived on the same block, and I couldn't pass him or slow down on those quiet, narrow roads. When he turned off into his driveway, he beeped the horn at me, two times in jaunty succession; I waved again and continued home.

I took the paper along with a cup of coffee out to the front porch, and read the business section in the cool of the shade. I was in the middle of a rather sexy story about a coming management shakeup at Ogilvy & Mather when I heard the front door open and looked up to see Ellie emerge from the house with a broom. To my eye, the porch never really gets dirty in the summer; it sits under the big elm tree and behind a row of hydrangea bushes, so that in the autumn it really is a struggle to keep it from looking as if the house has been abandoned. But Ellie is someone who does things according to a fixed routine, so every few days she sweeps the dust off the porch whether—at least in my opinion—there is dust there or not. I went back to the paper; but the steady, long, approaching whispers of the straw broom—turning to short rapid kisses when she came to a trouble spot—invaded my concentration, and after reading the same sentence four times I closed the paper, picked up my coffee, and went back into the living room.

I tried to do this as quietly as possible, without making a show of the fact that I had been disturbed; but I heard the broom silenced behind me for a few telltale seconds before the whispering resumed.

Fifteen minutes later, as I read the player statistics in the sports section (Jack had pitched too few innings to qualify for inclusion in the list), Ellie returned to the living room—that is, her return to the living room was heralded by the nerve-fraying clatter of the upright vacuum cleaner she was pushing ahead of her. She got down on her hands and knees to plug it in behind the end table. I stared off above the paper and tried to decide what was going on here, in lieu of losing my temper. This was fighting territory, and I do not like marital fights; perhaps my dislike of them is too strong, and I work to avoid them when I shouldn't. But there seemed no point at all in a fight over a little matter like this—even though she was clearly trying to disrupt me; there were, after all, empty rooms in the house that were presumably equally dirty. I tried to be delicate about it, but if she was trying to goad me into objecting, then anything I said, I realized, would do.

"Are you through on the porch," I said, "so I can go back out there?"

She straightened, one hand in the small of her back, and glared at me.

"Don't use that tone with me," she said.

"What? What are you talking about?"

"That patronizing tone."

"All I wanted to know was—"

"Was where do I get off disrupting your Sunday-paper reading by merely doing the housework?" she said in an edgy voice.

She had succeeded in making me lose my temper. I folded the sports section and put it down on the couch. "No," I said. "What I'd really like to know is why you deliberately follow me around to disturb me, when there are several comparably dirty rooms that I am not in. If you resent having to do housework, we can have someone come in to do it. Don't take it out on me."

"I see," she said, switching to a tone of mock-reasonableness. "So what you're saying is that the schedule you've worked out for yourself for today, what order to read the paper in, and where, before you go in and turn on the television, is inviolate. Any plan I might have to do work has to fit around that."

Do I have to say that this is an argument we had had, in one variation or another, perhaps a hundred times? Though we could easily have afforded it, Ellie—who grew up in a house with servants—was adamant about not hiring a cleaning lady; it's sexist, she would instruct me in her up-to-the-minute way, it's classist, it's lazy, and in any case she did not like the idea of a stranger poring through the rooms of our home whom she would have to feel guilty about distrusting. Every marriage, I think, has battlegrounds of this sort that husband and wife can return to when they need to work off something more important—or less important, as well, something as simple as a formless angry mood. It's when previously demilitarized zones, as it were, start to become unexpected sites for fighting that a marriage gets into real, often irreversible, trouble.

"Your schedule," I said, "seems to include annoying me for no good reason. Besides, I've never seen you sweep the porch on a Sunday. Don't you usually do this work during the week?"

"During the week? You mean when you're not here? Do you suppose I have absolutely nothing to do when you're not here? Do you suppose I go into a cocoon, until you come home from work?"

I closed my eyes. "No, I don't suppose that. Isn't it *true,* though, that you usually do this kind of housework during the week?"

"Well, you'd better get used to it," she said. "The concept of weekdays and weekends isn't going to be very useful to either of us for much longer." She switched on the vacuum cleaner.

Here, I realized, was the true source of Ellie's irritation—irritation and worry. One of the great changes in our married life was coming, at a time when, at least subconsciously, we believed we were too old to have to accommodate change. To be honest, though I had been concerned about my life in retirement, my concern had all been focused on myself, my own private adaptation. But the whole question of my relationship with Ellie—like any long-term marriage, both strong and idiosyncratic—had to be considered as well. We had built our marriage on a model that was common in our generation, though I believe it is less so now; the portion of each day that we spent together was, though important, quite small—in fact, important because it was small. I worked long hours, though not as long as in my younger days. And our sleeping schedules have always been different, even back when we lived in Manhattan, before Jack was born. Except for a very rare trip to the city to shop or see an exhibition at the Museum of Modern Art or the Whitney, Ellie was home in Belmont or the environs every day. If you asked her what she did for a living, she would tell you she was a photographer. This was a subject I had learned to approach with great delicacy, for though her employment by the *Advocate* was freelance and voluntary, and she sold just two or three other prints a year to neighbors and friends, she would not be contradicted, at least not by me, when it came to the question of her career. And, of course, she had her own society of friends in Belmont, mostly female, to whom I was certainly amicable, but not close. I quite frequently had to, or chose to, entertain clients and associates at night; sometimes there were more purely recreational pursuits with my own circle of friends, among whom she was comfortable, but not in her element. It was not unusual for me to arrive home after she was asleep. There had even been discussion, though it never came to anything, of my taking a pied à terre in the city for late nights. I knew she didn't mind this arrangement, as long as we weren't apart for too long at a time; and it gave me a measure of freedom as well, to know that what I wanted or needed to do wasn't done at her expense. Our life together consisted, in large part, in the ability to respect and maintain our separate societies.

What was coming, then, was one of the real watersheds in our lives as husband and wife. There wasn't any question, after thirty-seven years, of seriously threatening, or even weakening, the marriage; it would grow around such difficulties like a tree around a spike. But the stakes were all the higher because of it. Any bitterness, any standoff, was going to become part of the foundation of our declining years. All this, as I say, at a time of life when we each might well resent having to learn new strategies for happiness.

I could think of only two other developments that compared to this one, that had changed the terms of what it meant to be married to one another. The first, as for any couple, I suppose, was the birth of our first and only child, and the second was nineteen years later when he left home for good. Perhaps the latter would have been easier to handle had it been an actual event, something for which we could have prepared—as we had prepared for his arrival—and in which we could have taken part. But it happened in a more abrupt and unresolved way.

Baseball had taken Jack away from home on many occasions throughout his teenage years—road games, state tournaments, a pilgrimage with teammates to the Hall of Fame in upstate Cooperstown—but never for more than four or five nights at a time, and almost always just for one. (We did allow him to go to a special baseball-skills camp for four weeks when he was fourteen.) Then came the final semester of his senior year in high school, and his eligibility for the major-league draft. It would be nice to look back at those as exciting days, filled with the pleasures of fantasy and anticipation, but in fact they were a miserable trial. Jack became convinced, and not without reason, that each game he pitched in the last month of the high-school season was a make-or-break situation for him—so that winning a district championship game but giving up four runs, or striking out only five over seven innings, was cause for private panic. It was difficult to watch him, surrounded by teammates with much less at stake, in the midst of those ecstatic postgame celebrations at the pitcher's mound, struggling to control his own emotion over his personal performance, until he could get home, run up to his room, shout abuse at himself, and throw pillows against the wall. And it was only marginally less difficult to see him trying to share his teammates' grief after they lost the regional final in Ronkonkoma, 1–0, despite Jack's one-hit, fourteen-strikeout performance, with several major-league scouts in the stands.

Draft time in June was a festival of forced optimism and jangled nerves. Jack stood stock-still in the kitchen about eighteen inches from the phone; Ellie and I sat in the living room and pretended to read. A major-league baseball draft, keep in mind, takes place over two days. Somehow my most moving memory of that time of our boy's passage into adulthood, of his realizing his exclusive dream, is not the moment on that second day when the Phillies called up to offer him a minor-league contract; it is of the six or eight times earlier that day when the phone rang, Jack leaped on it, and from the living room I would hear him explain softly and politely to a neighbor or local well-wisher, his voice shaking with restraint, that no, there was no news yet, and he was very sorry but he hoped they understood that it was important to keep the line free. At last, the real call came, and the celebrating began.

He packed up and went off to Martinsville, Virginia, home of the Phillies' rookie league team, for the summer. He was back, tanned and nonchalant, at the end of the minor-league season, around Labor Day. There would be no more baseball until spring training began in February. Ellie and I tried to sell him on the virtues of starting college. Perhaps I didn't push it as strongly as I might have; after all, the most convincing reasons —what if your arm gets hurt? what if you're not good enough? —were dark possibilities of the sort I could not get myself even to mention to him. In any case, he was having none of it. He did take a job driving a soda-delivery van, just to pacify us, I think; but he quit in less than a month, citing his fear of hurting his arm. For the rest of the winter, he went to the Dewey High gym every day for a two-hour workout with his old catcher, stayed out at night with his friends, and slept till eleven. As far as he was concerned, that was his job. His contractual payment from the Phillies organization was small—about eighteen thousand—but when you consider that his room and board were paid for, he really didn't, as he readily pointed out, need to work. The winter passed, though not without some minor eruptions of temper from Ellie and me over the whole matter, usually directed, for some reason, not at Jack but at each other.

In March he was assigned to the Phillies' Class A team in Clearwater, Florida (Class A is the lowest of the three minor-league strata, labeled A, AA, and AAA). This time he was gone from home not two months but six. He still called us with some frequency, usually after he had been in a game, to let us know how he did. He had an average year—seven wins and eight losses—but it mattered little to anyone but him; at that level, a team's professional development staff relies more on radar guns and standardized psychological tests than on the usual statistics. They have certain characteristics, either positive or negative, that they are on the lookout for, and the games themselves are really just a pretext for flushing those things out. Toward the end of August, Ellie began to hum as she worked, readying Jack's room for him, making an occasional, non sequitur reference to some food item we were going to have to remember to buy more of now that Jack was coming home.

Then he called us one night—a little nervous, the way he always was when he was trying to be casual about something he knew we wouldn't want to hear—and said that since he had signed a year-long lease on his apartment in Clearwater, which he shared with two teammates, he had decided to stay there in the off-season. The team would be holding some informal workouts; besides, he was talking to the manager about possibly traveling to the Dominican Republic to play winter ball, to try to work on a new pitch. "But you don't know Spanish," Ellie said on the upstairs extension. Not hearing, he went on to say that he expected to move up to double-A the next season, in Reading, Pennsylvania, and so he would need to head out there at some point and find a new place anyway. This momentous conversation wound down somehow with a minimum of drama or emotion; it would have been different if he had been there in front of us, but he was already gone, and so there was nothing to be gained by trying to make him reconsider, except to make him feel angry or guilty. Baseball, it seemed, had finally completed the process of severing him from us. He was nineteen years old.

I hung up and, after a minute, went upstairs to see Ellie. I found her sitting in the desk chair in Jack's room, surrounded by all of his garish school trophies, his posters of Vida Blue, Tom Seaver, Steve Carlton.

She looked up at me. "I was just thinking what to do about his room from now on," she said. "It'll get dirty—everything gets dirty. But when I come in here to clean it, I'm going to feel like Norman Bates."

"Oh, now," I said. "Aren't you overreacting a little bit?"

True, I was feeling a little depressed by what had just taken place—by the realization that there would be no second opportunity to send my son out into the world with the dignity such an occasion seemed to owe me (or perhaps I owed it)—but Ellie seemed to be having a hard time controlling herself, which was not like her. "It's not like he's never coming back."

"No, he won't." There was a slight unsteadiness in her voice. "It's all over now."

I went and stood behind her. I put my hands on her shoulders, and, to my surprise, she flinched, as if I had had my hands in ice water. I put them back in my pockets. Ellie had left her job as a photo research assistant at *Life* magazine when she discovered she was pregnant with Jack; when we moved out to Long Island, there were no jobs in a town this small any more interesting to her than motherhood, and obviously we couldn't both commute to Manhattan when we had a school-age child.

"How could you let this happen?" she said, tearfully.

I put my hands gently against her hair, and this time she did not react. "He'll be fine," I said. "He's in a very structured environment, you know, when he's with the team. They wouldn't let anything happen to him."

She said nothing. I couldn't see her face.

"Besides," I said, "he's very mature for nineteen, at least in most ways. Kids grow up a lot faster now than when—"

She turned on me, red-eyed, her expression one of impatience and fury. "Oh," she said, "I'm not worried about *him!*" And she stood up and hurried out of the room, leaving me to sit in the vacated chair for a while and try to decide what was meant by that. Fifteen minutes later, when I left Jack's room, Ellie had already gone to bed; I went downstairs. I thought then —as I think now—that Ellie had run away from me not simply because she was angry or about to cry, but because her last remark had, perhaps unintentionally, brought us to the border of some understanding of the complex terms of our present happiness, of the benign but still surprising manner in which the features of our marriage had aged, over the last twenty years, while our eyes were on our son. It is possible to know too much about the secrets of one's own contentment. We never spoke of it again.

Now, by the time we were through with the vacuuming altercation, it was already close to one o'clock, and so I retreated to the TV room. The Braves had a doubleheader against the Dodgers, which greatly increased the likelihood of Jack's getting into one of the games. Sure enough, he relieved in the opener, pitching decently—two innings, one run on three hits and a walk. It made no difference in the game, which the Braves lost. But I knew he would be encouraged. Later that night, a couple of hours after the second game ended, I called his apartment in Atlanta to congratulate him, thinking I would find him there. But I got his answering machine instead; I left a short message telling him that I'd seen the game, that I thought he'd pitched well, that one of the three hits could just as easily have been scored an error, and that he didn't need to call me back, though I hoped we'd talk soon.

Several days later I awoke with a mild flu; both my muscles and my concentration were weak and uncertain, food as simple as buttered toast appeared to me as a pound of uncooked bacon must appear to a vegetarian, and I had a low-grade fever. Still, I thought I could make it to work, but it didn't take much prompting from Ellie for me to take off my suit and ease back into bed, glad to cede the judgment of my fitness to someone else. I took some aspirin and fell asleep, dimly hearing, at some point when I was barely conscious but not sensible of time, Ellie talking on the phone to Caroline, telling her that I would see her tomorrow.

I woke at about ten-thirty, and again at quarter to one. The house was quiet. My body, as I stood and slowly put on my bathrobe, felt emptied by fever and hunger; I was unsteady, a little light-headed, but better. I went downstairs. From the kitchen windows I could see Ellie out in the small garden in our backyard; she had her back to me and was crouched down near the dirt, working intently. The sun shone brightly off her white shirt, but I still felt a chill. I made myself some tea and, when that went down well, some toast and strawberry jam.

After letting some daytime television pass before my eyes for a half hour (nothing so embarrassing, so unsubtle, so brutishly old-fashioned as daytime TV advertising), I knocked on the window and waved to Ellie. I gave her the thumbs-up sign, but she dropped her spade and came in anyway. I let her feel my forehead and smooth my hair. She was pleased that I had eaten something. I told her I thought I might even go for a walk in the afternoon, since it looked so lovely out. She warned against it; but the older I become, the greater the impatience with which I tolerate sickness.

Around four o'clock, convinced I was feeling better, she drove off to do some grocery shopping and drop off some film; and so, after a quick shower, I dressed and left the house. It didn't take long to seem like a bad idea; the sunlight on my skin, still cooling from the shower, soon had me shivering again, and I had that slight dizziness and muscle ache that come with fever. The neighborhood was silent, with most of the parents off to work and the children a few miles away at the beach. Birds whistled invisibly in the trees; high overhead I saw a single gull.

They sometimes come this far inland, though what they might be tempted by I don't know. Mindful of the lecture I would have to endure if Ellie got home before me and saw me return looking pale and sick, I was thinking of turning back when I saw Ferdinand out walking, heading toward me.

He was still a hundred yards away, and I recognized his dog before I could make him out. When we were a little closer, Countess came trotting up to me, her tags jangling, and offered me her face to scratch. I rubbed behind her ears, and she lowered her head in supplication. I didn't know if she was a show dog, but when she sat, she sat as straight as a figurine, like something found in an Egyptian tomb. Ferdinand caught up with us and smiled approvingly.

"Such a beautiful dog," I said.

"Yes, she is. A little too eager to make friends sometimes. Not everyone appreciates it. I think she could tell you were a likely target, though."

He smiled. I was trying to gather myself together for this encounter, but I was feeling almost drunk; the sunlight was painful to me, and I had to look at him, at his friendly, melancholy, composed face, through a terrible squint. I pulled my hand away, but Countess batted at my palm with her long nose until I relented and scratched her some more.

"Do you take her out every day about this time?" I said, thinking this might be an opportune way to run into him in the future.

"Usually. It varies a little, now that she's gotten older. Everything takes a little longer. As we know, eh?"

"How old?" I said.

"Ten. Gene?"

I raised my eyebrows.

"You look pale. Is everything all right?"

"Yes, fine," I said. "I'm home sick from work today, with a little touch of flu, I think. But I'm feeling better, really."

"Well, you don't look it. Is your wife at home?"

"She's out shopping."

"Then why don't you wait in my house for a few minutes and at least get out of the sun? Have something to drink. Will you?"

I hesitated, then nodded.

"Good. Come," he said sharply, to the dog.

And so, in this chance way, I was to see for the first time where Ferdinand lived. I wished that my senses were keener for it, though I wasn't at all sure what I hoped to see there. Some key to a mystery, something that might explain, or explain away, the suspicion with which others—and I, too, now, unable to help myself—looked at him. Countess trotted alongside us as we walked the half block or so to the corner of Fairly Avenue.

"Besides, you should be wearing a hat," was all he said on the way there.

We went through the side door into his kitchen. Countess nudged me aside to get to her water dish. "Go in and sit down," Ferdinand said. I went through the hallway and into the living room, which was painted a kind of deep, undersea green, with a large picture window that faced his yard, fenced in to keep the traffic out of sight, and the handsome old maple tree that spread out to shade half the property. The room itself was handsomely furnished, though clearly by a man alone; everything was plush, simple, and large. The only decorative touches—though of course that wasn't the proper way to refer to them—were a small, exquisite painting of the Madonna in a black frame on one of the end tables and a small, dramatic statue of the cruci-

fixion that hung on the wall next to the picture window as if (or
such was my blasphemous first impression) He were hiding
from the gaze of someone outside. There was something else
about the room, something I couldn't immediately put my finger on, that made it seem oddly temporary, like a long-term
hotel room or an apartment a man might find after being kicked
out of the house by his wife, though I knew Ferdinand had been
there for seven years.

He joined me in the living room and handed me one of two
glasses of orange juice.

"Feeling better?" he said, sinking into a chair across the
room from me.

"Yes, thank you. It's nice and dark in here. Feels cool."

He nodded, pleased. "The old owners," he said, and laughed
briefly just at having reminded himself of them, "had this room
painted white, and no drapes over the big window. And they
told me that I could always cut down the maple tree if I wanted
more light."

"The Harpers," I said. "They weren't very subtle people, it's
true."

"Oh, my God, that's right," he said. "You know them. How
embarrassing for me—I forget how long you've been here."

"No, that's quite all right. We weren't close friends," I said,
though the Harpers, who still sent us Christmas cards from
Arizona stuffed with two-page family newsletters, might have
been surprised to hear me. "It is a lovely place, though. The
traffic noise isn't bad?"

I was annoyed with myself for indulging in this kind of sub-
urban-macho real estate banter, but I couldn't think of any entry point for a more personal conversation. In any case, Ferdinand seemed to take it as a matter of course. "No, it's fairly

quiet," he said. "I've grown very comfortable here. At the time, I was disappointed not to get something right on the water, but even at those hideous prices there was nothing on the market."

"Really?" I said. "I thought one of the attractions for everyone who lived here was that it was a little inland. Maybe it's just me."

"Oh, no. Sometimes I still entertain the idea of moving there, you know. But I think it's probably too late for me. I don't really want to move again, even if it's to the next town."

"Wouldn't all the summer people bother you?"

He waved his hand. "Yes," he said. "But the summer people are there for two months out of the year, and the ocean is there for twelve. All I'd be interested in is the view, and so it doesn't really make any difference to me whether it's summer or winter. It's too late to take up bodysurfing anyway, eh?"

I smiled.

"I drive over there a couple of afternoons a week with the Countess, year round, if the weather's nice, just to walk on the beach," he said.

"No kidding," I said. "That's admirable, really. I should do that more. It's ridiculous to live this close to the shore and never go. I've just become, I don't know, immune to it."

Countess walked in from the kitchen, still licking her lips, and, with a glance at me, lay down across the tops of Ferdinand's shoes.

"Well," he said. "You'll have to come with me sometime, that's all. Though I suppose it could only be on a weekend for you, which is when it's most crowded."

"Actually, I'll be home pretty much permanently before long. I'm retiring this fall."

"Ah. From what?"

"Advertising."

"And why are you retiring? Not your health, I hope?"

"No, nothing like that. I am turning sixty-five in a few weeks."

"So it's mandatory?"

"No," I said. "Symbolic. Voluntary."

He nodded, and seemed to think about that for a moment. He pointed to himself. "Sixty-six," he said.

"Retired?"

"Yes. For some time."

"And what did you do?"

"Well, many things. Real estate, principally. I was lucky enough to do well in my later years, so I was able to take my savings and come out here."

"From where?"

The feverish shaking in my fingers had been supplanted by nervousness in asking these questions, which sounded, I feared, like an interrogation, and a clumsy one at that. But in fact they were just the sort of questions any two men with friendly intentions always ask each other; and that seemed precisely the spirit in which Ferdinand was hearing them. He was a pleasant man, obviously smart, and, most perplexing of all, he had a sense of humor. What came off as aloofness when you passed him on the street seemed instead, in his own home, an appealing dignity. It seemed odd that someone so unshy in a situation such as this should have been a stranger, with a recluse's reputation, to me and to most of the town for these seven years.

"From Cleveland. Near Cleveland. A suburb called Pepper Pike."

"But, I mean, you can't be from Cleveland. I'm a little embarrassed at not being able to place your accent, but where are you from?"

"South America," he answered readily, if somewhat ambiguously.

"Where in South America?"

He smiled. "Brazil," he said. "I lived there until I was twenty-two, just after college, then I came to America. Not to Pepper Pike, you know. I've lived in a number of places, mostly in the Midwest. But somehow, the accent out there never rubbed off on me," he said, in a passable imitation of a flat Midwestern accent.

I laughed. "Bet you had an ocean view there," I said. "In Brazil."

His face softened. "Quite beautiful, yes. I do still think of that sometimes. I'm sure that's where I developed my love of it, you're right."

We listened to a car pass on the other side of the fence, slow for just a second at the yield sign at the intersection, and speed off.

"Enough about all that," he said. "Tell me about yourself. I know that you're married, I've met your wife in town several times."

"Yes, thirty-seven years we've been married, thank you."

"Really? A vanishing breed, don't you think?"

"I suppose so." I was surprised to feel uncomfortable at being asked about myself, so instead I talked about my family. "We have one son, Jack, who's twenty-six."

"And where does he live?"

"Atlanta. He's a professional baseball player."

This never fails to produce a reaction. Ferdinand looked astonished, almost reproachful, as if it were bad manners of me to have waited so long before telling him this. "How remarkable!" he said. "How proud you must be!" I smiled. In truth, I was surprised that no one in the neighborhood had ever told him this, since to strangers it was always, for some reason, the key piece of information about me.

"Did your son play at Dewey?" he said.

I nodded.

"Baseball is a beautiful game," he said. "In the spring I go down to the field at Dewey from time to time and watch practice."

"Practice?" I said.

"They're more pleasing to me than the games. The games are too emotional, too chaotic, at least when kids are playing. In practice, there's nothing at stake, and everything is very formalized, very structured, the coach points to the right fielder and then hits a ball to him. Very relaxing."

Though I had seen at least the tag end of perhaps dozens of Jack's high-school baseball practices, and found them completely unremarkable, I enjoyed this heretical thought; it made Ferdinand seem all the more endearingly foreign.

"Do you have children?" I said.

He shook his head.

"Were you married?" As soon as I asked this, I realized it might be an insensitive question, since there had never been any evidence, since he had lived in Belmont, of a wife.

"No," he said. "Never."

And I had a sudden idea that perhaps he was gay; it would not have explained anything about reporters asking questions about him, of course, but it would have explained to some extent his absence from the social life of a small, conservative town like ours.

I have of course met many outwardly gay people through work, and I'm sure many more of whose homosexuality I was unaware. While I consider myself quite free of prejudice, I must admit that I am frankly uncomfortable alone in a room with a gay man. I'm sure it shows. I don't know what it is I am afraid will happen, and I am conscious that my guarded behavior and my feelings are absurd; but I consider this attitude so much a part of my generational breeding that it is like a lisp or a tic, too difficult ever to truly correct. I couldn't stop it any more than I could stop myself from standing up in a restaurant when a woman leaves the table.

"Just never fell in love?" I said.

"Oh, yes, I've been in love," Ferdinand said. "But one thing or another interfered."

Now I felt as if I were prying. Nervously I glanced down at my watch and saw how late it was.

"How are you feeling now?" Ferdinand said.

"Better," I said. "In fact, I should really go back home. I've inconvenienced you enough."

I rose, and as I waited for him to cross the room and see me out, I understood what it was that I had first found peculiar about the house. There were no photographs anywhere in it. You don't realize how rare this is, I suppose, until you see it. Perhaps it is a more distinctly American custom than I realized, decorating a home with photos of one's family, or of vacation spots, or homely events like graduations and weddings. Or, just as likely, my idea of what a home should look like was too informed by the walls of my own house, which were covered with Ellie's prints of everything from family snapshots to ocean sunsets to Manhattan street scenes. Still, it seemed peculiar to me that in the home of a man my age should be absolutely no residue of a past. Another man might have taken Ferdinand's place in there the next day and not have felt that anything was particularly amiss. Even the large painting on the wall across from the picture window was a handsome abstract, a peaceful confusion of blues and reds, rather than a portrait.

Ever polite, Ferdinand held the kitchen door and then walked out behind me. It was around five-thirty, and the day had cooled just slightly.

"Well, I can't thank you enough for your hospitality," I said. "Who knows, you probably saved me from making myself even sicker."

"I hope you feel better," he said. "It was a nice excuse, though, for a little visit."

"We should do it again sometime."

"Absolutely. Any time. Before long, we'll both of us just be two old men with nothing to do all day."

"True enough," I laughed.

"Really, though. We have quite a bit in common. It's shocking that it's taken us this long to meet. After all, here we are, arrived at the same point in life, and in the same place."

I believe he winked as he said this, standing just outside his door, on the step above me. He looked healthy and at home in the sunlight, which was noteworthy only because he seemed to have gone to such lengths to reproduce, in his living room anyway, the atmosphere of a cavern. I smiled, shook his hand, and went through the gate. I heard the kitchen door click shut behind him as he went inside.

Our homes were no more than two hundred yards apart. Still feeling a feverish chill, I walked back slowly, to give myself a chance to reflect on what had just passed. Ferdinand was a neighbor, a good man, if a little affected, with whom I had passed a pleasant hour; I tried to bring out of myself, then, the reason for my undeniable feelings of guilt and unease. What came to the surface was a sense of shame—shame for knowing that I was trying to obtain information from Ferdinand, even though it was innocent, rudimentary information, on false pretenses, and shame for that very falseness, since it meant that I had at least subconsciously given in, decided that he must be hiding something, and approached him from that perspective. Perhaps it was that very shame over my dishonesty that led me, when I arrived home, to tell Ellie only that I had gone out for a walk because I was bored. I endured a slight scolding and meekly had my temperature taken.

What was my original interest in the cultivation of this friendship? For although I had a dim ulterior motive, friendship is what it became—I looked forward to seeing him (though our encounters were usually dictated by chance, the size of Belmont greatly reduced the odds of our running into each other), and when I did see him, I enjoyed the level and the tenor of our conversation. It was altogether relaxed and natural, if a bit more formal than I was used to—though I suspected that no matter how close one became to Ferdinand, his manner would always remain somewhat formal. Still, charming as he was, we had been neighbors for seven years without developing more than a nodding acquaintance. Why was I pursuing it now?

Of course it was the *Newsday* reporter, and the hint, false or not, he had given me of a secret life for the reticent Ferdinand. This acknowledgment accounted for the general guilt I began to feel, not only when Ferdinand and I were talking but, increasingly, in any moment of idleness, at work, at home, on the train. Still, I would not let this investigation go. My career in advertising—a form that I had to admit had outstripped my own creative powers years before—was ending, and my absence would not create a ripple among my younger successors, who did not even consider themselves my successors; my presence at home after my retirement was going to leave me, I knew, bored and psychologically weakened, and all at the expense of my wife's private life; I felt estranged from my only son, not by anger or resentment or anything at all personal but by a peculiarly modern American force that had caught him up and begun sweeping him away from me and my meager powers of assistance about the time he threw his first Midget League curveball at the age of twelve. I meant to get at this secret about Ferdinand, not because I meant to expose him but because, at that time, I desperately coveted the empowering feeling of knowing some important thing that nobody else knew.

I was sitting in my office with the door closed, with my back to the work on my desk, when my thoughts were interrupted by the long, high beep of the intercom. I pushed the button.

"Mr. Trowbridge?" Caroline said.

"Yes?"

"Jack."

I switched lines. "Jack?"

"Hey, Dad, how are you?"

His voice had a stuffed-up quality, as if he had just woken up. It was about eleven-thirty.

"Where are you?" I said. "Are you home?"

"Yeah, it's a travel day. I have to be on the team flight to Chicago in about an hour and a half. Hey, I got your message, I'm sorry I didn't call back before."

"No trouble. That's what happens when you work nights, eh?"

"What? Oh, yeah. I guess you're right."

There were noises in the background on his end.

"Do you have company there?" I said.

"What? No, nobody's here. Just me."

There was a pause.

"So I thought you threw well against L.A. the other day."

"Yeah, that wasn't bad. I just need the work, you know? If I

73

start getting some regular innings, I can stay in a groove. This once-every-ten-days thing is no good for anybody."

"You're sort of permanently rusty, that way," I said.

"Exactly."

"And how's your shoulder feeling?"

He didn't answer right away. "A little stiff," he said. "Don't tell my manager."

I laughed. "Okay, I won't."

"So what's new with you?"

"Not very much. I'm only here for another month or two, you know, before I'm put out to pasture."

"That's right, that's right. I keep forgetting that."

"And there's a big retirement bash for me on October first, at the Park Lane Hotel here. I checked the schedule, and you're in Cincinnati that night, so don't worry, you're excused from coming."

"Oh, hey, I'm sorry I'll miss it."

"You shouldn't be. But the end of August, you know, you're in to play the Mets. How about if your mother and I come in and see you?"

"Sure, absolutely. Just tell me what night and I'll set aside some tickets."

"Well, we'll talk closer to the date," I said.

"Okay. Listen, I should go, I'm not packed or anything. Say hello to Mom for me, all right?"

"Sure will. Good luck in Chicago. I'll be watching."

"Okay, great. Bye."

"Goodbye."

I hung up and tried to imagine that apartment, with a woman in it or without, it didn't make any difference to me. I pictured it as a mess, with clothes on the floor and the shades down, dominated by a television; but I realized that these few details were drawn from his adolescent years, which was the last time I had had a good enough idea of the circumstances of his life to be able to set it in my imagination. I hadn't seen any of Jack's homes since his Philadelphia apartment in 1985; he had lived in five different cities since then, and, within my mind, it was as if I'd lost the scent of his trail. I had large sections of the Braves schedule, which I kept folded in my wallet, committed to memory, because it was the only certain, if vague, way to keep track of him—Chicago, then Pittsburgh, then Philadelphia, then back to Atlanta, then to San Francisco, and on and on. He had not been back to Belmont at all in five years. I tried to make a regular but not too persistent effort to keep in touch with him by phone when he was home in Atlanta; and he always responded, though not right away, if only out of a desire not to hurt my, and Ellie's, feelings. We were very careful of each other's feelings now, in fact; perhaps it was a useful measure of the tenuousness of our bond that a fight between us would have been a very serious risk indeed.

I went to get myself some coffee. In the hallway where the machine was kept, along with the water cooler and the bulletin board, which was tirelessly annotated by young creative-side employees awaiting more fruitful ideas, three of the firm's copywriters, Joe Schultz, Davis McKinney, and Theresa Herbst —an attractive young woman, unusually prim and conservative for her age, who was known, though I believe she was unaware of it, as the Naughty Librarian, an irresistible reference to that something about her that was strongly suggestive of a secret life, a life of sin and daring—were having an animated, caffeine-fueled discussion, which they brought up short when they saw me.

"As you were, people, as you were," I said, pouring milk into the bottom of my black Glencairn mug.

"How's it going, Gene?" McKinney said.

"Okay, for a lame duck," I said.

They stood around uncertainly. They had the unmistakable look of writers on deadline, a kind of misapplied energy in every little thing they did, shifting their weight, jingling change in their pockets. McKinney was flapping the bottom of his tie between his fingers, as if trying to brush something off his shirt.

"Listen," I said, "don't let me interrupt you. I'm not your principal. What were you all going on about?"

They looked at one another. "Nothing work-related, I'm afraid," Schultz said finally. "We've been having this kind of informal competition for a while, to see who can come up with the one thing it would be the most difficult to create an effective campaign for."

"We went through all the hard products," the Naughty Librarian said. "Adult diapers, douches, septic systems, all the stuff no one wants to hear about. But products are all too easy."

"Davis came up with home rectal exams," Schultz said, "but we decided that imaginary products are disqualified."

"Not in the Olympic spirit, or something," McKinney said, in a mock sulk.

"So we moved on into the realm of the abstract," Schultz said. "Somebody suggested the seven deadly sins. But you know what?"

"Piece of cake?" I said.

"Utter *gâteau*. We had about ten great tag lines for greed in the first five minutes. 'Survive with the fittest.' "

" 'You've got it coming to you,' " the Naughty Librarian said.

" 'Dow lets you do great things,' " McKinney said.

"So where does that leave you?" I said, amused.

"Here's the beauty part," Schultz said. "We finally realized that the hardest thing to sell is virtue, because you can't create a need for it. So we're just putting a note on the board here, inviting entries for the best PSA campaign for each of the Ten Commandments. A true brainteaser, no? Want to enter?"

I laughed. "By some chance," I said, "you all wouldn't be working on the new spots for Van Allen?"

"Well," Schultz said. "Technically."

"And when is your deadline?"

"Davis?" Schultz said.

McKinney looked at his watch. "Four hours and six minutes," he said. "But we are fully confident."

"He speaks for us," the Naughty Librarian said.

I shook my head reproachfully, but I wasn't really worried, though Van Allen Electronics was a big account, nor was I surprised. Some people can only do good work the way these three were doing it. It's a common phenomenon in advertising, and always has been. These three were good at their job, and what was more, they knew themselves; in another hour or two, when they were riding that wave of giddiness just before it broke into panic, they would come up with something perfect precisely because they couldn't afford to think too hard about it.

It had been many years since I myself spent late nights— sometimes whole nights—in the office; but even in memory, to see people engaged in the creation of a new campaign, or to be engaged in it yourself, is a remarkable thing. Every night, in some agency or another in New York, young men and women go through consuming, rapturous, intensely personal creative agonies, in search of the most accessible aesthetic achievements. Despite the air of fearful urgency—the belief, often and paradoxically enough, that it is already too late to come up with anything—people still have their own creative pathologies, their pen-counting and desk-arranging rituals, the set of procrastinations they must exhaust before getting any work done. (Chief among these is the invention and subsequent mastery of ridiculously arcane "sports"; there is one man at AAK who can shoot a rubber band at a distance of twenty-five feet into an empty pencil holder seven out of ten times. Everyone in the agency knows this, and yet whenever he's on deadline, he rushes around the office trying to get someone to bet him he can't do it.) They are ecstatic when they come up with something that pleases them (for in that happy hour of the early morning, there is no one to please but each other), and when they know they have failed, their suffering is genuine and terrible, far greater than the simple fear that their job might be imperiled. It may seem ridiculous to those who don't know, but the stakes for these people are very high. The stakes are artistic, nothing less.

What are these if not the raptures of creation, of art? There are a few significant differences; for one, ad people tend to work in pairs or threesomes, so their solitude is not quite complete. Everyone in the business thinks, when he starts out, that he would prefer to work alone, but you find out very quickly how grossly you can deceive yourself when you are both artist and audience. The essential difference, of course, is in the copywriter's or artist's relation to the product he is promoting. But this relationship, in the age of advertising's dizzying ascendancy, is harder and harder to locate. The increasing obliqueness of the connection between advertisement and product was changing the language, as it were, of my business—changing it into a language I was too old to learn. This was no doubt one of the reasons why I had evolved, over the last ten or fifteen years, into a kind of agency figurehead, so valuable in public and administrative roles, yet creatively, as it were, left behind—as these three employees knew. In the parlance of my own generation of ad men, I was an extinct volcano, once mighty, but with my own creative fires burned out forever.

The Liberty Campaign

When I was in the position of McKinney and Herbst and Schultz, the self-imposed parameters of advertising were different; while it was all right to be clever, being too clever was frowned upon, forbidden in fact, as an elevation of your own importance over the importance of the product, its virtues, and its identifiability. The client was your boss; the relationship was quite clear, and it informed the work that you did. Now the elevation of cleverness, of art, is complete; both clients and consumers have been swayed to play the game just as ad men wanted it to be played all along. The quality of the ad, rather than of what it advertises, is the important thing. The high esteem in which people hold, say, a Nike basketball sneaker is simply a matter of reflected glory from the spectacularly creative ads for it; I'd go so far as to say that Nike's sales are directly a reward for the pleasure given by the ads they have commissioned. As a consequence, most of the hot young creative people today do what they do with almost no regard for the product—or the product's existence gives them a form to work in, like writing a sonnet. The idea is to come up with a flashy look, a capsule drama, an often self-referential joke, or a pop philosophy, with which the fortunate product might then be juxtaposed. It seems useless to deny that these young people have in the process come up with a new, if miscegenated, form, one that is at the center of our culture.

As in any discipline, eighty or ninety percent of advertising is the worst sort of crap. But when we speak of the people who make the best ads, is it useful to distinguish them from artists? True, they serve a master, but that service is to them a sly joke, a necessary condescension; you might as well complain that Mozart served the king. I've come across many people who think it tragic that America has siphoned off so much of its artistic capacity into the business world in this way—that some of its best creative minds were harnessed to a handful of people's desire for profit. But I don't think the ad people themselves look at it that way, at least not anymore. They do what they do, more or less anonymously except to their peers; their client is merely an opening night audience, their client's profit a pure, pleasing gauge of their own success. And even if you impute to them the least cynical point of view possible, if their aim is to shape the culture, to please and divert the greatest number of people (as was Mozart's aim, as was Dickens's aim), then for a Schultz or a McKinney or a Naughty Librarian is it more greatly to be desired to be the person who wrote a respected novel, or to be the person who wrote "Just Do It"? It's true that some ungraspable instinct, some snobbery perhaps, keeps me from agreeing completely with all this; but it's hard to argue why, and in any case, one mustn't begrudge the young their point of view. It might also be born of the fact that I cannot live in this world of supreme self-belief because I am just not an artist.

When I was in my twenties, before I was married, I wanted, like many in advertising or publishing or other word-related trades, to be a novelist. I would have had no stomach for obscurity; I wanted to be widely read through the sheer contagion of respect, like John Steinbeck or Irwin Shaw or Hemingway. But there was no particular book I yearned to write; even my daydreams about writing ran mostly toward postpublication fame and admiration. I never even made any false starts. Eventually, I admitted that, while I could write well, I really had nothing valuable to say. For a while, this seemed to me the tragic, central secret of my own existence. But it doesn't trouble me anymore. It would have shamed me greatly to write something mediocre. With the conservatism of old age, I find, comes an increasing belief in aristocracy, particularly the aristocracy of genius.

My retirement dinner was to be a fancy gathering of about one hundred and twenty people, industry bigwigs, friends, past and present clients, and the like. I knew little else about how it would be organized; while it was not meant to be a surprise to me, of course, the details were kept from me as a courtesy. I did know that there would be speeches; my old partner Dana Bradley from Ogilvy & Mather would say something, Tim Kellogg, one of the firm's two surviving founders, would get up to bore us interminably, and no doubt they would dragoon a few others. Tim is a good man, and in casual conversation he is quite witty and charismatic, but depth of character does not correspond to a person's ability to deliver an entertaining speech. It was this cruel fact that haunted me as I spent my last, increasingly formless weeks at AAK trying to decide what I would say to the assembled myself.

Since I dreaded the thought of a teary, sentimental evening, overemphasizing our own and our business's importance and too redolent of death, what I would have liked most was to give a funny speech, full of jabs at myself and the other speakers, disarmingly, even bravely flippant. But what a happy few will even dare to try to be funny in a room filled with one hundred and twenty people! Far easier to be maudlin, to exude sadness and lack of regret. To go out with a series of unfunny jokes, to have people smiling weakly and looking at their watches below the table as I struggled through my farewell, was too undignified even to imagine.

In my lifetime, I had delivered five or six speeches to groups that size—at industry lunches, at awards banquets, once, in fact, at the memorial service for Jim Acker thirteen years ago—and, if pressed, I would have had to admit that I wasn't much good at it, and disliked it for that reason. My deliberations now were complicated, though, by my remembering that the one truly successful speech I ever gave was the one occasion when I tried to be funny. In 1966, when AAK was just breathing regularly again after its fast ascent to the top decile of the advertising world following several years of struggle (ad agencies, like the products they represent, suddenly and mysteriously get hot, and those are heady days indeed), I was asked by Jim Acker to coordinate an agency-hosted convention in the Bahamas. Billed as a kind of informal think tank for agency people and their client representatives to discuss how they might be better served, it was in fact a large-scale, spendthrift, tax-deductible party, a way to thank all our clients in the lustiest possible fashion for helping us get over the top, and to maintain their positive feelings toward us in order, as Acker put it to me, to keep the wave from breaking. I think he also conceived it, in a more personal light, as a bonfire to the gods of business—it was, tax-deductible or no, a monstrous expense—and we conducted ourselves in the most bacchanalian way, in keeping, or so we liked to imagine, with the spirit of the times.

Jack was not quite three, so Ellie stayed at home in Manhattan with him. Like so much in the business world, regardless of the essential frivolity of this undertaking, it was vitally important to the agency that the whole thing go off well. It went off splendidly. By planning for weeks, arriving in Nassau two days early, and running like a Greek messenger from event to event to shepherd things along, I managed to give the weekend just the right tone, just the right slightly breathless pace, so that everyone could enjoy themselves to the limits of their capacities and still be able to say to themselves that they had gotten some work done, had learned something. Various seminars were held in the late morning and early afternoon; cocktails and dinners constructed around island themes were scheduled for the evenings, and I made sure to leave plenty of free time. I knew that everyone flying home on Sunday with a hangover would feel indebted to AAK, and I knew that on Monday, when the congratulatory phone calls began to come in, I would be sitting in my office overhearing them, if only in my imagination.

It was one of the great triumphs of my career, and thus of my young life, and if it had a slight whorehouse quality, it didn't bother me then and it doesn't much bother me now. And so when, at the gala dinner in the hotel ballroom on Saturday night, I was summoned to the dais with much whistling and foot-stomping, I had no reason not to feel all confidence in my abilities. Fueled by alcohol, as was everyone in the ballroom, I managed to give a funny, mostly impromptu address, gentlemanly, bawdy, replete with references to unnamed attendees' drunken exploits or embarrassments, any one of which only a few people could have understood, but at which everyone roared. I remember less of the speech itself than of the reaction to it; but that was probably as true the morning after as it is today.

In Nassau, then as now, it was legal to gamble. When the dinner wrapped up at about eleven-thirty, very few men were ready to retire. So we repaired to the hotel casino, where, scotch in hand, I camped out at a craps table. I was not a complete rube—I knew some rudimentary gambling strategies, some basic odds—but I had had very little high-stakes experience, on top of which I was drunk. In the next four hours, I won just over three thousand dollars.

Everyone should be, though perhaps not everyone is, entitled to at least one such moment in life, when it seems that all the world's attentions and all of fortune's favor have converged upon you, and all you can do is win. Only those who have been through something like it, I think, would understand how literally invincible I felt. At the back of my mind was the thought—absurdly premature, but correct, as it turned out—that I had gone a long way in the past two days toward sewing up the job as creative director of AAK. Around five A.M., though not at all tired, I somehow had the good sense to stop and cash out. The Bahamian woman who had been replenishing my scotch glass was giving me, and my winnings, looks of increasingly fervent and open admiration; and there was nothing to stop me from claiming her, really, because I felt that anything I might want was mine to claim. But I had an impulse of a more solitary sort.

I stuck my money in my pocket, walked off the hotel terrace and down to the beach, just twenty yards or so away. Leaving my shoes on the patio, I walked along the sand until I was just out of sight of the lights of the hotel, behind some palm trees and empty cabanas, their bright colors washed out by the darkness. The moon, at least in memory, was full, and threw a rope to me across the water. I felt on the verge of everything, in touch for the first time with my adult capabilities. I had a wife and son at home, I was admired by strangers, I was of sufficient importance to have this moon, this sand, this ocean, brought to me just at the moment when I was most able to appreciate them. I took off my suit and walked into the water. Never far from shore, because I have never been a strong swimmer, I did a slow crawl back and forth, loving the light on my arms, loving the lights of the hotel when I came in sight of them. I swam until I was exhausted. I stumbled out of the water, fell on the sand beside my clothes, and passed out.

Never mind that I was awakened rudely some six hours later by the toe of a hotel security guard. Never mind that my back was so painfully sunburned that I couldn't even step under a shower for a full week. That was in some areas the apex for me;

that mysterious foreknowledge of my success in life was sweeter to me than the success itself, when it came. But as I sat in my office, twenty-four years later, and replayed it all for myself once again, it only encouraged me to discard the idea of delivering a humorous speech to mark my own retirement. The elements of its success in Nassau were youth, carelessness, egotism, and innocence, and I felt I had exhausted my claim to all of these.

I could never think for long about what I might say at the Park Lane dinner without working myself into this sort of nostalgic stalemate. Most often I would fall to staring out the window or reading *Adweek;* and sometimes, feeling entitled, I would give up and go home to Belmont an hour or two early. The trains were marvelously empty at that hour as they rocked along the spine of Long Island, the air conditioner cooling the sweat beneath my suit as July turned into August. I would call Ellie from the Belmont train station before driving home, wanting to lessen the surprise, to accustom her gradually to the idea of seeing me at all during hours that normally belonged to her.

I saw Ferdinand several more times, always by chance, though I suspected that we both somewhat shyly made efforts to maximize that chance by going for walks at the same hour, and along the same or intersecting routes. Countess got so she could recognize my scent around corners, and frequently would surprise me by running around a hedge to greet me, heralding the approach of her master. Typically we would stand and talk amiably for a few minutes, critique the weather, compliment the dog, before Ferdinand would invite me to continue the discussion in his home, always politely, always as if for the first time. It fit some sense of propriety, some male reluctance to admit affection, that we never arranged these meetings in any tacit way beforehand. We never phoned each other; or rather, he never phoned me, for his own number, I discovered in a moment of spontaneous interest, was unlisted.

Of course it was not possible for all this to go on without Ellie's knowledge; I had never been in the habit of leaving the house for an hour or two in the evenings for some unspecified location, and it wasn't likely to go unremarked upon now. My disclosure, however, was not full.

"You know who I ran into?" I said to her in the front hall, returning from an evening walk and my second trip to Ferdinand's house. "Albert Ferdinand, from the corner."

"Hmm," said Ellie, unimpressed.

"But I don't just mean I saw him. I was walking by there, and ran into him out with his dog, and he actually invited me into his house."

"Really? Did you go?"

"Sure I went. That's why I've been gone so long, if you were wondering. Who could pass up a chance like that? It's like seeing the inside of Skull and Bones or something."

"Was it nice?" She was less interested than I thought she'd be, considering neither of us had been in the house since the Harpers moved out eight years before.

"It's all right. He lives alone, so it has a bit of a bachelor look to it. But you know what? He turns out to be really a nice man."

"If you say so," she said.

"I do. Quite interesting. He told me he used to live out near Cleveland. Very polite, very droll. I don't know why we never made the effort before to get to know him, you know?"

"He could be a little friendlier." She walked back toward the TV room.

"He's from Brazil," I called after her, a little miffed.

So, while I still hadn't ever mentioned to her the questions asked by the reporter, I didn't have to feel like I was sneaking around, at least not to the same degree. At the same time, I was able to keep the relationship private. In this way I was obliged by Ellie's conspicuous lack of interest. We always met at his place, never at ours; I wondered if he thought this impolite of me, but he never brought it up.

We talked about perfectly ordinary matters, there in his subdued living room, and in retrospect I'm sure these conversations divulged more about my character than his. When it came to political affairs he seemed quite conservative, perhaps a little too much so for my taste but by no means out of step with the rest of the town. He seemed especially fascinated—as was I, to a less passionate degree—by the throes of Eastern Europe in the wake of the stunningly quick and nonviolent collapse of communism that had taken place that past fall. We spent some time debating the future of the Soviet Union in that regard, though he was far better versed in such things than I.

Although he seemed as pleased as I was to run across someone with whom he could seriously discuss such matters, most of our chats concerned topics much less lofty and closer to home. He gossiped, for instance, about our neighbors with a surprising expertise—I had assumed he knew as little about them as they did about him. But he was very observant. He got me to talk more about Pittsfield, and Columbia, and my days in the army, than I had talked in years. He wanted to know about Jack's childhood; one of the traits I most liked in Ferdinand was the sensitive way he seemed able to discern not only the lack of undiluted enthusiasm behind my recounting of all of Jack's triumphs, but the guilt behind that as well.

As for his own background, when I asked him about Brazil he responded freely with unfailingly happy stories about his childhood, his parents, his brothers, his schoolmates, his nanny. They were all entertaining stories, and he told them well, but it was curious to me how they didn't seem specific to what to me was an exotic culture and a foreign land. Most of these boyhood stories could just as easily have been set in New England. Perhaps it was our age that gave our childhoods so much in common, or perhaps the veneer of memory works in similar ways the world over, but I wondered instead if these upbeat stories didn't serve to conceal other hardships, emotional or economic, which he was too proud to recall.

In any case, I didn't think Brazil held the key to the mystery about his past, if only because he was too young when he emigrated to have done anything really notorious. I had a fleeting idea that maybe he had some connections to the Nazi-exile community said to exist there, but I quickly decided that this was a ridiculous conceit, born of ignorance about Brazil and a disgraceful lust for tabloid fodder rather than of even the slightest evidence. I had decided that the suspicions about him had to center around his real estate dealings in Pepper Pike, or perhaps in one of the many towns he had lived in prior to that. Real estate swindles, on the face of them, were disappointingly mundane; but it had to be a sexy one, I thought, if there were newspaper people after him even here at the edge of the country. I did not want to come right out and question him about all this. He volunteered quite a bit anyway and, in one way or another, over the course of a couple of weeks, seemed to account for his whereabouts for the last twenty or twenty-five years.

Even though I was careful to acquire any information about Ferdinand in the most honest and passive way, digesting only what he gave me on his own, the puny and trivial nature of real estate crime exacerbated my guilt over listening to him in that duplicitous way at all. He was being, as far as I could tell, perfectly open with me, and I was deceiving him every moment we were together. Finally, the dishonesty of it became too much for me. I decided that our friendship now outclassed any business indiscretion he might have been accused of. There was only one way to give that friendship its due.

On the night of my fifth or sixth visit to his home, as I rose to go and he rose to see me out, he said something to the effect that it was never too late in life to make new friends. He was sometimes given, unfortunately, particularly after a couple of drinks, to speaking in homilies like that, though his accent did impart a touch of seeming wisdom to them.

"Albert," I said, "there's something I have to tell you, that I should have told you already."

"Oh?" he said.

"Yes. I hope you'll forgive me for not mentioning it right away. There was a newspaper reporter in the neighborhood a while ago, from *Newsday,* and he asked me some questions about you, about your background."

Ferdinand's eyebrows went up, but otherwise he didn't register any great surprise. After a few moments, his face returned to its usual composed, melancholy cast; he looked more thoughtful than worried, so thoughtful in fact that he seemed to have forgotten I was there. I waited nervously beside him, my hand on the open door. The dog walked back and forth between us, expectantly. Ferdinand put his hands behind his back and stood as if at parade rest.

"Of course I didn't tell him anything," I said. "I wouldn't have had anything to tell him, really. But I just kicked him off my property. I thought you should know. You don't have to say anything to me if you don't want to."

"How long ago was this?" Ferdinand said.

"A week," I lied spontaneously. "A week or so." I simply wasn't able to admit to him, for both our sakes, at this crucial moment, that these strange inquiries had come before we knew each other at all, that they had in fact been the basis of our relationship.

He deliberated for another minute, and I wasn't sure what to do. It may have been, I thought, that he was weighing the evidence of my betrayal, deciding whether or not I could be trusted.

"What were the questions?" he said finally.

I repeated them as best I could remember: where was Ferdinand from, what did he do for a living, where did he live before he moved to Belmont.

"Are you sure he was a reporter," Ferdinand said, "and not a policeman?"

"I'm sure," I said, alarmed. "He gave me a business card. I doubt a policeman would go to the trouble."

He took that in and was lost to me for a minute longer. Then he reached out and grabbed me by both shoulders in a comradely manner.

"What a difficult position for you, Gene," he said. "I'm sure it made you suspicious, as it would have anyone. I can't tell you how grateful I am that you came to tell me about it. One has few enough friends in this life, and I have fewer than most, as I'm sure you're aware. I can't tell you what this means to me."

"Do you know what it's all about?" I said.

"I think so. I think so. It's essentially a case of mistaken identity. Despite this country's reputation, you know, people aren't always as fair, as willing to believe foreigners as they ought to be."

I shrugged in agreement.

"All the more reason for me to be grateful to you. You're not an ordinary man, I hope you know that."

"Can you tell me anything about it?" I said.

He pondered for a moment. "Yes, of course," he said. "But it's a long story, and it's late now for both of us. Better to save it for another time, soon. For another night this week."

He held the door open for me. Countess squeezed past him, took two steps outside, and sat down to watch me go.

"I know I can trust you," he said as I walked up the path. "I know you will understand."

Bewildered as I was by this exchange, I felt quite pleased with myself as I walked home, in the middle of the silent street, just beyond the light spilling from the houses on either side. It seemed that I was going to have everything both ways: I had cleared my conscience with Ferdinand by telling him about the reporter, and I had gained his greater trust in the process. It seemed I was very close to being the sole possessor of whatever was Ferdinand's, and thus our neighborhood's, deep secret.

Even that dubious pleasure, though, was to be denied me, for the *Newsday* story appeared at last on the very next day.

I discovered it during my obligatory glance through the paper at the train station, while waiting for Salvatore to pour and seal my two cups of coffee, as he had done every weekday morning for years without needing to be asked. The papers then were full of breathless news about the Middle East, and even the index on page two had been redesigned to give more weight to Persian Gulf news and analysis; local news was crowded into a corner, given little room for summary. Hence the line read only "Belmont man focus of inquiry, p. 17." I flipped quickly to page seventeen and was confronted by a small, grainy black-and-white photograph of Ferdinand's house.

"Two regular," Salvatore said.

I slapped the paper shut as if Salvatore might know what

was in my mind. For some reason I felt great, heart-pounding fear at this point, as if I were complicit in something without ever knowing what it was, as if there were anything at stake for me at all. I reached into my wallet, the paper under my arm, and gave him three singles. "And a *Times,* and a *Newsday,*" I told him, as nonchalantly as possible, as if any noticeable break in my routine would appear suspicious somehow.

The train was already in sight when I reached the platform, and I decided to wait until I was settled, coffee in hand, before looking at the paper again. I can only explain this by comparing it to the way you will go through all the rest of the day's mail before opening the important envelope you have been waiting for, in an effort, usually vain, to collect yourself. Once on the train, I spread the paper open to pages sixteen and seventeen on the seat facing me, opened my first cup of coffee, leaned forward, and read.

The headline was "Belmont Man Suspected of Torture Past: Brazil Officials Say He Lied Way Into U.S.," and with that, my worst, most dimly apprehended fantasies took their first step forward.

A Belmont, L.I., man is a former captain of the Brazilian Army, responsible for the torture of civilian prisoners during the rule of that country's repressive military government of the 60s and 70s, a human rights group says.

Brazil: Never Forget, a group of activists many of whom were jailed and tortured themselves during the years of the military dictatorship, claims that retired real estate developer Albert Ferdinand, who has lived in the quiet suburb for seven years, is in reality Capt. Joao Carvalho da Silva. Capt. da Silva ran a so-called house of horrors—an interrogation center in which detainees were routinely tortured and sometimes executed—in a suburb of Sao Paulo from 1964 until his own mysterious disappearance in 1969. It was widely believed then that da Silva had been murdered as a result of internal struggles within the army.

"Da Silva was a man of casual, well-documented brutality," said Edward Casemiro of BNF. "As part of our effort to track down and identify all of these criminals, we have been searching for him for nearly ten years. We were never satisfied with the rumors about his execution. And now we are positive that we've found him, that the so-called Ferdinand is he."

Despite Casemiro's branding of da Silva as a criminal, the Brazilian government granted amnesty in 1985 to all those accused of human rights violations under the military regime.

Ferdinand himself could not be reached for comment. Suffolk County police said while they were aware of BNF's allegation, this was not a criminal matter and therefore they had no intention to pursue an investigation of their own.

A military junta, believed to have acted with the permission and the support of the United States intelligence community, overthrew Brazil's president, Joao Goulart, on April 1, 1964. The military maintained complete control of the government until 1979, when they were voted out of office in the first free elections held since the coup.

Stunned into thoughtlessness, I carefully folded the papers and put them into my briefcase; when we reached Penn Station

I walked without seeing along the familiar route to the subway. As I ascended the steps into Grand Central terminal, I was startled to realize that I couldn't hear anything—and, of course, an instant after this realization the noise of the cavernous place came bearing down on me again as if on wings. It seemed a deafening babble, every one of the thousands of voices warped by sheer numbers and by the acoustics of the place into a lost sentiment, an incomprehensible, loud clamor that served only to raise everyone's temper to dangerous levels, my own included. And then, as I escaped into the bright sunlight on Lexington Avenue outside the station, I saw that a vocal crowd of twelve or fifteen people was gathered in a circle on the sidewalk, around a woman in a business suit who sat down on the pavement, supported by a mailbox, bleeding from the head. Also within the circle, a man, black and apparently homeless, was being restrained by his arms by two other men, one in a suit and one in the candy-striped shirt of an employee in a pizza or ice cream place. When I asked one bystander what had happened, he told me—over the shouts of the three men and of others in the crowd—that the young woman had been struck by a cab while crossing Lexington and had been knocked unconscious; the man under restraint had been seen going through her purse as she lay in the street. I looked at the middle-aged woman; her eyes were open, but she appeared not to know where she was. Suddenly the volume of the arguing rose abruptly; the man in the suit released his grip on the black man and punched him in the face. The crowd surged forward, on the verge of a brawl. An invisible siren was approaching. I walked away, not anxious to see how it would end. Such street events were not unheard of—the summer heat in particular seemed every year to bring ugly impulses to the surface—but on this morning, it only contributed to my sense that all the demons had been released. I was relieved to reach the lobby doors of my office building.

Over the course of the day I was able to recover, as I imagined it, my equilibrium: this was a small story, I told myself, which few people would see and even fewer remember, concerning a wild and unproven accusation. For the more I thought about it, the more certain I felt that it could not possibly be true, that my own wariness about investing the media with too much trust had turned out to be right, even though I myself had not been consistent in that wariness. I had wanted to know, out of human curiosity, what Ferdinand was believed to have done. Now I knew, and that should be that. It was simply not credible. He was not that sort of man. The whole thing was bound to blow over. I took as evidence of the relative unimportance of the entire matter the fact that my wife hadn't called to ask me if I'd heard about it. Of course, I had no impulse to call her either, because I knew she would only ask me questions that would force me into lying again.

In the most general sense, I was right; but of course the *Newsday* story caused a storm of titillation and pompous outrage within the town of Belmont itself. Some regular *Newsday* reader probably saw it in her kitchen late that morning, going through the paper thoroughly after first scanning the front page, the gossip page, and the afternoon TV listings; and by noon, everyone who spent weekdays at home knew it, and everyone who worked in Manhattan (except me) had been phoned and briefed on it. In fact, I had an idea of what had transpired in town almost the moment I stepped off the train that night. Walking across the cooling asphalt toward my car, listening to the tentative return of birdsong to the trees surrounding the station now that the sense-dulling sun had dropped to the horizon, I ran into Ted Winton, my next-door neighbor, and a passenger on the same train.

"Gene," he said, by way of greeting. I nodded to him, as I stopped and put down my briefcase to look for my keys.

"So," he said. "Hear about our neighbor?"

I tensed just slightly. It is a wonder to me still how quickly I had taken the psychological position that this was my secret, too, that people were after, and I felt on edge, careful not to be caught out in it, even though twelve hours ago I hadn't had any more inkling of it, really, than Ted had had.

"No," I said, trying to look surprised.

"No?" He was pleased. "It seems that that guy Ferdinand, in the old Harper house, has got the law on him. Apparently he's some kind of fugitive, wanted in Brazil for war crimes or something like that, for torturing civilians. Ferdinand isn't even his real name. He's what we used to call a lammister. There's a story about it in *Newsday* today."

It is very difficult to look shocked on cue, but I did my amateur best. Ted looked at me closely, feeling proprietary about this news and its impact, wanting to achieve the maximum effect. I could imagine him already looking forward to telling people about the look on my face, and thus to have even that tiny, private share in an important event. No critic, he seemed well satisfied by my expression.

"Can you believe it?" he said. "A guy like that living right on our god damn street? I suppose now they'll deport him or something."

"No," I said. "I can't believe it. Are they sure it's true?" "They" is a helpful pronoun for conversations such as that one; it can serve to fill great chasms of ignorance.

"Apparently they're sure," Ted said. "I don't know how they know."

I shook my head and stuck my key in the car door.

"I haven't said ten words to the guy since the day he moved in," Ted said hastily, anxious to work that in. "I don't know the guy at all. Really keeps to himself, I think. Ever talk to him?"

In an instant I ran through all the subsequent questions that a truthful answer would lead to, and decided against it. "No," I said. "Just to say hi to."

I drove home the long way, in part to avoid seeing Winton in my rearview mirror the whole time, but mostly in order to come up Fairly Avenue the back way and thus pass by Ferdinand's house. I knew I wouldn't spot him outside, and I didn't expect anything to be different, except maybe my own perception of the place. I just wanted to have a look. What I saw when I turned the corner should not have surprised me, I suppose, had I taken the time to think about it, or known what to think. But there are certain sights that, though commonplace elsewhere and thus familiar as televised or photographed images, are revealed, when they touch down too close to your own home, as the bizarre, frightening, otherworldly violations of the landscape that they truly are.

A dozen or more vehicles of various natures—including two police cars and two television vans, one all the way from Manhattan, marked with expensive logos and topped with satellite equipment—were parked outside Ferdinand's white house, on the far side of the street across from his hedge, in a line that extended around the corner. Nearly everyone who had come in those cars was outside of them now, talking to one another, talking to the policemen, leaning across the hood to stare at the house's dark windows. I slowed down to near walking speed, both to gawk and as a precaution with so many people on the shoulder of the road. The revolving lights of one of the police cars had been left on, as a warning to oncoming traffic; reds and blues flashed down the thick hedge in the dusk. The police stood in a relaxed manner and spoke amiably to the press; their purpose here seemed merely symbolic, to make sure the peace was kept. But there was nothing unruly about this group. No doubt some, if not all, of them had ventured to the front door of the house, but Ferdinand either was not answering or was away from home. They were simply waiting, without knowing what for; they were at a place where something might conceivably happen, and thus doing their jobs.

A painfully bright, portable arc light snapped on near one of the vans; a young, coiffured woman holding a microphone stood in the white glare and taped a piece of her story, just ten seconds or so, perhaps something she had flubbed a bit earlier. When the light snapped off, her whole manner seemed to change; her hands fell to her sides, and her director took the mike from her hand seemingly without her noticing.

This is what it looks like, I thought. This is the American eye. Suddenly I noticed that the crawling pace of my car had begun to attract some attention of its own. Some of the media people were looking back at me; then, as if some sensory alarm were passing inaudibly among them, a few more. As if at some mysterious, invisible signal, some residual, animal instinct of which natural selection has deprived the rest of us, they began to walk toward my moving car, already bending down, their faces already forming expressions of polite intrusion, of apologetic inquiry. Among them was the television reporter, who had grabbed back her microphone. Genuinely frightened, I stepped on the gas and shot past them, around the corner and onto

Fairly Avenue. As I watched in the rearview mirror they fell back quickly, not that interested, apparently, in pursuing me.

Nearly everyone on Fairly—Fran, the Walshes, Bob Locke, the McClements—was standing out on their lawns, watching the commotion from a safe distance. They looked odd and lonely, each of them, standing there in the sunset, as if their houses were on fire. Even Ellie was outside, though in a more reserved posture, sitting with a drink out on our porch, in jeans and sneakers. She shook her head and smiled at me as I got out of the car and walked up the flagstones toward her.

"Can you believe it?" she said. "Did you hear about all this?"

"Just heard about it. Ted Winton told me at the station about the thing in *Newsday*."

"Just incredible," she said, looking back up the street. "What a sight. I was down having a closer look just a couple of minutes ago." From our porch we didn't have a view of Ferdinand's house, but we could see two of the strange cars and the rolling of the police-cruiser lights down the hedges and the pavement in our direction.

Ellie turned her gaze back to our bewildered neighbors lining the street. It was hard to guess what she was thinking; she seemed more grateful for the general diversion than anything else. I think she may have been feeling an ambiguous jealousy toward the legitimate-press photographers and cameramen gathered at the corner—more of their professionalism and air of consequence than of the actual, unimaginative job they were doing, in which, so far as I know, Ellie has never had any interest.

"It's like that John Demjanjuk thing," she said. "Do you remember?"

I watched with her for a minute. Nothing was happening. "Well, I'll go change," I said. "Could you use a drink?"

"Gene?"

"Yes?"

"You didn't have any idea about any of this, did you?" She looked sweetly at me as she said this in her most nonconfrontational tone, trying to make it sound as tossed-off as possible. She wanted to look as if she already knew the answer was no.

"About Ferdinand? No, of course not," I said, a trifle too defensively—conscious, even then, that in terms of dishonesty I was getting in as deep with her as I had ever been. "My God, how could you even think that?"

Caught up in the human appetite for scandal, I had thought—if somewhat guiltily—that I was ready to believe anything I might have clumsily uncovered about Ferdinand. But instead it developed that, in declining to turn away from the unknown, I had taken on more than I could handle; the secret, once out, eclipsed what I thought of as my daily inner life, a source of shadow impossible to look at closely or to escape. The stakes—for him, of course, but in a different way for me as well—were much higher than I had ever supposed. I had entered into a friendship with this man. That friendship had now become a trap for me. Giving way to my own chain of fears, I began to worry that neighbors had seen me go in and out of Ferdinand's house lately—I was certainly unique in doing so—or that Ellie had innocently mentioned somewhere in town that I was becoming good friends with that aloof Hispanic gentleman.

More than that, though, I was haunted by the thought that Ferdinand had not been trying to fool me at all. I don't mean in terms of the facts of his life, but in the matter of his personality.

He was not acting, I felt that instinctively; the way he was when we were together was truly the way he was. What would it mean, then, if someone capable of such beastly, sadistic, dispassionate activity as the newspaper article had hinted at was in fact a pleasant fellow, with various, fairly common charms and foibles, someone to whom I could feel a bond? What did it mean, in a more personal vein, if I was capable of forming a friendship with such a man? Was my ignorance of his past really an excuse, or did it merely miss the point—that I could look into the eyes of a man who represented such extremes of evil and see nothing, absolutely nothing, about him? Or did such behavior, contrary to what we would like to believe, leave no mark on a man for even the most discerning person to spot?

The more I thought about it, over the next few days, the clearer it became that my one hope for recovering my emotional balance lay in the thought that Ferdinand was perhaps totally innocent of all these charges, that it was—as he had hinted to me—a case of mistaken identity. In this spirit, I tried to rekindle my distrust of the powers of knowledge others invested in the press. It did not take long for me to talk myself wholeheartedly into this proposition; my doubt could be characterized as instinctive, in fact, a product of my equally instinctive fear of all that believing Boyd's contentions would lead me to. Even here, though, there was cause for uneasiness; for now Ferdinand's own hopes for salvation were rather too closely allied with my own.

How is it that one human being is capable of inflicting torture on another? This child's question, even put privately to myself, sounded so naive and hollow that it made me ashamed; yet I kept coming back to it. Part of the trouble, I realized, was that I didn't really even know the terms of my own argument; an American citizen, even one who has lived as long as I, has no real call to learn them, after all. What was physical torture, specifically? To what end was it employed? To gather information, naturally, but what sort of information? And who were the victims? What were they accused of? Justly or unjustly? Did that make a difference? My ignorance of Brazil, in political terms, was near absolute. Was the government of this nearby country —presumably an extreme one, if torture was one of their methods—run by extremists of the right or of the left at the time under discussion? Surely I was not alone, at least in my own country, in not having the vaguest idea about this. What had been at stake then, for both torturers and victims, which had led them to such a hellish confrontation? Or does such cruelty necessarily take place in—or even create—a kind of political and moral vacuum?

I had no experience of these things. While on the one hand I could only feel grateful for that, it was galling—as I sat wondering about these matters, in the evenings, in my living room—to think that, at age sixty-four, these fundamental questions of life and death, of good and evil, of the infinitesimal sliver of world history encompassed by my own lifetime, were too hard for me. I kept a book open on my lap, because I did not want Ellie to break my concentration by asking me what I was thinking about, a question I couldn't really have answered. In my mind's eye— just two hundred yards or so away, but out of sight from our windows—was Ferdinand's quiet house, from which I had not seen him emerge since the story had broken. He was in there, though, as one could see lights behind the curtains in the evenings.

The more magnified and distorted these issues became in my own mind, the smaller their significance (as I had originally predicted) to the world at large. Anyone who regularly reads a newspaper knows the neuronlike speed with which media interest shifts; nonetheless, this was a new perspective on it for a town like Belmont that had, as it were, slept for centuries. To the papers and local TV, this was no more and no less than a human interest story, substantially identical to stories from the weeks before about a man arrested for abusing his foster children over in Islip, or a Mineola teacher who was fired for deflowering one of his tenth-grade students. These stories could be ground down and poured into the same mold: the message they tirelessly conveyed, regardless of details, was that you can never know your neighbor, that there is delicious weirdness going on all around your house. On the day after the *Newsday* article, the vigil of a dozen or so vehicles outside Ferdinand's home had dwindled to four; on the day after that, to three; and on the next day, and every day thereafter, there had been one lone blue Dodge van, unmarked, parked near the intersection. This was creepier, to me, than the original onslaught had been. No one ever seemed to occupy the driver's seat of the van; presumably the back contained some people, whether policemen or reporters or electronic surveillance experts it was impossible to know. Perhaps it was filled with guns. Or, maybe, at any given moment, it was simply empty—only very late at night, and through careful vigilance, could you see some perfectly ordinary-looking man knock on the back door of the van and switch places with someone equally nondescript. The blue van, whose engine was never heard, was to remain opposite Ferdinand's house around the clock for the next two weeks.

I could learn the necessary history anywhere; but the more I thought about it, the clearer it became to me that the only possible source of answers to all the gaps in knowledge and the confused self-recriminations that were really plaguing me was Ferdinand himself. There were questions, of course, that I wanted to put to him. But beyond that, I thought optimistically that just in seeing and hearing him again, this time with full attention and sharpened senses, all that had escaped me before, all that pointed to his true nature, would be laid bare; and thus I could attribute my prior ignorance and lack of discernment to simple laziness, to the kind of automatic pilot of one's faculties that is engaged in any normal social interaction. I would, now that I was paying attention, surely see instantly what I had missed before. What I wanted was to be able to judge, confidently and accurately, his innocence, for that would take me off the hook completely. But if I saw the opposite in him, so be it; the important thing was to reestablish my ability to see.

It irritated me to know that I couldn't just wash my hands of him, that my own self-knowledge depended on him now even to that small degree; but I was not long in accepting it. What inhibited me in a more practical way was the presence of Ellie, and more particularly of the blue Dodge van parked at the end of Fairly Avenue. Whoever was inside there would not look upon my knocking on Ferdinand's door, and being admitted, in a kindly light; and I could not risk being exposed by them, being questioned—however satisfactory and innocent my answers—in front of Ellie or the neighbors. In fact, my whole aim, at least until I could get everything sorted out in my own mind, was not to be questioned by anyone at all.

Then, on a Saturday afternoon, I heard the sound, on the street outside our house, of an engine struggling to move in low gear. I stood up from the couch to look out the windows and saw the blue van creeping up the street. For a moment I thought its occupants were brazenly looking in on me and the other neighbors. But I leaned a little forward and saw, a hundred feet or so ahead of the van, Ferdinand and Countess, walking at their usual stately pace. They moved as if unaware there was anything behind them; Ferdinand stopped, hands behind his back, and examined the sky with a sailor's squint as he waited for the dog to urinate in the gutter. He was not conceding anything, it seemed, at least not to the extent that I had taken it for granted he would. I made a mental note of the time.

Sunday, at around that same hour, I went out for a walk, along the route that I knew Ferdinand and Countess would take. As long as I appeared nonchalant about it, I reasoned, no one looking on—from the van, from a living-room window—could interpret our running into one another as anything but a chance meeting. Excited and nervous, feeling clever, I walked around the corner and down Smallwood Road.

My cover, such as it was, was of course instantly blown by the dog, who ran ahead to greet me like a long-lost friend, her behind wagging crazily. I stopped in front of the Baldwins' house and scratched her head as Ferdinand, looking pleased to see me though somewhat drawn as well, approached. The sunlight reflected off the windshield of the van as it idled, far up the street, visible to me over his shoulder.

"Gene," he said. There was something in his voice—past gratitude, past dignified apology for the trouble he'd caused— that set the tone for that conversation by instantly making me feel sorry for him. Reading about him, discussing him with my wife, had been one thing; but confronted with the sight of the man himself—sixty-six years old, blinking in the sunlight, idiosyncratic, trying to relax, perhaps too neatly dressed to walk his dog, being openly followed in his own neighborhood by one or more strangers in a menacing blue van—how was it possible not to feel for him? I said nothing, only smiled and, not wanting to commit myself in any way, returned my attentions to the dog.

"I've been wanting to talk to you," he said. "I know you

probably felt you couldn't come over. I wanted to call you, but I didn't know if that might make things awkward for you at home."

"Well," I said reflexively, "I appreciate that." Then, wanting to say something just to deflect the stare—patient, knowing, weary, waiting for me to reveal myself—which he had fixed on me, I said to him, "Who's in the van?"

He frightened me for an instant by turning around and staring at the blank vehicle along with me, as if to include its passengers in the conversation. "I don't know," he said. "They haven't chosen to show themselves. My only concern was whether they might want to kill me, but since they obviously don't, I don't really care who they are, because I have nothing to fear. I am innocent."

He had worked in that last, I felt, as a gesture of friendship, to get me off the hook, to relieve me of the burden of having to ask the question that hung between us. It was touching, in fact —all the more so because he did not declare his innocence in any impassioned way, but unobtrusively, so as not to call attention to the favor he was doing me.

"You are innocent," I repeated. "All these things being printed about you are untrue."

He looked a little annoyed at my apparent objectivity, at the fact that I did not take his innocence for granted. "For believing such things about a friend," he said testily, "for being as susceptible as the average man to the fearsome power of the newspapers and of hysteria in general, I forgive you."

I couldn't help smiling at this locution, but only for an instant. "Then why all this," I said, aware that I was mouthing some *National Enquirer*–like party line, but pressing on all the same. "Why would they say all this about you if it wasn't true in at least some measure? It can't all be just a coincidence?"

The wind rattled the leaves as we stood there on the side-walk, under the hot sun. Countess lay down on the small strip of unkempt grass between the pavement and the white fence of the Baldwin house.

"I have to apologize to you for one thing," he said. "It's one of the reasons I was so anxious to see you. I did lie to you about something, or rather, I haven't told you the whole truth about it. I hope when you hear it, you'll understand why." He paused, wanting, I think, to force me to show some sign of engagement.

"What's that?" I said finally.

"About the circumstances under which I came to this coun-try. I told you that I came here after college, which is true, but I came illegally. I come from a wealthy family, and at that time, in the late forties, after the war, there was a lot of persecution of the higher families in Brazil. Perhaps you know about all this?"

"No," I said. "I don't really know anything about it."

"Ah," he said, smiling, "well, that's common enough. I can certainly see how that kind of life, the constant worrying about governmental change, worrying about falling out of favor with political sentiment, must seem very far away to someone who grew up in this country. In any case, suffice it to say that at-tempts were made on the lives of members of my family. I didn't want to stay there and be killed, but since Brazil and America were war allies, I couldn't be granted political asylum here. So I entered this country illegally, and have lived here ever since. Ferdinand, by the way, is not the name I was born with. But by now I have lived with this name twice as long as with my given one."

"But that was forty years ago," I said. "What does all that have to do with these accusations? I understood that the things they're talking about happened in the sixties."

"Well, unfortunately, there isn't as much of a connection as

either of us would expect. As far as I can tell, these leftists from
Brazil are searching for a man of roughly my age and roughly
my physical description, in spite of the fact that he is generally
believed to have been killed twenty years ago. They suspect that
in reality he fled to the United States. In their researches, they
uncovered the fact that I am a Brazilian, living here illegally
under an assumed name. And from this they have concluded
that I must be this da Silva."

He looked at me, intently but calmly—the calm of a man
who knows he is untouchable, either because of his innocence
or for some other reason. The soul of him, which I had imagined I would coax out in his face now that I had cause to look
hard enough, was as hidden from my sight as ever. I didn't know
what to believe. It cheered me to think he might be innocent.

He placed his hand softly against the center of his chest. "I
am not he," he said. "Of course, you see how difficult that basic
fact is for me to prove, not only as a philosophical problem but
because I can't risk exposing myself as an illegal alien."

A car turned the corner and rolled past us down to the end
of Smallwood Road; and as suddenly as that I was frightened, I
had been out here far too long, I realized that what I thought
was a safe, private way for me to learn more about Ferdinand
and his past was in fact going on in public, in plain sight of the
neighbors or of anyone who happened to drive by. On top of
which, I wasn't sure what, if anything, I had learned. I felt
exposed; I wanted to bring this conversation to a stop, and get
away.

"Of course, I understand their need for revenge," he said. "I
understand it perfectly. The Brazilians, I mean. That was a terrible, brutal period in Brazil's history, and it ended a relatively
short time ago. I understand their need to catch all the da Sil-
vas, their psychological need to catch and pronounce judgment

on their own jailers. Death cheats them of this. But that thirst has caused them to go too far. I try to maintain my sympathy for them, even though I am the victim, temporarily, of their zeal. It was a bloody, hate-filled twenty years or so, and one can't expect them to emerge from it with their charitable souls intact. That much I know, even just from following it in the papers here. I'll tell you more about it when we see each other again."

He looked at me. "But I'm sure you have to get back home," he said.

I nodded.

"I'm glad we ran into each other," he said. "But, you know, I need to know that you forgive me for having lied to you, and about something so very fundamental as my name. But I hope you see why I needed to do it. Besides, it's been so integral to my life for so long now that it hardly qualifies as a lie anymore."

I smiled weakly, looking furtively over his shoulder to see if anyone else was on the street.

"Do you forgive me?" he said again.

Desperate to break away, I said, "Well, sure."

He beamed. "Ah, well," he said. "Then it's been a good day after all. Come," he said to the patient dog, and the two of them continued up the street. A few moments later, as I stood there, the van came by, its driver turning to stare unabashedly at me as it crept past.

The next night, Monday, there was a Braves game to watch, in the course of which something curious happened. The Braves had played a fifteen-inning extravaganza the day before, in which every pitcher except Jack was used; this made it much more likely that he would appear in the game that night, at least if the Atlanta starter got into any trouble. With the Braves behind 3–1 in the seventh inning, their starting pitcher, visibly tiring, walked the leadoff hitter for the Cardinals. On the television appeared a brief shot of Jack taking off his indigo warm-up jacket and beginning to toss a ball lightly in the bullpen.

"Ellie," I called.

She came dutifully into the living room, still carrying a *Time* magazine folded open to a story she was reading, and sat in her chair, touching me affectionately on the shoulder as she passed. She cared little for baseball, but came as willingly to the TV at times like this as she had come to his more important high-school games, sometimes secretly reading in the stands when Jack wasn't on the field.

The Atlanta pitcher got the next man on a fly ball all the way to the base of the wall in left field, but followed that with another walk, on four straight pitches. The Braves manager emerged from the dugout, hands in his back pockets so that his stomach preceded him as he moved steamboatlike toward the mound; halfway there, he turned in the direction of the bullpen and tapped his right arm with his left hand. At that signal, Jack stopped throwing and trotted across the field toward the mound.

"Here he is," I said, nervous as always. As the broadcast went to a commercial, I could hear in the background the noise of the crowd in Atlanta's Fulton County Stadium—a kind of prolonged, not entirely amenable mutter—that followed the stadium public-address man's announcement of Jack's entry into the game.

During the commercial, Ellie went back to her reading, and I went into the kitchen to replenish my scotch.

Our son's familiar expression, the squint of concentration he had had since the age of about six, filled the television screen. The first batter got a lucky hit, an infield single deep in the hole

110

between shortstop and third base, to load the bases. Three pitches later Jack delivered a curveball that bounced in front of the plate and rolled all the way to the stands, allowing a run to score. A kind of moan went up from the crowd, which was much larger than usual because it was a promotion night at the stadium, at which every paid attendee received for free something called a "sports watch." Two pitches later Jack had walked the second batter. The next Cardinal singled cleanly, scoring two runs and making the score 6–1. The moaning, which had never really abated, grew slightly louder, and angrier, at the spectacle of Jack's failure. The camera showed a close-up of his red face as he stared in at the catcher, trying to concentrate and to tune out the threatening noise. The announcers agreed with each other that Jack seemed to have absolutely no movement tonight on any of his pitches. He walked the next hitter to load the bases again.

At that point, if not before, the Braves manager would normally come disgustedly out of the dugout again, take the ball from Jack, slap him on the butt, and turn things over to a new pitcher. But now, with the game probably already out of reach for Atlanta, their manager did nothing. The camera showed him leaning stoically against the side wall of the dugout, his hands in the pockets of his warm-up jacket, looking as if he were trying, between the cap pulled low over his eyes and the folds of flesh around his neck, to make his own face disappear. Jack appeared to be trying resolutely not to glance over at him, though he was probably wondering as much as anyone why he had been stranded out there. Perhaps it was because the game was effectively over and things couldn't get any worse; perhaps the other Atlanta relievers were so arm-weary from Sunday's game that the manager didn't want to risk an injury by bringing any of them in; or perhaps there was a more perverse, sacrificial purpose, to let things proceed to their awful conclusion, for the woeful team, for the fans, for himself, and for Jack in particular.

The catcher came out to try to calm Jack down. By this time, the crowd of 45,000 or so was in a paroxysm of anger; many were streaming toward the exits, but a surprising number were staying, filled with bitterness and with the thirty-ounce cups of beer that are the staple at ballparks everywhere. The drama of the game itself had ended; now, finding their strength in night and anonymity and numbers, they were intent on venting their darkest passions, joyfully. What these passions were, from what place they could have grown, it was impossible to know. The TV cameras showed shots of the crowd, their faces twisted, many of them smiling with pleasure at finding themselves a part of this rare festival of bad feeling. That it was impossible to hear clearly any one of these individual shouts in the forest of sound only made the scene appear all the more ominous.

Utterly unhinged now, Jack hit the next Cardinal batter in the leg with a wild fastball. Determined to throw the next hitter a strike, he grooved one right over the plate, and the bat met it with the sound of an ax. By the time the ball landed in the right-field seats—a grand slam home run—the bowl-shaped stadium had become filled with screams of execration, and the Braves manager had finally ascended the dugout steps and was on his way to get Jack.

A close-up showed us the muscles spasming in Jack's jaw as he waited. He had allowed eight runs to score without getting anyone out, to make the score 11–1. He and the manager avoided each other's eyes as Jack handed over the new baseball. He trotted toward the dugout, head down.

At first, it appeared to be raining on the field, out of no-where—a development so surprising that Jack stopped dead and looked up. There were a few more flashes of silver in the air around him, and in the grass by his feet, and then, as if we were still connected by the empathic cord between father and son, Jack and I appeared to understand simultaneously what was happening: the fans were throwing their promotional watches at him. He ducked his head and ran into the clubhouse. With a sound that is hard to characterize, in an orgy of misdirected passion, the forty-five thousand began to throw their watches onto the field, at anybody.

This is the land that I live in, I thought. This is where we consider the emotional stakes in our daily lives to be at their highest—at the ballpark. If nothing is at risk in our own lives, if most of us know nothing of real danger or real violence or real fear or real lust for cruelty, then why do we invest our games with them? If we have purged civil life of such base instincts, maybe that isn't all to the good, for we can never banish, it seems, the instincts themselves; and if they are brought out in such pointless, isolated arenas, will we not be warped as well? Will our understanding of our own characters not be inevitably skewed?

The manager, still waiting on the mound, saw what was happening (the new pitcher was hesitating to take the field) and ran in his ungainly fashion toward the home-plate umpire. The two of them conferred quickly and then began waving frantically at the fielders, who ran in to the dugout, covering their heads with their gloves, a shower of cheap plastic pouring down all around them, glittering under the arc lights of the stadium.

"Turn it off," Ellie said hoarsely.

I did as she asked; but after she had gone to bed, I turned on the news, unable to quite believe what I had seen. The sports report carried a condensed version of the story, this time with a conclusion (the game had been resumed, needlessly, after a delay of fifty minutes to clear off the field) and a coda: after the game, a small group of young fans had gone out to the parking lot and slashed the tires of my son's car.

As the midpoint of August passed, the heat did not let up, but there was nevertheless a strong whiff of fall in the air, as the handful of summer people in Belmont began to refer to the problems of packing, and the drugstore window was papered with the Booth sisters' hand-stenciled signs advertising back-to-school specials. Football practice began—formally designated as "informal"—at Dewey High. I had about five more weeks of work and about three more weeks of being sixty-four years old; Ellie considerately, and wisely, asked if I would enjoy a little neighborhood party to mark my arrival as a senior citizen. The answer was no; I told her that the retirement dinner would no doubt provide all I could countenance in the way of self-celebration.

There is always a strange rush to socialize as the end of summer looms—having to do, one fancies, with some remnant of our selves that is still distantly in touch with the rhythms of nature, since nothing in our modern lives changes with the seasons. Whatever the reason, Ellie and I were invited, as every year, to a spate of cocktail or dinner parties around the neighborhood, at the Campbells', the Wintons', the Deckers'.

The chief topic of conversation at these soirees was always Ferdinand, and the rush of indignant excitement, of which everyone was reluctant to let go, that had come when the media had turned its awesome, fickle stare for a moment on our little community. Not surprisingly, just about everyone assumed Ferdinand was guilty, without really understanding what it was he had been charged with. The very fact that he had never been a part of this little chain of dinner parties was already enough, in most people's minds, to classify him as the Other. The one exception was Warren Decker, but his dissent had less to do with a belief in Ferdinand, whom he did not like, than to his locally famous, congenital distrust of anything that gave off even the faintest stink of government involvement, to which he was able to impart no good motive. When pressed, he would often mutter something about Orwell; one had the suspicion that Warren didn't read much, notwithstanding his fondness for the words "Orwellian" and "Kafkaesque."

There was an unsavory contradiction, though, in their blithe, chatty assumption that their mysterious neighbor was guilty of such scarcely imaginable crimes against humanity. If they really believed what they were saying, it seemed to me, then they should have had to act accordingly; instead of sitting, say, on the Campbells' cedar back deck, drinking gin and tonics and eating off of paper plates, shivering secretly in the ocean wind but unwilling to go inside, arguing inexpertly about Ferdinand's rights and about the history of his native country, they would have been hiding in their bedrooms with the doors locked, or storming his house to force him out of town, or asking themselves in solitude what it revealed about their own lives that such a monster could have lived undetected for years in their midst. But none of them, to my silent consternation, seemed alive to this fundamental problem. Where did these people, most of whose lives had never known danger, come by their blasé response to evil? More interesting to them—and, at least in their own minds, more threatening—was the invasiveness of the media; I heard Rachel Bright tell several versions of a story wherein she was sitting at the bar of the nearby Saw Mill Restaurant, and the talkative man sitting next to her, whose questions were so relentless and intimate that she assumed he was trying to pick her up, turned out to be a tabloid reporter looking for someone who was friendly with Ferdinand.

"Well, that's the way it is with the press," Fran said, brushing her silver hair out of her eyes. "They want what they want, and if they think you might have it, they're relentless."

"And now look," Anne Winton said. "They're gone. They get bored quickly and move on to the next thing."

"Gee," Devin Campbell said, "any coincidence most of them are men?"

Everyone laughed; no one made mention of the fact, though, that the "thing," as Anne referred to it, had not packed up and moved on along with the reporters, but was still very much with us, for us, privately if not publicly, to resolve.

Not wanting to make small talk about it, I stayed politely mute during these conversations—even on the night when we took our turn, at Ellie's insistence, as hosts. I was worried, though, that Ellie, who was more sociable than I under any circumstances, would offer up the fact that I had actually been on friendly terms, of late, with the criminal in our midst. But she kept mum about it, talking instead, in the skillful, outgoing way I've always admired, about these friends' home improvements or their children or some other topic in which I find it so hard to maintain interest during the second between the question and the answer. She has always thrown a smooth party—it was a part of her upbringing, which was significantly more upper-class than my own. While I was grateful for her discretion, I also saw that it was not done just to spare me. Though she certainly did not blame me for anything and looked upon me as, if anything, too innocent, she was embarrassed by my acquaintance with Ferdinand and was afraid of being shamed should it get out.

Then one evening, just at twilight, soon after I had gotten home from work, I was turning on the lamps in the living room when I saw, through the front windows, an unfamiliar man walking furtively, in a kind of crouch, across our lawn. I went to the window, but he was out of sight. Where just a few weeks before I might have concluded, from the man's behavior, that he was a burglar, now I could only assume, from the way in which he was trying to avoid detection, that he was either a policeman or a reporter.

Then the figure appeared again, coming into view from the other direction this time, moving in a difficult, sideways fashion, to enable him to look behind him, back up the street toward Ferdinand's house, as he retreated. He stood there on the sidewalk in front of my house for a moment, looking around him, still in his cautious half-stoop, seemingly ready to flee. I saw that he was not dressed the way any newspaper reporter would dress; he wore a light, beige windbreaker over a short-sleeved white shirt, gray pants that looked as if they belonged to a suit, white athletic socks and black sneakers. I couldn't get a good look at his face, as he kept his eye on the street. Slowly, surreptitiously, he started back down Fairly again, toward the corner; and I realized that his clumsy efforts to escape detection were not those of a man on some official covert operation, but of someone who was frightened.

I decided to go outside and have a look. I found the man at the end of the block, across from Ferdinand's, several steps back from the sidewalk in front of the Tyler house, one hand resting lightly on the elm tree in their front yard, the lowest branches of which served to partially conceal him. There was still enough light to see by. He didn't hear me walk up behind him, so, when I was still ten feet away, I said in a soft voice, "Hello."

He whipped around, startled. I saw right away that there was something slightly off about his face; his right eye drifted a bit, giving him, I thought, an involuntary expression of fear. He gazed at me warily, though for a moment, until I registered what was wrong with his eyes, I thought he was looking behind me.

"It's all right," I said, unsettled myself. "I'm just a neighbor."

He seemed to relax, though not completely. "I'm sorry," he said. "Is this your yard? I'm sorry." His voice had the same accent as Ferdinand's, though it was thicker and harder to understand.

"No, no," I said. "I live up the street there." He did not look where I pointed. He nodded once, then turned back to look at Ferdinand's house. Out of some hard-to-explain impulse—to convince him that I was to be trusted, I suppose—I went over and joined him under the limbs of the tree. Once there, I saw that he had chosen that spot not only because it was out of sight from the house but because it was out of the line of vision of the untrustworthy blue van, parked in its customary spot on the opposite corner.

He kept rising up on his toes and then crouching again, and I understood that his problem was that, being a shorter man, he could not quite see over the hedge to Ferdinand's lighted windows. I looked around and tapped the man lightly on the shoulder.

"From back there," I whispered, pointing to the shrubbery one property back down the street toward my house, "I think you can see in through the gate in the hedge."

He looked at the bushes, then at me, then the two of us rather ungracefully—for, though twenty or so years younger than me, he was no longer a youthful man—scampered over there. Sure enough, we had a clear view of Ferdinand's kitchen windows, though the white curtains were drawn tightly across them. We sat watching the bright, empty windows, like a movie screen after the film has run out, for a minute or more.

"Do you know him?" the man said to me. His eyes were still trained on the curtains.

"Yes," I said. "A little."

"And is it him?"

I looked at his unaligned eyes, his desperate expression. He seemed to be trembling slightly.

"I don't know," I said. "I don't know if it's him or not."

There was a long pause.

"I had to come and see," the man said.

In the silence, I thought that enough had now passed between us that I could begin to ask him the questions I felt piling on top of one another—when had he left Brazil? Why? What had happened to him there? What was he believed guilty of? Did he think of himself as a strong person? More so than before, or less? How far had he come tonight?—but it was hard to know where one could begin with any tact. Just then Ferdinand's shadow appeared in the kitchen. The little man's body tensed immediately, with such force I could feel it; in another few seconds, he started to shake, his whole body, so violently I thought he was going to give us away.

Here it is, I thought, excited myself. This is the identification. But looking back at the window, as Ferdinand moved back and forth, as I could deduce, from the sink to the counter, I realized that all that was visible to us was a blurred shadow, distorted further by the folds of the curtains, so that not even a profile would have been at all distinctive. It could have been the shadow of anyone. I could see, though, that it was fruitless to point any of this out to the man beside me. He was still trem-

119

bling uncontrollably, prodded, I was sure, more by memory than by what was in front of his unfocused eyes; I have never seen anyone so visibly terrified, and his fear began, for some reason, to infect me.

Countess started to bark at something; Ferdinand's shadow moved away from the window, and a moment later the dog was quiet. The shadow did not return. Now that he had seen it, not knowing where it was seemed to panic the little man all the more. He began to glance nervously all around him, ready to run; then his glance fell on me.

"Please," he said.

I looked at him questioningly.

"Please," he said again. "You won't tell him I was here."

I very nearly laughed. "But how could you tell anything from that?" I said. "How do you know that's even him?"

He was near tears. "Please," he said. "Promise me. I beg you."

"You're in no danger here," I said softly.

He reached out and grabbed my forearm, with a surprising force of which I'm sure he was unaware.

"Promise me," he said, less coherently now. "Promise me."

I tried to tell him that I didn't even know his name, but he was near hysteria, well out of reach of any appeal from logic. So I promised. With that, he let go of me, and he stared up into my face; though it lasted just a second, I thought I saw in his expression that he was trying to convey to me some sense of his great shame. Turning his back to me, he walked hastily back up the street, finally breaking into a trot; he turned the corner, and was gone.

———

The next morning, from my office, I called *Newsday* and asked to be connected with Sam Boyd. After a few rings, he answered with a curt, pessimistic "Boyd," straight out of a movie from the generation preceding his. As I expected, when I told him it was Gene Trowbridge calling, he gave a noncommittal "Hi," trying to remember if he should remember who I was. I told him I was the neighbor of Albert Ferdinand to whom he had spoken on the Fourth of July.

"Can you hold on a minute?" he said. He put the receiver on his desk; there was a loud shuffling on his end of the line, the sound of a drawer banging shut. I heard him hiss "Later," presumably at someone who had come to ask him something. I had those few moments in which to think better of having called; but I only felt the great weight of my own uncertainty, and so I waited patiently for his voice. My own office was empty, the door shut; it had darkened with the sky, which was promising one of those summer lightning storms of which I had a dramatic view.

In another few seconds, Boyd was back on the line, a little breathless. "Sorry," he said. "Just finishing up something. What can I do for you, Mr. Trowbridge?"

"Well, first of all, I don't want to get your hopes up. I'm not calling to offer any sort of scoop for you. I only mention it in case you were setting up to record the call."

"Ah. Well, yes, I am recording it. Do you mind that I'm recording it?"

"I suppose not, no. Still, I'm afraid I have to specify that anything I say is off the record."

"Okay," he said, a little frustrated. "Okay."

"Not that I anticipate saying anything you'd be interested in. But I just need to make sure."

"That's fine, sir," Boyd said. His manner was easy, more confident and yet somehow less impudent than he had been when I met him in his broadly drawn fake persona. "So what have you called to tell me that's so uninteresting?"

"Well, I saw your story, of course. Actually, I wanted to ask you some things, rather than tell you anything. I realize that's not what your time is for. But I thought maybe if you had a moment."

Boyd made a sound of long exhalation, which struck me as unnecessarily rude until I realized he was smoking. "Well, you're right," he said, "that's not really my job. But maybe we can work something out. Maybe someday I'll have a question that you'll be able to answer?"

It was easy to agree to such a nakedly mercenary proposal; I felt no honor would be lost if I ever had cause to back out of it. "Agreed," I said.

"As it happens, I'm not too busy right now," Boyd said.

"Did you talk to anyone else in Belmont besides me?" I said. "Did anyone else know anything about this?"

He laughed, though not happily. "Nope. You were the first. I did such an awful job with you, I was sure my cover was blown, and everyone would be keeping an eye out for me. I was afraid I'd lost the story. Why, you didn't mention it to anyone?"

"No, actually, I didn't," I said.

"You didn't? Why not?"

"How do you know all this is true?" I said. "What is your proof? Your story, if you'll forgive my saying so, was a little thin on evidence, I thought. A little thin period."

"Can you believe they put that on page seventeen?" There was a false camaraderie in his voice now, same as there had been on the Fourth of July, as he tried to draw me out. "The original version of the story was a lot longer, a lot more detail. Then they cut it, and buried it behind all the Gulf coverage. I didn't speak to my editor for two days."

"So what was cut out of it?" I said.

"It's a bit long and involved, but basically it gave a short history of Brazil during the years of the military dictatorship there, including some examples of what civil rights consisted of during that time. It described the detention and interrogation center da Silva was in charge of in São Paulo, where it was, what it looked like, what it did and to what kinds of people, et cetera. Plus, it followed da Silva's career up until his disappearance and then traced Ferdinand back as far as I could trace him. The two lines converge roughly in the same place at roughly the same time."

"How roughly?"

"Da Silva was last seen in São Paulo in 1969. I can only trace the existence of Ferdinand as far back as a town in California in 1974."

"That's it?" I said, a little loudly. "That's all?"

Boyd sighed. "In terms of a paper trail, yes, that's as good as it gets. If I had more, I'd have run it. But no, that's not everything. The people at this organization BNF have been after this guy, after about a hundred guys just like him in fact, for a long time. When I say after him, I'm just talking about positively identifying him, not arresting him or executing him or anything like that. When they first came to me to ask for my help with this, they gave me more than two hundred depositions from some of the surviving victims of the torture in Brazilian jails, describing in detail what had been done to them. Many of these documents, about two dozen I guess, ended with testimony in which victims from the São Paulo area were shown a recent photograph of Ferdinand, taken secretly, and all but a few of them testified that they were certain that he and da Silva are the same man."

"All of these people were relying on their memory of the man's face more than twenty years ago, right?"

"These are pretty indelible memories, keep in mind. It's not the same as being asked to recall somebody you met at a party twenty years ago, you know what I mean?"

There was a knock on my office door. Without waiting for a response, Tony Hobson, our art director, stuck his head inside and raised his eyebrows. I held up my hand with fingers spread apart to indicate he should give me five more minutes, and he withdrew.

"But wouldn't they say anything?" I said to Boyd. "Think how badly they must want this da Silva to be caught—to be alive, for that matter—so they can pay him back. How reliable can they be?"

There was a pause, and when Boyd resumed speaking it was in a different tone, as if he were thinking about something else. "If it was one or two people," he said, "I might be inclined to agree with you. But I'm talking about fifteen or twenty people. Mr. Trowbridge, can I ask you something?"

"Of course."

"You said you didn't know Ferdinand very well, isn't that right?"

Aware, suddenly, of the tension in my hand, throughout my whole body in fact, I leaned back in my chair and relaxed my grip on the receiver. "That's right," I said.

"Well, you know what?" Boyd said. "I don't believe you anymore."

There was a short silence, which I tried to think how to fill.

"I think you know him better than you're letting on," Boyd

continued. "I think you're friends with him, not that that's a crime."

"What makes you think that?" I said, trying not to sound concerned.

"Because," Boyd said, "if you aren't friends, then I can't possibly think what your interest might be in defending this man."

"I'm not defending anyone, I just—"

"Certainly you're defending him. Why did you call me? No one else from Belmont has called me."

"I just can't stand to see people tried in the media, on no evidence, that's all. It's barbaric. Of course I assume he's innocent. This is America."

"Well, that's a noble sentiment, Mr. Trowbridge. But I've met the people from BNF myself. I've talked to a couple of da Silva's victims. You know what? I've seen the photographs, too. It's him. It's him."

"Why not just run the photos?" I said.

"The legal department here told us not to. There's no criminal proceeding going on, so it's too risky for their taste."

"Did you ever talk to Ferdinand yourself?"

"Of course. I told him where I was calling from, and he hung up on me."

I felt very tired and foolish. "I'm not saying it can't be him," I said.

"I'm saying it is him. You know, I think part of the problem is that we're talking in such abstractions here. I'm sure you don't really know what's meant, specifically, by the word torture. Or by the word Brazil, for that matter. You're probably just like I was, you think it's where string bikinis and coffee come from and that's it."

I didn't answer.

"So I'll tell you what I'm going to do. To help you out, I am going to have copies made of all the material that's been supplied to me by BNF and by Human Rights Watch, all the histories and the testimonies of the prisoners. You look it over. Maybe then you'll remember something that you might want to tell me. Maybe then you'll understand that community spirit is all very nice, but is it really worth protecting this sort of man?"

"I'm not protecting him," I said.

"Then you're protecting yourself." He made that smoker's noise again. "I have your home address already, actually. I'll just send it off."

"No," I said glumly. "Not at home. Send it to me at the office." I gave him the AAK address.

"You read it," he said as he wrote. "You think about it, and about what's the right thing to do here."

"I swear to you," I said, "I don't know anything."

"You call me when you've read it, okay? Mr. Trowbridge?"

I hung up.

Seeing on her switchboard that my line was clear, Caroline buzzed me to let me know that Tony Hobson was still waiting. I had her send him in.

At thirty-two one of the younger art directors in the business, Tony was still in his young-hotshot days, and had a brash manner with his elders that, for the time being anyway, was charming and served him well. In fact, his work was consistently terrific, and surprising in the way only the young can be. He was on a long roll. Winter and summer, he walked around the office with no jacket and his sleeves rolled up, colorful inkstains on his forearms.

"What can I do for you?" I said.

Trying, for Caroline's benefit, to keep any nonprofessional lilt out of his voice, Tony said, "Gene, we're starting to audition

for the Glencairn shoot. You said you wanted in on it, so
we're—"

"Yes, right, here I come," I said. "Thanks for waiting, Tony."

"*De nada,*" Tony said. Pulling my jacket on, smoothing my
hair with my hands, I walked behind Tony past Caroline's desk,
down two corridors, and finally to the door of the conference
room at the north end of the floor. Glencairn scotch was one of
AAK's oldest and most steady accounts, one that I had been
instrumental in bringing to the agency more than fifteen years
earlier. I felt very close to it, and the people there placed great
trust in me and in my willingness to oversee every facet of their
advertising. They had never been among our most lucrative clients, but they were unrelievedly loyal, the kind of pillar upon
which any agency that means to survive for the long haul must
be built. The one downside to the relationship was the constant
infusion of scotch they would send me, two or three cases a
year, in spontaneous displays of good feeling. I never dared,
naturally, to tell them that the stuff—a blended scotch, a kind of
lowest common denominator in the brand wars—is far too dull
for my taste; my own brand is a hard-to-find single-malt called
Talisker, which I pick up at a liquor store between the office and
Grand Central. I was constantly foisting the Glencairn on colleagues, or placing bottles of it on the bar during office parties.

My interest in attending the audition of a group of young
female models might have seemed prurient, even taking into
consideration my duties as steward to the Glencairn account.
But thousands of these sessions, over a period of almost thirty
years, had rendered them, in my mind, not more commonplace
but rather more bizarre. These women, whatever the more prosaic qualities of their characters, are natural phenomena, gifted
with forbidding beauty; and one never becomes so jaded that
one is not moved by the sight of them. But they are not attrac-

tive, somehow. Their beauty puts you at what you yourself feel is an appropriate distance. Gorgeous though these women may be, you wouldn't think of holding them, or kissing them—it would be as fitting, and perhaps as pleasurable, as kissing or fondling a museum piece. In fact, it's vaguely embarrassing even to entertain the image of it. No doubt that has to do not simply with their flawlessness but with the self-consciousness they produce in an outsider, particularly when they are in a group. One does not like to be confronted, even in such an oblique way, with one's own imperfections.

When we reached the conference room, Tony, whose feelings were not similarly clouded, looked at me with mock solemnity. "Praise God," he said, then opened the door.

There were fifteen of them in the conference room, which had only ten chairs, so that a few of them were seated on the floor with their limbs folded like those of a sleeping colt, or perched on the edge of the table with one long leg reaching to the floor. The oldest was probably around twenty-four, and the shortest was probably five-seven. All of them were dressed in black, to accentuate their thinness—black stretch pants, black miniskirts, black boots, black turtlenecks, faded black jeans. They turned their perfect heads to look at us; some smiled, some did not, but none of them was in true repose around us. It was an odd thought; just sitting there, motionless and silent, they were working. It was quite a tableau.

"Girls," Tony said, "this is Mr. Gene Trowbridge, vice president of AAK. Unfortunately, Mr. Trowbridge is a busy man and hasn't time to sit in on the individual tests, but he wanted to have a look at you all and say hello."

I looked from face to face, trying to be struck by something that would make one of them more perfect for the Glencairn campaign than the others. All of them were aware that this was their opportunity to impress me. But how? Any one of them would have been fine for our purposes, as they may well have known. (I've often thought that those ad executives who do sleep with models do so not as an exercise of their power, but because they're so desperate for any criterion, even a corrupt one, by which to favor one girl instead of another.) Still, they were forced on virtually a daily basis to live through this sort of capricious competition, never knowing why they lost, or why they won. It was no wonder they were, as a profession, so famously neurotic. It would have been interesting to see them sometime in some other setting, more relaxed, more natural, more native, where they might be the unself-conscious natural wonders that they ought to be, as free to be beautiful as the animals they so often strikingly evoke—not trapped in the relationship between viewer and object, between themselves and the American ideal. But perhaps, for such creatures, there was no such setting, no escape even in solitude, like animals whose habitat has been destroyed. As they offered themselves up, I looked around again, from face to face, from image to image, at all the beautiful young women who had dressed themselves in the color of death.

They looked back, eagerly, seductively, ready, like us, to sell anything.

On the train home that night, a light rain spotting the windows, I was consumed with thoughts of Ferdinand and with reminiscences of my conversation with the reporter Boyd, whose accusatory tone had struck me as surprising and unfair. I settled upon the thought that it was, above all, my uncertainty about what one might as well call the facts of the case that was the cause of all my pained deliberation. I decided what I would do about it, then waffled, then decided again; but, in this as in so many other matters, my course was eventually determined not by me but by events, more specifically by the reception I was astonished to get from Ellie when I arrived home.

She was sitting in the living room, half in shadow, with a glass of white wine in her hand, facing the windows. She turned when she heard me come in the door, looked at me without expression for a moment, then turned to stare outside again.

"Hi," I said. She had to decide, it seemed, whether to engage me even to that extent; finally, after enough seconds had passed to alert me that something was wrong, she said "Hi," in the kind of shallow voice that comes out of you when you are awakened by the telephone.

"What's the matter?" I said.

She didn't answer.

"I'm not that late, am I?"

She looked at her watch. "It's seven-thirty," she said.

"Yes," I said, "I have a watch too, but what I meant was, I didn't ruin dinner, did I?"

"I haven't made anything," she said.

"Were we going someplace tonight? Did I forget?"

Again, she seemed not to want to talk, but finally uttered a barely audible no.

I have, I think, an honest idea of the faults that I bring to our marriage—a lack of patience, a tendency to hold a grudge, an excessive (at least in earlier years) concern with work. But I have always counted it in my favor that when I am mad, I get mad. There is no tactic of Ellie's that gets deeper under my skin than this business of forcing me to guess what it is I've done wrong. She may not do it on purpose; on the other hand, she certainly knows by now that it annoys me. Seeing that this was how the evening was going to play itself out, I went into the kitchen, poured myself a drink, and took it upstairs, to nurse while I changed out of my suit. I looked around the bedroom, just to confirm that everything appeared normal, as if there might be some physical evidence of whatever was darkening the atmosphere downstairs. Then I went back down, bypassing the living room, and turned on the television.

Small domestic victories, as petty as they are revealed to be later, can be tremendously satisfying at the time. Ellie finally got up from the couch and came into the TV room.

"Could you turn that off, please?" she said. I turned the sound down.

She sat on the very edge of her chair, across from me, unable or unwilling to relax. Her jaw was set in a way that accentuated the lines around her mouth.

"I had a long talk with Peggy Baldwin today," Ellie said. I reached back in memory to try to discover what might cause this to be said in such a dramatic tone; I caught up to it just as Ellie spoke again.

"She said that last weekend she saw you and Albert Ferdinand having a long talk, in the street, right outside her front yard. She said the two of you were there for a good half hour."

I had some scotch.

"Is this true?" she said.

"Yes, it's true," I said, mocking her solemn manner. "Peggy wouldn't lie about a horrible thing like that."

"Very funny. What did you talk about?"

I considered trying to tell her that it was none of her business, but it was too late for that; besides, it would sound mean and self-incriminating, and I was guilty of nothing. "What did we talk about?" I said. "I asked him if it was true what was being said about him, if he was the famous barbarian da Silva. He said no, it wasn't true."

"And did you believe him?"

"I didn't know what to believe. I still don't."

She weighed that for a moment. "So that's one question and answer," she said. "What did you talk about for the other twenty-nine minutes?"

"He explained himself in some detail. Listen, I don't really like this tone. What is it exactly that you think I'm guilty of?"

"Who used the word guilty? I just—"

"You implied it."

"I just am curious why you didn't consider this particular conversation worth mentioning to me."

"For God's sake, I ran into him on the street!" I said—forgetting, as one often does in domestic arguments, that I was not telling the truth, and focusing instead on the fact that she was jumping ahead of the flimsy evidence that was available to her.

"The man is accused of brutalizing hundreds of people," she said. "It's not every day you have a conversation with such a person, whether you just ran into him or not."

"All right," I said, anxious to end it. "All right. You win—I should have told you about it when it happened. And now I've told you about it. I apologize."

She shook her head slowly. "No," she said, in a softer voice, as if talking now as much to herself as to me. "Not good enough. It's too much of a coincidence, you getting to know this man after seven years, just as all this is coming to light. I really can't help thinking that you're concealing more than just this one thing from me. I think you know more about this man than you're telling me."

She looked genuinely hurt, and I was surprised that all this could have affected her so. She also looked—and I very seldom had this sensation, having spent nearly every night with her for the last thirty-seven years—old; and in her old age and confusion, I suddenly recognized my sense of partnership with her. I was reminded that there was no one in this world who had repaid my trust more, who had loved me so unconditionally. I decided to try to explain it to her, if I could.

"That's just it," I said. "I don't know. I don't know anything. And I can't bear it, I have to know."

"And you've asked him," she said. "And he's told you. And you don't really believe him. So where are you?"

"What do you mean?" I said.

"What do you expect is going to happen that will suddenly make it all clear for you? I'll tell you what. This will all be decided elsewhere, by politicians or in the courts, and we will read about it. You're not going to make that happen any faster by obsessing about it."

"So what's your point?"

"My point is that you must know that. So all you're left with is your fascination with the whole thing. That's what disturbs me. It seems so unlike you."

"You don't understand what's compelling about any of this?"

"It's morbid!"

"It is the opposite of morbid," I said.

"What is that supposed to mean?"

I closed my eyes, in despair, and gave up, submitting to nastiness. "You know what I think this is all about for you," I said, "is being embarrassed in front of a neighbor. You care less about what I think, or for that matter about a man's right to be presumed innocent, than you do about your standing with your god damn gossiping friends."

"If you want to talk about that," she said, "yes, I was embarrassed, but not by your associating with this guy. I was embarrassed to have to learn something important about my husband from a relative stranger, and more or less by accident."

"You haven't learned anything about me," I said.

She put her palms together. "Maybe I haven't," she said.

Sitting across from her, both of us mute with emotion, staring into her brown eyes as they shimmered with inappropriate tears, I felt I was seeing more than I wanted to see. I know that Ellie's life has not turned out the way she feels, in retrospect, it should have. Among the expectations of class and culture, of her generation, of the family she came from and the family she held together, it has escaped from her, somehow. In her sixties, she finds herself devoted to a slapdash kind of self-improvement, to adult education weekends at Bryn Mawr, library groups, most especially to the impossibly compressed project of her artistic development as a serious photographer. When she looks back at her life, Ellie sees a conspicuous lack of product. I know that I bear some responsibility for this. And, though she doesn't blame me for it, she expects me to know it. She expects some consideration. I could see her equation now, incorrect though I felt it to be, of my keeping a secret of this magnitude from her with my trampling of the idea of the sacrifices she had made, of the sacrifice that her life, at least in times of stress, represented to her.

I turned off the television and stood up from the chair.

"Where are you going?" Ellie said.

I walked to the hall closet and got out a jacket; it was still cool outside following the rain.

"You're not going over there?" she said, standing at the end of the hall. "Gene?"

I was too worked up to speak.

"Gene? Listen to me. There is no need for you to get involved in this. There is nothing at stake for you here. Do you hear me? He's not your friend. He's a dangerous man for all we know. What does any of this have to do with you?"

I went out the door, cut across the lawn, and continued down the street. The black pavement shone with rainwater and the light from the houses on Fairly Avenue. Muttering rejoinders to myself, to Ellie, perhaps to someone whose demanding existence I had forgotten was only imaginary, I reached Ferdinand's door. He peeked from behind the curtain to see who was knocking; a moment later he opened the door with a look of confusion on his tanned face.

"Gene!" he said. "What a surprise."

I walked past him into his living room, which was nearly dark. Countess trotted along behind me, sniffing at the backs of my knees.

"Is something wrong?" Ferdinand said. "Can I get you a drink?"

"A scotch, thank you, if you have it," I said.

He returned with two scotches, and handed one to me as he crossed the room to his chair. "You know," he said, "I'm aware of what small towns such as this are like. I know the prejudices, and the pressures that can be put on people. So, under the circumstances, the fact that you would still come into my house means a great deal to—"

"Please," I said. He stared at me, curious, unoffended. While I kept expecting him, at some moment of clear vision, to stand revealed before me as a horrible brute, cruel and satanic, I saw him now only as an almost unbearably silly, foppish, pathetic old man, with his aristocratic yearnings and his stilted way

of addressing me. Everything in his manner seemed to make fun of me, of my ignorance, and I couldn't bear to be made fun of by such a ridiculous personage.

"What is it?" he said. "Sit down, please."

We both sat down. There was only one table lamp turned on in the long living room, beside his chair.

"Are you who they say you are?" I said.

His eyebrows lowered. "I have already told you," he said. "I am not he."

"I don't believe you," I said. "I think you're lying. I think you're mocking me."

"I understood that we were friends," he said darkly.

"We're in a relationship. That much is true."

"If you have already made up your mind about me," Ferdinand said, "why do you bother to ask?"

"Because you have to help me," I said, and something within me gave way with those words. "I've lived to be nearly sixty-five years old, and I don't know anything. I don't know the difference between a good man and an evil one. My own life, apparently, hasn't taught me anything. I've lived in the middle, I don't know what the extremes of life are like. Everyone thinks I know all about you, newspaper people, my wife, maybe the police, too, for all I know, they all think I'm hiding something, but they all don't get it. I don't know a god damn thing. I feel stupid, and it's one thing to be stupid as a young man, but I can't tolerate it now. There was never anything more for me to work for, to worry about, than comfort, and now, maybe as a result, I find I have no anchor, do you see? If I have to find that anchor in the knowledge of evil, so be it. I have to know what you know."

Ferdinand's face was lit by the lamp; his hands were folded

in front of him. The dog's tags jingled as she walked through the darkened room.

"Who sent you here?" he said.

"No one sent me here. I'm here on an idiot's errand. Only my wife knows where I am. But it makes no difference. Because even if pressed I would never turn you in, never betray you to anyone, because if I do that, then I'll lose my chance, I'll never learn what I need to learn. Do you believe that I'm telling you the truth?"

He stared at me for a while. "Yes," he said finally.

"I need to know what you did," I said. "And then I need to know how it was possible for you. How did you do it. How did you *decide* to do it. How could you not kill yourself knowing what you had done. The unimaginable. You saw, you were responsible for, moment after moment of horrible physical pain. I don't even have the vocabulary for it. The extreme, the extreme, of human experience. What was the point of it? How could you convince yourself to do it. How did you feel at the time. How do you feel about it now. How could such an outwardly civilized man be at the same time such an animal."

"Not an animal," he said. "Never an animal. Take care how you speak to me. A man. Just like yourself."

"Yes," I said. "Fine. All the better. A man, then, just like myself. How could you do it. How could you."

A car drove by outside. Something was changing in Ferdinand's sad face, something was draining out of it. His gaze drifted off to the left of me. The mask of good cheer, of formality and perpetual gratitude, was disappearing as if in a fire; but what was behind it was not what I expected. It was blankness: not the blankness of an automaton or an executioner, but the focused expression of a man listening to some sound that no one else in the room has heard yet. I could hear his breathing. After a few moments, he looked back at me—though, it occurred to me, I was now sitting in nearly complete darkness; and I wondered whom, at that moment of converged time, he was speaking to.

"It was war," he said.

Two

A city contains the visible seeds of its own destruction; anywhere you go, amid the fury of growth and the anxiety of prosperity, you see as well the harbingers, sometimes small, sometimes hard to miss, of an almost biblical decay. In a taxi on your way to the World Trade Center, you see through the window abandoned, graffiti-covered town houses, earth-brown, unused warehouses, the smashed windows covered over with plywood that is in turn smashed through to shelter those hardy citizens who know how to extract a living from the blasted landscape, the ones who will outlast us all. From the window of a commuter train you see, on the little-known fringes, the most frightening sight of all, apartment buildings ten, twelve, twenty stories in the air, blackened, burned out, gutted, so that speeding past you may see for a vertiginous instant through the front and back windows all the way to the blue sky beyond, and imagine the air whistling through the upper floors, and reflect that there are most likely people living in that building still. Walking to work in midtown, you often pass by a thin blue fence of plywood, with windows cut into it, through which you may contemplate the grim, yawning hole in the ground that is the site of a future skyscraper, an artist's rendering of which is posted outside. To those whose livelihoods are pinned to the project, this wound is a symbol of optimism and the endless improvement of human endeavor, but to you it appears, with the men and the trucks and the cranes moving back and forth over the submerged, irregular dirt floor, as something out of Brueghel, and as a surprising visual reminder that here in the forest of highrise buildings the actual earth still breathes beneath the thick skin of pavement. It is important that these things should exist side by side. It is possible, with a small effort of the imagination, to envision the distant but certain generation when these holes in the fabric will spread, when all the tall monuments to wealth will be abandoned, then looted, then left to decay. Any patient person can hear how much of city life, even now, speaks of collective doom.

Whereas what seems to me the most enduring material symbol of the social life of man, curiously enough, are these even-keeled suburban communities like the one in which I live. When I look around Belmont, or, less often, when I close my eyes and imagine it, I am struck by the connection between its modesty and its permanence. It is hard to conceive of anything that might displace these solidly built, reasonable, two-story homes or change the character of these secure streets. There is no industry that Belmont is tied to. It consists, with gradations of course, of one class of people. There is no real threat to it, either external or internal; it even has a decent volunteer fire department. I wonder if part of the reason that well-off people continue to move here isn't the subconscious understanding that such places are immune to deterioration. Of course, this refers to the town as an architectural phenomenon. I would never make such a bold claim for the people themselves. Like people anywhere, they will come and go, their fortunes will rise further or begin to decline, they will be driven out of their homes by divorce or illness or death. The properties will change hands; sometimes a house will be razed to accommodate some young man's dream vision, but a change like that is an insignificant detail, to all but the people directly involved. In fact, I even came to think of the affluent people of Belmont more or less as spirits moving through the town, temporarily occupying this material incarnation of the notion of human comfort, then making way, insubstantial, ghostlike.

Ghostlike, my wife and I orbited through our own house, cordial, rarely speaking or touching, quietly alone with our thoughts. It was the evening of the day of my sixty-fifth birthday. Both of us, I'm sure, were glad in retrospect that Ellie had honored my wish not to have a party, though it made for some awkwardness to have to celebrate it by ourselves. For the past two or three weeks, I had been spending the better portion of my evenings, Saturdays, and Sundays visiting Ferdinand. It seemed to me, in some way I was always struggling to define, that real life was in that nearby house, and that to hole up in my own home—particularly with its new atmosphere of pointed silence—was to hide from that life, at great, if indistinct, personal peril. I didn't tell Ellie where I was going, though obviously she knew; sometimes I would say I was going for a walk,

sometimes I would just slip out, avoiding the sight of her, without saying anything at all. I took no satisfaction in defying her; I
felt terrible about it, actually, and would stay up for hours sometimes after coming home late from Ferdinand's simply to increase the chances that when I got into bed I wouldn't have to
listen in the dark to the breathing that told me she was still
awake. We didn't discuss it—I think she recognized, as I did,
that I was going through something that put me, for some indeterminate time, out of her reach; but the matter hung between
us, and made the kind of common daily exchange of minutiae
that normally takes place between husband and wife seem self-
mocking. I was not angry with her—in fact, I felt for her quite
deeply, and mourned her inability to understand, or mine to
make myself understood. She was afraid of scandal, certainly,
but more than that she was unsettled by the idea that after so
many years I was capable of doing anything that could confound
her.

Still, a sixty-fifth birthday is a momentous thing, and any
marital difficulty, no matter how serious, was bound to seem
reversible and temporary in the shadow of such a milestone. We
were both resolved to be as cheerful as we could manage. I
arrived home a little early from work, carrying a small shopping
bag filled with modest, mostly humorous gifts from colleagues
and employees. The younger ones, in particular, had seemed
touchingly intent on softening the blow to me represented by
my official passage into senior citizenship. "It's a government
number," Tony Hobson had said dismissively of my new age.
"Doesn't mean anything." Ellie came into the hall to greet me,
and insisted that I narrate as she looked through the bag.

All the restaurants in Belmont and its environs are quite
ordinary—places you go to when you're too tired to cook, rather

than indulgences for a special occasion. Ellie hadn't even suggested going out for dinner, and neither had I. She was preparing one of our favorite summertime dinners—swordfish and corn on the cob—and insisted that I relax out on the porch for another twenty or thirty minutes until everything was ready. I don't know why there is so much coddling involved with a birthday, as if the day itself would be too exhausting for you if you weren't constantly attended; I suppose we do it, as we do so much else, because of our awkward need to make use of the recognized symbols of affection. I went upstairs and changed—pulling a light cotton sweater over my shirt now, for fall was in the nights, if not yet in the afternoons—and went back down to the porch, where Ellie had placed a lowball glass of scotch and ice on the broad, flat arm of the wooden chair.

Scotch is a wonderful thing. I settled into the chair and sat still in the twilight, my eyes roving over the houses across the street, some still dark. The Walshes' boy, Richie, was visible in his tiny second-floor bedroom window, head in hand, assessing the leap in homework required of him now that he was in the ninth grade, which he had begun that week. Most houses across the street had curtains or blinds drawn to keep out the setting sun, which shone directly through their front windows. Our house faces almost dead east; as the sun set behind it, the long shadows of the telephone poles, the elm trees, the bicycle in the Wintons' driveway, our mailbox, our house itself, pointed straight out across the street and up Frannie's lawn, directing my vision, it seemed, all the way out past the Hamptons toward Montauk and the open water beyond.

The shadows were merging with the darkness when Ellie came to the screen door and invited me back inside. The dining-room table was candlelit; in my customary chair at the head of it was a large, oblong, awkwardly gift-wrapped package. I looked from it to Ellie, who said, "Well, go ahead." It was a Spalding tennis racket, very up-to-date and expensive; it was called, with the fine elevation of sound over meaning shared by market researchers and surrealist poets, the Paradox. I already had a perfectly good racket, as Ellie knew, but she had caught me taking a few admiring practice swings with this one in the aisle of a sporting goods store on a trip to the Patchogue mall a couple of months ago and had made a note of it. With its aerodynamic design and its ridiculously overengineered frame made from materials that sounded more appropriate to a space shuttle, it was the kind of thing I never would have dared buy for myself; even though I could have afforded it, it was an extravagance. Consequently, it made an absolutely perfect birthday gift. I could see the gratification in her face as she watched me trying it out, and I went to her and kissed her—surprising us both, I think, with the realization that such moments of contact were rare enough lately to have become unexpected.

"I was thinking about a set of golf clubs," she said, "what with you retiring and all, but I thought this might be better."

"I loathe golf."

"I know," she said. "Just kidding."

"Ty Cobb, the great old baseball player," I said as she went back into the kitchen, "was once asked by a sportswriter if he enjoyed any other sports, like golf. He scowled and said, 'Golf's not a sport. When I hit a ball, I want someone to chase it.' "

She came back in with our plates, smiling at my story or at something else entirely, and poured us each a glass of wine. Sitting down with a contented sigh, she raised her glass and looked at me over the candle flames.

"Well," she said. "To the golden years."

I narrowed my eyes in feigned anger. "You just wait," I said.

"Forty-one months until you join me, I counted today. Then we'll see how funny it is."

We began eating. The meal itself had become associated, over the years, in both our minds, with our marriage; a shared pleasure, a private understanding.

"So, do you feel any different?" she said.

"No, not really," I said. "God, this is great, by the way. No, you know, I was thinking today, I've pretty much felt sixty-five ever since the day I turned sixty-four."

She smiled.

"But hey," I said, "as long as I can still eat corn on the cob, things can't have gotten too pathetic yet."

After that, dinner drifted into a near silence. I lingered over it, having already decided that, as my contribution to this rare evening of good feeling, I would not go to Ferdinand's house that night. But as the minutes passed, it became apparent to me, and I'm sure to her, too, how much of what had been exchanged between us was simply ceremonial; now that it was over, the sense of another presence, of something we weren't discussing, had returned to the air. Tonight, though, the whole affair with Ferdinand—the whole idea that it was possible to have lived as man and wife for so long and still, when it came to something fundamental and vital, not be able to reconcile our wishes—was not the central, shared, unspoken thought. Rather, it was, I think, the poignant drama of our aging. We were truly at the door to it now. It was easy to leave aside the question of death—I certainly felt very far from dying—but there are practical dangers in aging, the contemplation of which, as you draw closer, becomes a more and more private thing. I don't mean that such thoughts are restricted to concern for oneself; but how to mention the fears that had visited me, that day, of what might await either or both of us as our bodies began to wind down, how even to touch upon it? Everything that needed to pass between us on the subject, I think, passed in the shared acknowledgment that the whole matter was unspeakable.

"My father was a captain in the army," Ferdinand said, "a bit of a reactionary, though perhaps we all think of our fathers that way. A career military man."

"I've known a few," I said.

Ferdinand looked at me sharply, not pleased to be interrupted while talking about his father. "He was a visionary in one sense. He was staunchly, angrily anti-Communist. Now, it's one thing to be opposed to communism in our day, after Stalin, after Mao. But the Brazilian Communist Party was founded in Rio in 1922, just five years after the fall of Russia. It held a lot of romance in those days; it continued to hold that attractive promise for a lot of naive people well into my adulthood. The PCB was very active and influential, increasingly threatening. I know there was quite a bit of flirting with communism in America at that time, during the Depression, but it was confined to an intellectual elite, and therefore, believe me, quite a different matter. Some of my earliest memories of my father have to do with his fear of the Communist spread, and his bitter temper whenever anyone would dare to defend, even in part, socialist principles. He would even lecture me about it—this is when I was a boy of six or seven—when he was particularly drunk or frustrated. It would scare me quite a bit, to be honest, partly because he made Communists such horrible bogeymen and partly because his own anger was frightening to me. He was an imposing man. My mother would shout at him to leave me alone."

He allowed himself a smile, in remembrance. It was late on

a Saturday afternoon, in his cool living room; idly I scratched the dog's head as I listened.

"In 1935, in São Paulo, where we lived, when I was eight years old, Communists began to infiltrate the lower ranks of the army. There was great nervousness among the senior officers about it, including of course my father. In November, a group headed by a band of lieutenants led an armed insurrection in the São Paulo army barracks. There were pitched battles throughout the barracks compounds, in which senior officers led troops loyal to the president, and enlisted men, often men from the same hometown, fought face to face over this issue, over the issue of the country's future. The whole thing—though this is often forgotten now, as the day itself is still celebrated in Brazil—the whole thing was put down quickly, and there were relatively few deaths, less than ten if I remember right." He took a breath. "My father was shot in the head, but he survived. He was left partially paralyzed, and aphasic, but he lived. He was shot in the head by one of the men under his own command. I wonder if you can imagine what that's like."

I tried dutifully to imagine it, though I had never been an officer myself. "How awful," I managed to say.

Ferdinand looked at me with an expression somewhere between amusement and scorn. "He had to retire, of course," he said. "Full pension, full military honors. Upon his retirement he was promoted to colonel. He lived nine more years."

He shifted in his chair.

"Do you consider yourself an anti-Communist?" he said.

I did for as long as I could remember being able to distinguish what communism was, and I told him so.

"An anti-Communist, yes. I wonder what that means," he said, "to someone born and raised in America."

I bristled a little bit. "If you're trying to say that what happened to your father somehow justifies the worst thought about any person with Communist sympathies, anywhere in the world, I don't buy it," I said. "I certainly am sorry for you, and for him. But the man who shot him was just a man."

"And what does that mean?" Ferdinand said. "Do beliefs like his have some existence separate from the people who hold them?"

"I know that socialism has always been just a specter in this country, that we wouldn't know what a real threat to our way of life was about. But that doesn't disqualify me as an observer. And as for me, I certainly would never kill anyone, or even harm anyone, over an idea."

"Neither would I," he said.

On the Sunday following my birthday, I was sitting in the brightly sunlit dining room with a second cup of coffee, plowing obligatorily through the myriad sections of the Sunday *Times*. No amount of advertising could ever buy the kind of mind control the Sunday *Times* exerts over its millions of local readers, including me. No matter what remains to be done on a given Sunday (in this case, thankfully, nothing) in the way of chores or office work, it must all wait until the newspaper has been thoroughly read; why this anxiety over completing the paper's arcana is reserved for the day when it is ten times its normal size, I don't know. What a terrible anxiety bears down if the paper threatens to swallow the whole day! If I had read as superstitiously on Sundays when I was in college, I'd be an academic now.

In any event, I had a tennis game at the town courts that started in less than an hour, so I was pleased to have wrestled the paper under control. I sat in my tennis clothes, with my warm-up jacket spread on the chair beneath me so as not to show up at the courts with wicker marks printed on my haunches. Ellie was upstairs, at her rolltop desk in our bedroom, going over some new contact sheets. The paper sat on the table before me in three piles, unread sections on my right, completed sections on my left, and the viscera—Help Wanted, Real Estate, Weddings—tossed out of the way, into the center of the table.

The sports section was mostly given over to lengthy coverage of the newly begun football season. Though I like football well enough to fritter away the occasional autumn Sunday watching it on television, it seems to me close to sacrilege to start paying attention to it while baseball season is still under way. In fact, the word "season," as it pertains to professional sports, has become virtually meaningless; still, as my own private protest against these games' increasing disharmony with nature, I refuse to start watching football until the weather turns cold, which is about halfway into their schedule. I took a quick look at the writers' somber predictions (unable not to look, really, just as I had been unable not to look at the book review or the ads for forthcoming blockbuster movies or the endlessly recycled travel section) and skipped onward to the statistics pages.

These pages, as a sports fan will know, contain no writing— only a mad patchwork of box scores and season statistics and divisional standings and schedules and TV listings and results of everything from tennis tournaments to regattas. I find that they always repay careful scrutiny. Sipping my lukewarm coffee, holding the paper nearer my face to read the small print, I looked through the National League batting and earned-run averages. I glanced over the box scores looking for anything unusual and saw that in Oakland, the great Henderson had gone four for six, with a home run and three stolen bases.

The smallest square in this whole quilt is the list of official roster changes—trades, injuries, signings, promotions, demotions—which runs under the rather brutally honest heading "Transactions." My attention, skipping across this section, stopped in shock at the following entry: "ATLANTA (NL)—Waived Jack Trowbridge, p, for the purpose of giving him his unconditional release."

I read this item, in its tiny agate type, two or three more times before I could begin to think about what it meant. Given his uneven performance over the last few months, I had half expected—and I was sure Jack had, too—that he would be sent again to the minor leagues. But an outright release—baseball's equivalent of being fired—was much more severe and, I was sure, much more traumatic. He had been released once before, by Seattle in 1987, but that was in midseason, and he had been picked up again by the Braves' minor-league organization almost immediately. But the minor-league season was over now, and it was extremely unlikely that any other big-league team would be inclined to sign him. His baseball career, it seemed possible to conclude, was over. More dire, though, than anything I could reason out for myself about the situation was the fact that this had happened at least a day before and yet Jack hadn't called himself to tell us what had taken place, leaving me to discover his humiliation and panic by accident, buried in the small print of the Sunday paper.

"Ellie?" I called. Her steps resounded in the bedroom over my head, but evidently she couldn't hear me. Not wanting to herald such serious news by shouting, I folded the paper, stood slowly, and went to the foot of the stairs.

"Ellie?" I heard a drawer close, and she came to the upstairs landing in one of my old cardigan sweaters, smiling inquisitively, with the politeness that seemed to regulate our relations lately. In her left hand was a magnifying glass.

I gave her the news; in moments of stress, Ellie has a habit of asking insistent questions to which I could not possibly know the answer. She's aware of this, of course, and when she does it I know she's thinking aloud rather than genuinely trying to get information; still, it does put pressure on one. "Where is he now?" she said. I told her I didn't know; I had just that instant learned about it. "Is he at home?" she went on. "Is he all right? Does he need money? Will he be coming home?"

I broke in to reiterate that the reason I knew none of these things was that he hadn't called himself to tell us what had happened, and it was principally that which had me worried. She saw the logic in this, and it helped her become a little more focused.

"What should we do?" I said.

We stood in the narrow stairwell, unreached by the sunlight, Ellie high above me, and looked at each other searchingly. It was a kind of reversion to marital instinct—our child's well-being was threatened—and I don't think it is an exaggeration to say that, on some secondary level, we were grateful for it. I looked to her in such crises, just as she looked to me. Despite my worry for Jack, which had not abated, I was suddenly warmed by the realization that we had the chance now to operate as one, that, at least for the moment, our marriage was uncomplicated and everything was natural between us.

"Do you think we should call him?" Ellie said. "Maybe he's just too upset to want to talk about it yet. Maybe we should wait for him to get in touch with us."

"Well, you may be right," I said, "but I just don't think I can stand not calling. I'm too worried about him."

"Me too. All right. But just you call. If both of us get on the line, it might seem like we're treating it like too much of a disaster. I don't want to put any pressure on him."

"Good idea," I said. I went to the kitchen and dialed his number in Atlanta. Ellie came and stood in the doorway. On the fourth ring, the answering machine engaged. I wondered where he could be—if, in fact, he was in the apartment and simply uninterested in answering the phone. "Not home," I said over my shoulder to Ellie. As I listened to the raspy recording of his voice, I hurriedly tried to decide whether it would scare him off to have parental condolences left on his machine, or whether it would not be better to hang up. But the awful prompt of the beep was already upon me, and I had to say something. I knew it would be useless to play dumb.

"Hi, Jack, it's your father," I said. "Listen, son, I just saw a notice in the paper, in the sports pages, with the bad news, about your release. We're both so sorry. I'm sure everything will be fine. In any case, your mother and I are very anxious to talk to you, so whenever you get this message, please give us a buzz. Okay?"

I hung up, feeling unsatisfied with my message, wanting, as one so often does, to erase it and try again—though I couldn't think offhand of any better way to articulate what I was feeling to a tape recorder. Despondent, I caressed Ellie's thin shoulders as I walked past her and out the door, and drove off to the courts to play some distracted and uninspired tennis with my birthday racket.

In my remaining afternoons at the office, I would often read, never for very long at a stretch, through the dossier that Boyd had sent to me, as promised. It had arrived—courteously, I thought—in a common, padded envelope, marked in the upper left corner only with Boyd's initials and home address. I would close the office door before taking it out of the desk drawer; I had the impulse to close the blinds on the large picture windows as well, and would have done so if not for the fear of having to explain why to any impromptu visitor. The material itself seemed to inspire, if not command, contemplative solitude, a withdrawal from my world.

The two hundred or so pages—Boyd wrote on a yellow Post-it note that he had taken the liberty of condensing it, for me, to about one-sixth its original size—were assembled in a red three-ring binder. An introduction of fifteen pages sketched the history of twentieth-century Brazil—ideologically tilted, no doubt, but still a useful corrective to what I, in my ignorance, had been told by Ferdinand. But beyond that, this document, assembled by BNF and the Archdiocese of São Paulo, was surprisingly, and affectingly, simple: page after page of the testimony of those who had survived the brutally imaginative interrogations of the Brazilian military and police during the years 1964 through 1979. It was a kind of oral history of nightmare, each passage followed by the name, age, occupation, and city or town of residence of the victim, recorded with a matter-of-fact diligence. There were sometimes brief connective paragraphs—their author unidentified—but these served always to classify, in an even, almost bureaucratic tone, never to editorialize, because, after all, what was there to say?

I was stripped, a young lawyer told his transcriber, *and made to sit down in a large, extremely heavy chair, the seat of which was made of corrugated iron. In the back was a kind of outlet where an electrical wire could be attached. They told me this was known as the Dragon's Chair. I received repeated electrical shocks. . . . In addition, beneath the seat of the Dragon's*

Chair was a heavy wooden bar to hold the legs back; with each spasm caused by the electrical shocks I received, my legs would hit against the wooden bar, causing deep gashes . . .

Often there would come some interruption—a knock at the door, the buzz of the intercom—to break the trance, and I would put the binder on the floor behind my desk. Even when there was no outside intrusion, though, I found I could read no more than six or eight pages at a time—not because of unbearable horror or squeamishness (even after reading these detailed accounts, after all, they remained frustratingly hard to imagine) but because of the questions, both specific and general, that would mount up as I went along until I noticed that I had become lost in thought and had stopped reading several minutes before. Why, for instance, was there never any mention of the specific information the authorities sought from these people? Did they lead their lives with more caution in the years of the military regime, desperate not to hear anything that might be worth repeating? Or were they brave, if only because they knew that, in terms of the potential for suffering, bravery or cowardice seemed to make no difference? What happened on the day they were released from prison? What was it like to return home? Did they have to be coaxed to tell these histories to the documentarians, or did they gladly volunteer? Were they themselves more cruel, more indifferent, as a result? Were they weeping as they spoke to their transcriber?

I was overrun by questions of this sort in spite of the fact that I quickly came to understand that there is no way to truly contextualize such confrontations between man and man. No amount of detail would explain anything. Absence of context was in fact the true context. It was better to be left with one's questions.

During the course of my interrogations I had a heart and

respiratory stoppage. The doctor who was present during the session said that it was aerophagia, or the blocking of respiratory channels due to the electric shocks. The doctor administered Cepasol to me, and also muscular tranquilizers so that my body would once again become sensitive to the pain of the beatings, for after a certain moment, I had become insensitive to pain. . . .

I was subjected to electrical shocks to various parts of my body, including my arms, legs, and vagina. At one point in the interrogation, my husband was brought in to watch the administration of shocks; then he was taken into an adjoining room—equipped, I later found out, with a loudspeaker—and for the next phase of questioning, each time one police officer administered the shocks, a second held a microphone near my mouth. . . .

One of the tangential yet curiously relevant things I found myself wondering about was the character of the person, or people, who took this testimony down. There was a uniformity of tone in all these hundreds of depositions that simply had to have been the creation of the transcriber. Surely some of the witnesses ranted, while others mumbled, or swore, or delivered bitter apostrophes. What was the point of conforming them all to this flat, dispassionate monotone? After reading a few dozen accounts myself, though, I came to a kind of agreement with the anonymous transcribers. Even the strongest emotions are quickly spent; against the tide of citizens who had come to describe their "interrogations," one's ability to feel was simply overmatched. It's one thing to have your breath taken away; what lies on the other side of that? This dull, deadened style was perfect. In the face, the literal face, of such suffering, horror and sympathy must rapidly have been revealed as embarrassing luxuries.

I was ordered to stand, naked, on tiptoe, with my arms straight out beside me. Four telephone books were placed in each hand. I was already very tired, having gone without sleep for an indeterminate time, but I was ordered to maintain this position, even as they beat me with sticks on the chest and stomach. The officer told me that this position was known as "Christ the Redeemer" . . .

Without telling Ellie, I made three or four more phone calls to Jack's place in Atlanta; but he was never home, and I hung up before the end of his machine's recorded instructions. Finally, on the Thursday following his release from the team, he called us. It was just after dinner, and I was in the kitchen pouring myself a drink.

"Jack," I said, striving to put down any note of urgency or emotion even in that one word. "You got my message?"

Ellie fairly burst through the swinging door to the kitchen and looked at me anxiously.

"Your mother's here," I said lightly. "Okay if she gets on the other phone?"

"Yeah, sure," Jack said. He cleared his throat. I gestured toward the stairs with my head and Ellie hurried off toward the bedroom.

"Before she picks up," Jack said, laughing, "let me tell you that the reason I didn't call sooner is that this is the first moment since Friday I haven't been drunk, asleep, or hung over."

"Well, I think you're entitled," I said, flattered and surprised that he would trust me with anything he didn't want Ellie to know. "A good bender is not always a terrible thing. Just so long as you didn't do anything too foolish."

"Well, that's the great thing about memory loss," he said.

There was a fumbling click as Ellie picked up the bedroom phone.

"Jack," she said, "honey, are you all right? We've been so worried about you." This made me flinch, frightened as I was of saying the wrong thing, of scaring him into a sullen, prideful insistence on his own self-reliance; but people will accept things from their mothers that they would treat as an affront from anyone else.

"Yes, Mom, I'm fine. I mean I'm unemployed and a little depressed, and in Atlanta, but I'm okay other than that. I was just telling Dad that I've been staying at a friend's house, so I didn't want to call until I got back."

This was an unimaginative story, and Ellie must have seen through it, but out of concern for him she let it go. "What happened?" she said. "What explanation did they give you?"

I smiled, expecting Jack to laugh at this bit of feminine naïveté. But he didn't. "No excuse at all," he said. "They just blew it, that's all. I really felt like I was throwing better lately. I haven't had any stiffness in the shoulder for a while now. But that's why the whole franchise has been in the toilet for the last decade or so. They don't know what they're doing, and they panic when things go bad."

"And Dad was telling me that it's too late in the year for you to hook up with some other team?" I winced again.

"Well," Jack said, sounding a little hurt, "technically it's not too late, but it is pretty unlikely, I guess. Nobody wants to start rebuilding their pitching staff in September. Offers are much more likely to come around spring training time next year."

By this time I was grateful for Ellie's frantic takeover of the conversation, because it made it easier for me to conceal how bewildered I was by Jack's cocky attitude. When I read of his release, on the heels of his less than mediocre season with the

Braves, I had gone ahead and assumed that his career as a baseball player was finished. It seemed the only reasonable conclusion; and all my concern for him, all my worry over his disappearance, had been built on that. It was confounding to hear him talk now as if he had been treated unfairly, and I wasn't sure what to say.

"So," Jack said, with a slowed delivery that seemed to signal something weighty, "that's partly why I'm calling. I have no plans for the next few months, I hate it here, plus I'm in a little bit of trouble with my landlord. I don't want to put down money on a new place when I don't even know where I'll be next spring. And I'm having a little cash-flow trouble as it is. So I was wondering if it would be okay with you if I came back home for a while, for the off-season maybe, to live."

"Of course!" Ellie said immediately, delighted. "That's wonderful. Of course it will be all right. Wouldn't it, Gene?"

"Well, of course," I said.

We made some loose arrangements—he was, characteristically, unsure what day he would arrive—and hung up in a general air of forced anticipation, except, that is, for Ellie, who seemed disproportionately happy, perhaps taking into account the relief Jack's presence would provide from the strained dialectic between us. We were to be reunited as a family, it's true, for the first extended period in eight years; still, I couldn't help reflecting as we said our goodbyes that that conversation, wherein we all spoke with emotion and optimism without being able to see one another, unwittingly caught some of the repressed essence of our family character. I could hear Ellie scuttling around upstairs, looking in at his room, no doubt, and wondering what she could do to prepare the place for him. I stood still by the phone in the kitchen, puzzled and a little angered, in a fatherly way, by my son's remark about his money problems. The Braves were paying Jack only the minimum salary allowed in the agreement between the major leagues and the formidable players' union; still, that was the rather princely rate, in our era of the exaltation of sports figures, of one hundred thousand dollars a year. What did he mean, money trouble?

Oblivious to such nit-picking, Ellie came downstairs and into the kitchen. She looked at me, smiled warmly though distractedly, and then looked restlessly around the kitchen, with such thoroughness that I instinctively stepped out of her way, before moving on to the TV room. I had no idea what she was looking for, and raised my eyebrows in the hope of getting an answer, but she did not pay attention to me. I followed behind her as she unself-consciously repeated this process—staring critically, almost worriedly, deliberating, but finally doing nothing—in every room on the first floor of the house.

It dawned on me that while Ellie was being driven by a powerful instinct to get Jack's home ready for his return—powerful enough to obscure the fact that he wouldn't be home for days—she had no way, really, to act on this instinct, in part because at some point over the last decade this had ceased to be his home and in part because our long separation meant that we were not really acquainted with the adult Jack. She, and I, had surprisingly little idea of what he was like or what he would want. It was grotesque to imagine him with the same personality he displayed as a high-schooler, but that was the last complete image of him we were able to draw on. And it was watching Ellie's nervous excitement that made me realize that what was stirring me to uncertainty and worry was not, in fact, the question of what Jack had done to fritter away his generous salary. I had given myself that issue as a screen over what was really working on me: my only son, whom I had more or less consigned to benign estrangement, was now being returned to me, and I was going to have to find an authentic way to relate to him, whether he was aware of the need for it or not. Somehow, over that spring and summer, even though I had foreseen the end of his career and had even, on some level, congratulated myself for that unsentimental, clear-eyed assessment, this logical consequence of that end had escaped me; somehow I had failed to prepare, or even allow, for this perfectly simple scenario.

The testimonies of the tortured showed a marked fondness for the passive voice—"I was beaten," "shocks were administered," and so on. I supposed that the idea (which may have been the transcriber's) was to keep the focus on the victims, and not to grant the military and police even the metaphorical empowerments of grammar. Nevertheless, from time to time, like an extra in an old film who later went on to stardom, a certain Captain da Silva would inevitably wander through the tight frame of these reminiscences. Sitting in my office, I could remind myself at these moments, speaking of unwelcome empowerment, that the single link across the years and across the latitudes, between this misty figure of brutality and the unobtrusive suburbanite Ferdinand, was me.

I was thrown several times into a room known as the Ice Box. This was a small room with an insulated door like that of a freezer; the walls were painted black, and on the ceiling, out of reach, were a very strong light, a loudspeaker, and a partitioned opening connected to a system of cold air. Several different voices began to come from the loudspeaker, calling me dirty names. When I protested the treatment to which I was being subjected and demanded to see Captain da Silva, the voices stopped, and were shortly replaced by electronic noises so loud I could no longer hear my own shouts. Sometimes these noises were simple buzzing or banging, sometimes they were recognizable, an airplane turbine or an air raid siren. These were interspersed with periods of absolute silence. Together with the extreme cold, these sounds produced a great physical effect on my eardrums, and a psychological effect as well. . . .

It wasn't that outrage was an inappropriate response to these stories; but I was surprised at how outrage turned out to lead nowhere. Being indignant, after all, changed nothing; in fact, it only made one feel weak, laughable, naive. When feeling, so absent in the accounts themselves, was understood to be pointless and unthinking, one's fascination began to latch on to abstractions. What was most disconcerting to me was the remarkable range of imagination displayed by the torturers. One had imagined them to be stick-wielding brutes, able to do what they did only by connecting with some sleeping primal anger, with less capacity for invention than the average man; but it seemed the opposite was true. In what mind would be found the confluence of the barbarous and the poetic that would produce the Ice Box, or Christ the Redeemer, or a host of other methods? Were they derived scientifically, relying on medical knowledge of the most direct corporeal avenues to the mind? Or were they conceived on the basis of their strange, hellish beauty, and then adopted on a trial-and-error basis? Almost from the beginning, I had been unable not to wonder, though I knew it to be a self-indulgence, if I myself would have had the innate physical and mental strength (the tortured were, after all, ordinary citizens) to withstand that kind of pain; but a more complex question was whether I, as a human being, was not by definition equipped with the same ability to invent evil as these men.

. . . *the officer insisted that I look at him as a condition for receiving my meal . . .*

I read on through the binder, guiltily, slowly, trying to stare at every sentence until its impression had been formed on me, but there was no way to know if this was happening in any lasting way.

Understand that though I continued to seek out Ferdinand's company, I did not then have any sympathy for him, or identify with him, or anything so mundane as that. It was true that I was making an effort to work up some sort of revulsion toward him and was finding it difficult; but that had to be put down to the simple inconceivability, to me, of the whole subject, the great problem of reducing the things I was reading and hearing to terms in which I could converse—as well as to the fact that, when one is confronted with a human voice and a human face, things inevitably take on subtler colorations. In short, I treated Ferdinand as an emissary from the outside world, the real world; if this was the man that world had chosen to send me, then I was determined to make the best of it and learn as much as I could.

A large part of what helped me, in practical terms, to overcome my nervousness about talking to him was the abrupt disappearance from its perch across the street from Ferdinand's house, after three solid weeks, of the blue van. I asked him if he knew anything about it; he frowned contemptuously.

"That never had any real surveillance purpose," he said. "It was a harassment, a scare tactic, to see if I would panic and run,

I suppose. Once they saw I wasn't going to scare, they realized it wasn't worth the expense. I'm sure the surveillance does go on, but in a more conventional, hidden way."

"How do you know?"

He cocked his head. "I can feel it. They're waiting to see what I will do. I've developed a sense for it. You will, too, I'm sure."

"Me?" I said. "I doubt that."

He smiled. "How nice for you," he said teasingly, "to be watched and followed, to feel wanted and dangerous and at the same time know you have done nothing wrong. Like a courier with an empty bag, like a player in that game with the dart guns, Assassin. How thrilling and uncomplicated. How American."

Copywriting jobs, when I was a young man and advertising was still defining itself, were pretty easy to come by—in fact, there was a hint of something unfortunate in the announcement that you had accepted one—but that hasn't been the case for nearly three decades, and certainly is not today. Even at entry level, the competition is heated. It's no longer a matter of where you went to college, or to high school, or what your major was; at AAK, as everywhere, we had to design a rigorous sequence of interviews and evaluations for job applicants, to separate the truly gifted from the merely personable. As a result, prospective AAK copywriters have to produce a fair amount of work just to get inside the door, just to prove that they're serious.

The last interview for each of these young people was with me. Over the years, as I grew more stately, I had refined my technique in these discussions, which refinement had as much to do with controlling the applicants' impression of me as vice versa. I confess there was a charge in being—with a handful of exceptions—so unabashedly feared; it made it seem worthwhile to have survived in the ad business long enough to have become an eminence. I couldn't help but be pleased to see reflected in their nervous eyes an image of myself as both genial and terrifying, a man whose good side was a mysterious, shifting, El Dorado–like place of legendary benefits. One of the reasons I could afford to so amuse myself during the interviews was that, by the time a candidate reached that step on the interview ladder, he or she was virtually in; in twenty-odd years, I had rejected very few of those adrenalized young people who wanted to write advertisements and insisted they cared not for what.

That fall, in the strange limbo of my last weeks at work, one of these eager young people was directed by the personnel manager to make an appointment with Caroline for an interview with me, very likely the last I would ever have. He was my only appointment that whole day. Unbeknownst to me, Caroline nevertheless had him sit in the waiting room for a good ten minutes past the scheduled hour—exercising, to my delighted surprise, her own ability to sweat out these poor men (they were mostly men) who, she knew, would in a few weeks arrive as her seniors and in a few weeks more would have lost all compunction about ordering her around.

I had little to do in those final days. The preparations for the retirement bash slipped into a higher gear, and from time to time someone would stick their head into the office to ask me about a seating problem of some corporate delicacy, or about the menu. But I didn't give any more time than absolutely necessary to these requests because, frankly, I thought it would be immodest of me even to care. Certainly, I thought, it would have appeared to others that way. The great event had been scheduled for four weeks after my birthday. I was told that the Park Lane ballroom was booked solid until that day, but I suspect that the real reason for the delay was that the agency, bless its heart, didn't want it to look to me or to anyone else like it was hustling me out the door.

Caroline escorted the young man, whose name was Tom Freilicher, into my office. I stood and shook his hand, and motioned him onto the couch on the receiving end of my desk. "Coffee, anything?" I said; he smiled and said no—no one in his position has ever said yes—and Caroline took her leave.

The young man had the perfect posture of the very nervous. He had thick brown hair that was moussed back for the occasion, and wore a gray suit with a bold red tie. The suit itself had the earnest, conservative look of the first suit a man owns, and it put me in mind of how green he was.

"Just graduated this past June, Thomas?" I said.

"Yes, sir. From Kenyon."

"Graduate in that suit?"

He looked perplexed for a moment, until I cued him to laugh with a small smile. "That's right," he said. "Old Faithful. I got my diploma, so I'm one for one in it."

My smile broadened. I found myself thinking in the boy's head, trying to wring all the meaning out of this meaningless pleasantry, thinking how well it all seemed to be going so far.

"Did you bring a résumé, Thomas?" I said.

Failing again to correct me—no one in the world named Thomas is actually called Thomas, except by his parents—he handed it over almost before I had completed my sentence. Not so long ago, job applicants of any age had their résumés professionally typeset; now, in the era of the personal computer, Freilicher's meticulous, laser-printed, necessarily scanty c.v. had a homemade look to it. He was an English major; his senior thesis, on the Lost Generation, had won a departmental third prize. He had held some student Social Committee position and had played junior varsity squash for two years; apart from that, nothing much. The margins on the paper itself were conspicuously wide.

None of this counted against him—in fact, the contrary was often true; solitary, renegade creative types were often outsiders (though not sociopaths), and a traditionally impressive school record could actually work against one. But when I looked up at Freilicher, and frankly examined him, it was difficult to see any spark of real individuality, real intelligence, any of the detachment from the world a great copywriter needs. He looked amiable and eager to please me. What was wanted—and perhaps this was in him, though below the surface—was a little energy, a little restlessness, even a hint of impatience, really, with the interview itself.

"And what have you been doing since graduation?"

"Oh, well," he said, slightly embarrassed, "my parents gave me a trip to Europe as a graduation present. The usual, I guess. I mean not the usual, just it's not that uncommon. Maybe half the guys I know did the same thing. It was like America East."

"I had a European tour when I was about your age," I said. "It was called World War II." This was a pointlessly mean thing for me to say—I certainly didn't give a damn if the boy's parents were wealthy enough to pack him off to Europe—but he was getting too comfortable with me, I felt, before we'd even gotten to the meat of the interview.

It had its effect on him; I actually saw him swallow. "So anyway," he said—choosing to move on rather than try to apologize, which I noted with respect—"I've been in New York for about a month now, staying with some friends on their couch and interviewing for jobs."

As he was speaking, I picked up his book off the top of a pile on one side of my desk and flipped through it again. Applicants for jobs on the creative side—copywriters or artists—are required to produce a set of pseudo-advertisements, for real or imaginary products, as a gauge both of their inventiveness and of their dedication. Freilicher had produced a set of eight, which were impressive in terms of their professionalism, if not exactly groundbreaking. I frowned as I perused them, just to keep him on his toes.

"Who did your art here?" I said.

"My girlfriend," he said.

There was an ad for something called Colorado Beer, which featured a group of young adults whitewater-rafting above the tagline "Free and Easy"—undistinguished, perhaps, but a sight better than some authentic campaigns like the fascistic "It's the Right Beer Now," which is a proof of my own private maxim that you can say absolutely anything in an ad, no matter how stupid, if you set it to music. Facing that was a public service ad urging citizens to register to vote, dominated by a cleverly doctored photograph (taken, according to a credit in the margin, from an album cover) of a man with no mouth. "If you don't register to vote," the copy began, "you might as well send a letter to Washington informing them that your own opinion counts for nothing." The rest were along these same lines—an instant coffee ad featuring two people who appeared to have just had sex for the first time, a car ad in which the car itself did not appear, only a road with all the trees and telephone poles bent in the same direction as if by a hurricane, an ad for a credit card with the tag "Free At Last." The best of the lot was for a high-top sneaker; it showed two basketball teams at the tipoff. Only one center stood in the circle; he, the referee, and the rest of the players were all looking in amazement up at the unseen roof of the gymnasium. Splinters and dust fell to the floor around them. "Mercuries," the tag read. "They'll take some getting used to."

Freilicher watched me carefully as I looked through his book, obviously fighting his impulse to get up, come stand behind me, and look over my shoulder. "Television," he said meekly, "is my real field of interest, so the book may not really reflect my strengths, I think."

On the one hand, it's not at all difficult for anyone born in the television age to invent his or her own advertisements; they just imitate what they know, with a little variation. On the other hand, such imaginative and time-consuming effort just to get a job—just to get a job *interview*—is a very long way from the thinking of the executives of my own early years. Everything was different then; if the ads themselves were more nakedly scientific, then the ad agency's practices were similarly more intuitive. About four months after my return from Germany in 1946 —four months of sleeping, putting on weight, doing household chores as if I were twelve again, disinterestedly catching my parents' increasingly uneasy glances when I turned down one invitation or another—I agreed to go to work in Pittsfield for my father's small department store. He would have preferred to put me in an office job and keep me off the shop floor—as much to avoid embarrassment to himself as to make things interesting for me. But there were a lot of veterans in my father's employ, men who were grateful sometimes to the point of tears for the fact that my father had held their jobs for them while they served overseas; he already had more men working for him than he truly needed, and under the circumstances there was no question of laying off any of them to make room for his son, even the ones who deserved to be fired. He put me to work selling suits, and I quickly reassumed the useful army discipline of robotically doing as I was told.

It didn't take me long to discover that I didn't want to stay in the retail business, or in Pittsfield; but a lack of energy, as well as an utter dearth of ideas about what I wanted to make out of my life, kept me selling suits to hicks for close to two years. Everything was easy; my meals were cooked for me, my laundry done, and I was able to save a good deal of money, though for what I didn't know. I was in a kind of zero-gravity state; the slightest push, in any direction, and I would continue in that direction, either until I encountered some resistance or forever. And in fact that is what happened. An old army buddy (the designation is as hackneyed as it sounds, for it was someone I didn't particularly like) called me at home late one Monday night, from New York. God knows why he called; I imagine that despite all his oppressive cheerfulness he was having more trouble than he had anticipated in laying aside his existence as a soldier. His name was Howard Mills, and he was calling from somewhere noisy.

"How's it going, Trowbridge?" he said. "Hey, who'd have thought it, huh?"

"Yeah," I said, with no idea what he was referring to.

He asked me if I wasn't dying of boredom up there in the sticks, and I admitted that I was close to it. New York, he said, that was where it was all happening; that was the only place in the country where a man in his early twenties belonged. He was originally a country boy himself, he said, so he knew I'd love it just as much.

"I have just one word to say to you, Trowbridge," he said in lewd tones. "That one word is dame. Dame, damer, damest. You absolutely cannot imagine it."

I had to admit that Mills's one word had, at that time, great resonance for me.

"We were in Grenoble together," Mills said. "So I know you know what I'm talking about."

"Yes, I do," I said. I didn't want to elaborate any further on that memory since my parents were sitting in tired silence in the next room.

"So how fast," Mills said, "can you get out of Dogpatch and get down here?"

"I'll be there this weekend," I said.

He was delighted. I knew even then that he would be less delighted once I got there, that it was one thing to find an old army buddy's phone number in some jacket pocket and call him up from a bar and quite another to suddenly have him on your hands, but I didn't care. Nor did I care to analyze the expressions—half relief that I was doing something, half fright at the precipitous, dispassionate way I was doing it—on the faces of my mother and father when I told them I was leaving. I took out all my savings and traveled by bus to Manhattan, ready again for input, for the engagement of all my senses.

I stayed in a hotel near Gramercy Park, glad I could afford to, at least for a while. Howard Mills and I wound up spending two or three nights on the town together, in unsuccessful pursuit of dames, before again falling out of touch, this time for good. It was nearly 1948, and the job situation had become a little better. But I had come to a veritable fount of ex-servicemen my age, and as my savings were being quickly devoured, I was forced to take the only job for which I was genuinely qualified—selling suits, this time at J. Press. I cut down to part time in order to take courses toward a B.A. at Columbia, but on that demanding schedule I felt I was learning nothing, and after the second year I didn't bother to reregister. I bounced around a bit after that, traveling from my two-room apartment in Murray Hill to jobs as a loan officer at a branch of Chase Manhattan (my first office job, though loathsome otherwise) and as a jobber for the Scribner's publishing house.

In 1951, all of twenty-six years old, I stumbled into a job at the old magazine *This Week,* selling ad space. A fellow bachelor of the neighborhood—whom I met at least twice a week taking my laundry to the dry cleaner's to be done by the pound—who held a similar job at *Time* tipped me off about it. "Here's the secret," he said in his lordly way. He was two years older than I, a confident, unattractive man, and he loved to explain the world's workings to me. "When you get there, they'll have you fill out a questionnaire, four pages single-spaced. As soon as the door closes behind you they throw that thing out. I'm telling you. All they care about is your attitude, your personality—are you the kind of guy who can go out and sell advertising space all day? It takes a certain combination, and that's what they're look- ing for. The kind of guy who can call a potential client six times in two weeks and still have the guy be happy to hear from him. Charming yet persistent, smooth yet hungry. Do you feel hun- gry?"

"I feel bored," I said.

"Well, it's a short step from bored to hungry," he said. "And back again."

I don't think his theory about the questionnaire was accu- rate, but in any case I put on a good bright-eyed act for the personnel manager and was hired. It was a miserable tenure. I worked on commission, naturally, and that commission was kept low enough to wring the maximum effort out of you just in order to feed yourself. Other than the fact that it led me indirectly into advertising, the only good things I can say about my year or so there are that it taught me to handle job pressure and that it introduced me to Ellie.

She was working as a secretary to one of the photo editors at *This Week;* but that didn't facilitate things for me quite as much as it would seem, for she and I worked on different floors, and I never had any remotely legitimate excuse to drop by the photo department. We had never exchanged more than a hello in the elevator ("exchanged" may be the wrong word, for my own greeting to her, out of recent habit, apparently came out more wolfish than I had meant it) before I began going to the corner deli for lunch, when I had lunch free, at the nonsensical hour of eleven-fifty, just because I knew that's when I would catch her there.

Within a week or so, I had gotten this down to a science, so that I would be just two or three spots away from her on line at the delicatessen. The first two times I managed to return on the same elevator as she, I said nothing. I wasn't concerned that she would think I was following her—in fact, I wanted her to think that; for when the only time you ever see someone is in an elevator crowded with strangers and business colleagues, the only way to convey your interest must be a nonverbal one. Finally, after having gotten her to smile politely at me in the deli line, I waited at the door for her and made my pitch as we crossed the street.

The very fact that I would ask out a woman who had never even told me her name (I knew it from friends) forces me to realize just how long ago this was. Over the span of my adulthood, sex and conversation seem to have swapped positions on the intimacy spectrum; you'd as soon brand yourself a rapist as try to strike up a conversation with some strange woman in a public place, whereas I have actually walked in on people—

employees and clients, employees and models, employees and employees—having sex in the office during business hours. I can't say I disapprove of all this—if I'm honest with myself I admit that I'm a little covetous—but at the same time part of me is glad that I am too old and too married to have to catch up with these changes. Once or twice every year, some corner of the agency is thrown into chaos by the aftermath of some frantic, ill-advised, shooting star of an office fling. Still, no one thinks anything is amiss. The men at the agency speak of the Naughty Librarian, whose defenses have apparently never been solved by any of her co-workers, as the Holy Grail of such couplings.

In any case, as we waited for the light, I asked Ellie her name, just for form's sake. "Elizabeth," she said, not smiling, cautiously withholding her last name. "Well, Elizabeth," I said as we crossed, "my name is Gene Trowbridge. I'm in the ad sales department. How would you like to go to dinner sometime?" She didn't seem thrilled, though nor was she offended; this must have happened to her a lot. She walked a step ahead of me, not wanting to seem encouraging. She was slim, with her hair cut short almost in a 1920s style, and her elegant suit, I noticed, suggested that there was more money available to her than what she found in her pay envelope as a secretary. When we reached the far sidewalk, just outside the building entrance, she turned back to find me.

"Sorry, Gene," she said. "You seem like a nice guy. But I'm engaged."

"Oh really?" I said, smiling, crushed. "That's terrific. To whom?"

It was a silly question, and she laughed. "No one you'd know, I think," she said as we crossed the lobby. "He's from back home."

"And home is?"

"Gladwyne, Pennsylvania. Near Philadelphia."

We stood at the back of the group waiting for the elevator, our rolled brown paper bags in hand. On an impulse, I looked down to where she held the bag and her purse primly in front of her. My eyes ran over her fingers.

"Elizabeth?" I whispered, to avoid being heard by the others. She raised her eyebrows.

"You're not wearing an engagement ring," I said.

She blushed.

"Frankly," I whispered, "I think that someone with as much class as yourself deserves a fiancé who'll cough up for the ring."

She kept her eyes on the floor indicator arrow as it traveled slowly counterclockwise.

"Or maybe there is no fiancé?" I went on. "Maybe it's just a line you use to—"

"There is," she whispered, not looking at me. "Please stop."

"Then where is the ring?" I said. "Did he buy you one?"

"Yes."

"What happened to it?"

No answer. A woman standing in front of us cleared her throat, which seemed to embarrass Ellie even more.

"What happened to it?" I said, a little louder.

Deftly she undid the clasp on her purse, reached in, fished around, held a rather expensive-looking ring above the bag where I could see it for just an instant, then tossed it back in.

The elevator door opened. We squeezed in and I rode up staring at the back of Ellie's red neck, my mind working. This was too good to leave alone. Why would she take off her engagement ring? There were perfectly reasonable explanations for it, but the whole subject was obviously so upsetting to her that I was sure no simple explanation could apply. There was a mystery there, and it was the mystery of her vulnerability. She walked off the elevator at her floor without looking back. I gave her a day to think about it. I called her the next afternoon, and for the next eight working days in a row, until she agreed to go out with me. Five months later she came to my apartment in her best dress late one night after having broken off her engagement at dinner and sobbed until dawn. I held her in my arms and repeated, in a soothing voice, all the blandishments I had been saying for weeks in a much more insistent manner in order to bring us to this momentous evening: details of the life of love and riches and excitement that I promised her, a life that differed in one essential respect from that which the hometown fiancé offered her—it would be something other than the life her parents had led, the life she already knew. I was spinning a tale of my own ambition; it was not a lie exactly, but it was a subject I could warm to, I had noticed, only when looking into her face. Eight months after that we were married.

The fiancé was a wealthy fellow veteran from Gladwyne whom she had known since childhood. Her parents adored him. In the end, I think it was his very familiarity as much as her feeling for me that worked against him; he is, I don't doubt, a good man, and we know from Ellie's remaining family connections that he has gone on to great business success. Even now, in my weaker moments, I wonder jealously if Ellie ever wonders what might have happened had she chosen differently.

Pursuing her kept me at *This Week* longer than I might otherwise have stayed. On the other hand, once I began to contemplate marriage, a genuine nervousness about my lack of a regular salary began to take hold of me. My and Ellie's parents had not, respectively, the means or the inclination to help us out. I mentioned this over an alcohol-soaked lunch to John Bianchi, a man I did business with often enough to have become friends, from a fledgling ad agency known as Nagle Associates.

"Look," John said. "I shouldn't say this to you, because before you the last two sellers from *This Week* were pinheads, and if you leave they'll probably replace you with another pinhead. But you're on the wrong side of this whole racket. What can you get promoted to? Head space seller? Who needs it. Come on over to Nagle. I'll put in a good word for you, not that I'll have to—the place is growing so fast they'll hire pretty much anyone who speaks English and can tie his own tie."

I had one interview, with the president of the agency, Bill Nagle. He had gray hair in a brush cut, wore a heavy tweed suit, and held in his teeth a pipe with which he had filled his large office with sweet-smelling smoke. He did not invite me to sit down. He looked me over impassively for a full minute before he spoke.

"You were in Europe, Bianchi tells me," he said.

"Yes, sir."

"Where'd you serve?"

"Tenth Division, VIth Army Corps, in France and Germany."

He nodded. "General Truscott," he said.

"Yes, sir."

He stared at me again, exhaling small clouds of pipe smoke. "In the service a young man learns to follow rules," he said. "You haven't forgotten how to follow rules, have you?"

"No, sir," I said.

He opened the top drawer of his desk and took out a mimeographed sheet of paper. He handed it to me. "These are the rules of advertising," he said. "You can start in two weeks; that should give you enough time to give notice at your old job. My secretary will show you where your desk will be. Welcome aboard."

I was alarmed—pleased, but also a little spooked by this professorial-looking man's eccentricity. "I'm very grateful, sir," I said. "But don't we need to discuss, that is, I'm sort of obligated to ask about things like salary."

A look of real irritation came over him then, a look I was instantly sorry to see, and he leaned forward onto his desk. "Salary? Son," he said—I don't think he had registered my name—"you see that piece of paper in your hand? You tape that to your desk, and come to work every day, and don't drink to excess, and you are going to be a rich man. You're getting in on something here. Don't you see that?"

"Yes, sir," I said uncertainly.

He glared at me. Then he sat back and waved his pipe dismissively. "Well, it doesn't matter if you see it or not, I sup-pose," he said. "Just be here two weeks from Monday."

To this day I can only consider it a freak of nature that a man so obstinate and dim in every other respect (his "rules," derived from a science of his own making, were bizarre, though heaven help you if he came by your desk and they weren't in plain sight) could have possessed such mystical foresight in regard to business—in regard to American culture, really. I showed up two weeks later knowing nothing, and, as he had told me I would be, I was taken along for the ride.

How little I had in common, then, with the collegiate, over-prepared, preprofessional Freilicher, who watched with mount-ing agitation, trying not to lean forward, as I paged through his book. His work may have been raw in terms of its conception, but the execution of it was quite compulsively detailed and thor-ough. There was no way it could have been slapped together between the time we had contacted him and the day of his first interview; a great deal of thought, years of thought really, had to have gone into it. In the course of my lifetime, advertising had gone from a vocation to an institution, the perfect bridge for an ambitious young person between art and commerce, between creative satisfaction and material comfort. One did not, indeed could not, stumble into it; it was a life's work, and boys like Freilicher, apparently, began dreaming of its magic and of its riches from an early age. I could just imagine him and his fetching girlfriend in her dorm room at Kenyon, in the spring of their senior year, working back to back on this program for their future, collaborating on imaginary sales pitches in the small hours of the night.

I put the book down. "Thomas," I said, "why do you want to go into advertising?"

As many candidates did when I asked this question, he looked momentarily frightened; he had probably guessed that the only relevant question, to his prospective bosses, would be how *badly* he wanted to go into advertising. He folded his hands in his lap and fingered the bottom of his red paisley interview tie.

"Well," he said. "I don't know, how does anybody decide what they want to do with their life? That is, there's no one moment when you just know. As far back as—well, at least at the age when I first became even interested in reading magazines, I remember being as interested in the ads as anything else. From a creative standpoint, they're such a compressed form, you know? And not only that, but so much work goes into any ad, and yet you can tell in the first glance, the first split second, whether it works or not. That's a great challenge. I've always wanted to be in on it, because I feel like I could do it. I feel like I know the language."

There was no right or wrong answer, of course; I just looked for honesty in the respondent, and by that measure I thought young Freilicher had done all right, with one reservation. He hadn't mentioned the money. "And do you have any creative aspirations outside the field, Thomas?" I said. A lot of young people, aspiring writers or visual artists, made the mistake of taking jobs at AAK simply because they hadn't the stomach for being poor in New York. "You'll be working on the Great American Novel in the spare hours you imagine you'll have?"

"No, sir," he said firmly, shaking his head. "I don't have any aspirations like that."

"You seem quite sure about it."

"Well, Mr. Trowbridge," he said, ingenuously warming to his topic, "I flirted with it a little bit in school. I even took a couple of writing classes. Maybe it was just the people I was in them with, but it really turned me off. It's so much about ego. The ten people in the class were basically all writing just for each other, and for the professor, and I'm sure absolutely no one outside that room gave a damn whether we did it or not. I just decided I have greater ambitions than that. That whole atmosphere just seemed so *phony*."

This was a provocative answer, however casually delivered; it was all I could do not to smile. Advertising—refuge from egoism, from the phoniness of art . . . "And why AAK specifically?" I said.

He seemed more ready for that one. "AAK has a reputation for being a real cutting-edge agency," he said, "a place where there's a lot of emphasis on the creative, on breaking new ground, and that's the sort of place I want to work. I've been reading the trades, so I really follow who's behind what campaign."

"I see."

"And," he said nervously, "I know a little bit about the history of the advertising business, just from reading I've done, and I know it may sound like kissing up but I would look forward to the chance to learn from you in particular, because you're one of the giants, I think. I know a lot of the work you did back in the sixties, and it would be a real honor to work for you."

I sighed. "Thomas," I said, "two things. One, I'm afraid you won't get the chance to work under me, because I'm retiring in another month or so."

He looked concerned, as if I had told him I had some terminal illness.

"And two, and this is very important, even if I were staying on, you wouldn't be working for me. You work for the client. It's important that you go into it understanding that, rather than learn it later, the hard way." I continued, Cassandra-like, to give this admonition to job applicants, not because I was unaware of its diminishing relevance but because I didn't know what to offer in its place. "All the work you see on TV or in print that you admire, all of it was done to please the client, and if it hadn't, you would never have seen it. Do you understand what I mean?"

"Yes, sir," he said.

He would forget it quickly enough. "Good. Now, the work you've done here is very satisfactory, but before we decide on your application there are two more ads I want you to mock up for me. This is standard," I added, seeing his disappointment. "Everyone who comes through my office has to do this. The first is a PSA for AIDS prevention; the object here is not to test your civic-mindedness, but to see if you're able to find a new path over very well-traveled ground. Ads like these find themselves in the position of having to say the same thing over and over again, and there are already a thousand of them, so this will be a good test of your ability to create something unique. Got it?"

He nodded.

"The second is an ad for perfume. You can make up the name of it yourself. Perfume ads are an industry favorite, always have been, and I'll tell you why. Even if you wanted to, it is by definition impossible to relate any product information about perfume in an advertisement. So all the bonds are loosed; it's all image, you can do whatever you want. So I want you to really stretch, go wild, show me how imaginative you can be. I know you imagine your medium is TV, so you can submit them in script form if you want, but if so, I want you to have your girlfriend do storyboards for them. Okay?"

He was smiling slyly now, anxious to get to it.

"All right then," I said, rising. "I want to thank you for coming in. It's been a pleasure meeting you. I'll see you in two weeks or so?"

"I'll make an appointment with your secretary?" he said.

"Fine." We shook hands, and with my other hand I buzzed for Caroline, who appeared in the doorway to show Freilicher back to the reception area. I remained standing, waiting until Caroline returned so I would know that the boy was gone. When she reappeared, I went down the hall to the men's room.

On my way back, I passed the agency bulletin board, and stopped to look it over, having nothing pressing to call me back to my desk. A piece of regular typing paper was pinned to the board; at the top of it, in what looked like Joe Schultz's handwriting, were the words "Beer Campaigns (TV) in Which A Wet Woman Does Not Appear." Beneath it was written, helpfully, "1)". No one had thought of one, or, just as likely, they understood that the joke worked better if they left the list blank.

I thought again of the day of my own interview at Nagle Associates, how I felt waiting outside the office, how I felt afterward, how energetic and ignorant and aimless a young man I was, and I thought of the likable Freilicher, his future, as he saw it, hanging on my every frown. I tried to think of those two people—Freilicher and my twenty-seven year-old self—as having a lot in common. I tried to relate them; I tried, in a sense, to reach across time and introduce them to one another, hoping sincerely that they would get along. But even in the realm of fantasy, it was a fruitless exercise. The boy was of another generation, another world; and anyway, it was not possible for him ever to see me as I was. Everywhere I look, I thought, I see my sons.

After the Communist insurrection in the army barracks was put down in 1935, Brazil's president, Getúlio Vargas, used the erstwhile menace of socialism to justify his resistance to popular pressure for democratic reforms. Vargas, while in most respects what we would call a right-wing extremist, was an anticolonialist as well, who shared with his subjects a longing for a Brazil that could control its own economic destiny. His various programs for the nationalization of industry, which made him a hero to Brazil's middle classes, directly threatened many American economic interests there. American industry, of course, would not stand for it, and so prevailed upon their connections in the U.S. government to do something about it. Washington courted the Brazilian army in unambiguous terms, leading a General Monteiro to stage a coup deposing Vargas in October 1945.

President Marshal Eurico Gaspar Petra, who took office in 1947, was a sternly pro-American leader, on the right wing even on the skewed spectrum of the army. While he pleased his supporters in Washington, he was far less popular with his countrymen—who, at the first opportunity they were given, voted him out of office in 1950 and reelected in his stead the unfortunate Vargas.

By this time, the trick any president had to perform to stay in power was apparent, though much easier said than done: balance the interests of the foreign monopolies upon which the country's economy was dependent against the popular pressure for Brazilian control of Brazil's own resources. Vargas, failing for a second time to pull this off to everyone's satisfaction, was threatened with another coup from the right, and he headed it off in perhaps the only way possible. He committed suicide in August 1954.

This one episode alone, in spite of the fact that it took place in my own adult lifetime, is nearly enough to place the whole history of this people out of reach of my ability to understand it. What American can even fathom living in a country whose leaders are weak enough, human enough, to kill themselves in a fit of panic and despair? Think of the confidence with which we elect Presidents. Think of the air with which they carry themselves. American leaders embody a peculiarly American ideal of brash self-confidence, of invincibility, free from the cancer of introspection. It is what we elect them for, really. We are impatient with complex personalities, either in our leaders or in other nations. What stunted aspects of our national character have never been, perhaps will never be, represented?

Vargas's suicide touched off mammoth anti-American demonstrations of such passion that the army's right wing thought it prudent to call off its planned takeover of the government. The military fell into a period of internal squabbling; for the next few years the government was stewarded by a president named Kubitschek, an inconsequential figure as Brazilian leaders go, which at the time was perhaps not an unwelcome thing—a kind of Gerry Ford of Brazil.

A new wave of populism swept him out of office in 1960. He was replaced in a general election by Jânio Quadros. Quadros's administration, while not excessively respectful of generally accepted democratic rights, was still not to the liking of much of the armed forces, who felt he was overly liberal and nationalistic. In still another bizarre episode, Quadros resigned without explanation in August 1961. Perhaps he was afraid for his life— or perhaps he wished to further antagonize his opponents on the right by providing for the ascension of his constitutionally dictated successor, João Goulart.

Indeed, military members of the cabinet tried to block the ascension of Goulart, whom they considered a flaming radical. Goulart in turn organized massive popular demonstrations in his own support, and the opposition to his presidency was withdrawn.

The next two and a half years were the Brazilian equivalent, in some ways, of the Prague Spring; the country raced giddily toward democracy, all the time praying that their own happiness would somehow be shield enough when the tanks started rolling. This time, though, the enemy was internal. Goulart rewrote the country's labor codes, which had been based on those of Mussolini. Workers received raises to match Brazil's surreal inflation. Land and educational reform bills were passed. And legislation was introduced to control the expatriation of profits made by foreign companies in Brazil.

It was this last, of course, which was too much for the United States. It suspended all government aid to Brazil—with the exception of funds paid directly to state governors opposed to Goulart. The military attaché to the U.S. embassy in Brazil— Lieutenant Vernon Walters, who went on to become our ambassador to the United Nations—offered American arms to generals who were considering a coup. These expressions of American support were the final encouragement the army needed to overthrow Brazil's duly elected government yet again.

I am not a complete naif when it comes to the issue of secret American involvement in dirty business in other countries. I suppose I am as aware of what is now in the public record as the average person. I hope I will be understood, then, when I explain that I was, and am, profoundly uninterested in this aspect of the story. It's hard to get worked up about Vernon Walters and his like, precisely because they were so quintessentially American. All this was a game for them, which ran according to certain principles and strategies. The stakes, as they experienced it, were all either abstract or merely economic. Having grown up here, they had, I imagine, as little idea as I would have about what the true stakes were, about what it's like to know that every expression of your beliefs—even, under certain circumstances, the refusal to express them—could cost you everything, absolutely everything, on very little notice.

On March 13, 1964, Goulart, knowing that the jig was up for him, nonetheless engaged in one last act of hubris: in front of more than two hundred thousand people at Rio's Central Brazil Railroad station, he signed into law all of what had come to be known as the Basic Reforms, one after the other. On April 1, the military overthrew him, virtually without resistance. It was announced to the people that the subversive, Communist elements that threatened the life of Brazil had been supplanted by means of an "indirect election."

I learned all this from two sources—from the brief history appended to the testimony of the torture victims in the binder sent to me by Sam Boyd, and from Ferdinand himself, who was one of the officers who supported the coup and who received a promotion to captain for his good efforts. The two sources, as one might imagine, seldom coincided on matters of interpretation, but it proved easy, even for someone like me, to decode them both, to spot exaggeration when so little effort seemed to have been made to disguise it. Ferdinand spoke to me mostly on the beach; he would drive us there, along with Countess, on sunny weekend afternoons. He never mentioned it, but I believed he was worried his house was bugged. I didn't dare tell him how unlikely I thought that was. He spoke very rapidly, and it was as if he had rehearsed this all before, even though I was reasonably certain he had never delivered these speeches to any other person. They were mostly private recapitulations, delivered as much to himself as to me. They contained no pauses where a question might be put. But then I confess that this history, though no doubt necessary in some sense, was not that important to me; on the contrary, I felt it was pushing me farther away from what I really wanted to understand. Far from grounding Ferdinand's past in fact, or bringing it into relief, this broad social canvas threatened to abstract it; I didn't want anything from him I could get from a book. I did not really want to know what had brought him to those interrogation rooms, because I understood instinctively that the moment one entered those rooms, all that had come before was obliterated in any case. I wanted to be inside, and he was avoiding it. It was a struggle for me to be patient with him. I could see what he meant, though, about the lure of the quiet, empty beach, the sun and wind, and especially the ocean itself, now that the off-season was upon us.

Their task accomplished, and mindful of the mistakes they had made before, the military government made its primary task—as it would do for the next fifteen years of violent repression—the consolidation of its own power, to be achieved by the ferreting out of opposition in even the most private corners of the country. They took their first step just eight days after the coup when the First Institutional Act instigated the removal of 378 elected officials from office—including Kubitschek, Quadros, and Goulart—and revoked their political privileges; seventy-seven unsatisfactory army officers and more than ten thousand civil servants were also dismissed in one stroke. Several months later the second institutional act, or AI-2, outlawed all political parties, abolished presidential elections, and extended the jurisdiction of military courts to include the entire civilian population of Brazil.

Jack arrived home in a garish yellow Ryder van containing all his belongings; apparently he owned no furniture, nor anything larger than a television. He came on a Thursday, in the middle of the afternoon. The yellow van, so suggestive of the shock of uprooting, of transience, as to be glaringly out of place on Fairly Avenue, was still parked outside the house—against the curb, for some reason, rather than in the driveway—when I drove home from the train station that evening. It was the first thing I saw when I turned the corner onto our street. I'm obliged to say that my first sensation upon seeing it was one of embarrassment —embarrassment that our grown son had billboarded his return home in this way rather than go to the trouble of being unobtrusive, embarrassment that the stigma of the yellow Ryder van could be seen to have visited my household, and embarrassment, finally, that this moment for which I had had a week to prepare had still managed to catch me unprepared.

Nervous about going inside, I walked across the lawn to look over the van. He hadn't unpacked it yet; the waves of cardboard, old clothes, and stereo equipment still rose to the level of the windows. I took a step back and looked to both ends of the street. No one was outside in the chill air; lights glowed in every house.

Before I could close the front door behind me, Ellie came hurrying out of the kitchen with her finger to her lips. She wore an apron. She was unusually bright-eyed, though not smiling.

"He's asleep," she said.

"Upstairs?"

She nodded. "In his room. I think he made the whole drive straight through. He was just exhausted when he got here. I think he'll be out for a while. Didn't unpack or anything, just straight to bed."

I tried to conceal my relief at having this grace period to decide what to say to him, to get used to having him in the house. "When did he get in?" I said.

"About four."

"What about the van? Did he—"

"It doesn't have to be back until the morning, he says."

I had a drink, and we ate dinner. It was bizarre and, in some way, infuriating to notice how we tiptoed around downstairs, and spoke quietly, afraid to disturb Jack's rest, just as when he was a baby. Afterward, we sat in the living room and read. Since there was no more personal interest for me in watching baseball on TV, I seldom did. It seemed inappropriate, somehow, to go visit Ferdinand, though Ellie, I knew, was watching me to see if that was what I would do; or perhaps I was too sensitive to the imagined scenario of Jack coming downstairs while I wasn't there, and Ellie explaining to him where I had gone, in bitter and inaccurate detail.

We ran into each other in the kitchen the next morning. He was up early, having slept for some fifteen straight hours, and on his way to Patchogue to return the van. It was the first time I

190

had seen him (as opposed to the image of him) in my home in nearly five years. I believe that most fathers, though I'm sure not all, know what it is like to be afraid of their sons—not consistently, but at certain moments of stress. They pass a point in their adolescence (with Jack it came early, around age twelve, when we both realized that he now knew as much about baseball skills as I knew, and from then on he was going to have to find other men to learn from) beyond which they have the terrible, often unwitting ability to belittle you. I don't know what caused me to be frightened in this private way—in fact, to take a step backward—when Jack walked into the kitchen. Perhaps it was that sudden incarnation of the pressures of fatherhood, the expectation (or, maybe more to the point, his lack of one) that I would know how to say something comforting and constructive and loving to my son, in the face of his great disappointment, his unwilling arrival at a crossroads in his life. In fact, I didn't know what to say—those muscles, as it were, had been allowed to atrophy for ten years or more—and I was afraid of disappointing us both.

But then, he didn't look dissolute or scared or worried—he didn't look the way I thought he should look—at all. He smiled when he saw me, took one long step forward (he is much bigger than I), and we hugged. The strength in Jack is breathtaking. I felt the force of his shoulders and arms as we patted each other on the back; for a moment I had the sensation that this was what it felt like to be rescued from a burning building, or brought back to life in an emergency room.

"Jack," I said, a riot of emotion. If he had held me a moment longer, I might have started to cry.

He stepped back; his mood was positively jovial. "How are you, Dad?" he said. "You look great. You both look great." Ellie had come into the doorway to take in this scene.

Jack is about six-two, with blond hair a bit darker than Ellie's used to be, cut short and combed straight back almost in an old-fashioned brush style. There is tremendous strength visible in his back and in his haunches even when he is at rest. The sight of it brought back to me the faintly shameful feeling of pride I used to take, when he was becoming a man, in his appearance.

"Sorry I missed you last night," he said. "I was just beat. I drove straight from North Carolina on."

"You shouldn't do that," I said weakly. "It's dangerous. You should have stopped over somewhere."

"Yeah, I know. I don't know why I didn't. Just pumped to be out of g.d. Atlanta, I guess. Plus I was so anxious to get back home."

He smiled at me. I was paralyzed, in a way, by the tension between my amazement at his lack of seriousness and my relief at it. I said nothing.

Finally, he clapped his hands and said, "Well, I better get going. The van has to be back by nine, or I'm charged for another day, and I haven't even unpacked it yet." He looked at me. "Guess I'll see you tonight, when you get home from work? You'll be around?"

"I think so," I said.

"Slammin'," he said. "See you then."

I smiled wanly. It was as if he were using up all the energy available in the kitchen.

He took half a bagel off the counter, stuck it in his mouth, and trotted out the front door. Listlessly, unmindful of the time, I stood where I was, in the corner of the kitchen where the counters joined, and watched him make several loud, grunting trips between the van and his bedroom upstairs; until finally I became aware of Ellie's burning eyes on me. She had not moved from the kitchen doorway, other than to let Jack pass.

She stared at me angrily.

"What is the *matter* with you?" she said.

On one occasion, I was returned to the cell after an interrogation session to find three new people in it, one of whom was my brother-in-law, Edoardo. Upon seeing me, Edoardo became hysterical, weeping uncontrollably, rocking back and forth with his hands around his knees. The guards watched for a while, then lost interest and went away. I went to Edoardo, who I saw bore some marks of beatings, and before I could ask him what was the matter he grabbed me by the wrist and said, "Atilio, forgive me, may God forgive me, when they were torturing me I broke down, I denounced you, I accused you, just to make them stop. Just to give them what they wanted. I couldn't take it. . . ." I tried to tell him that it didn't matter, that they weren't really interested in our guilt or innocence, that he had not made things any worse for me. I did not believe that myself, but I wanted to try to calm him. Nonetheless, he continued weeping, and repeating, "I'm going to die, I'm going to die. . . ."

On the next day Edoardo was taken from the cell for further questioning. Evidently they were so pleased with his garrulousness under torture that they had resolved to get everything out of him that they could. . . . I remember vividly that this was on the day of a World Cup match, for there were several radios belonging to the guards which played at top volume. The guards and officers were fiercely dedicated to football—as we, too, had been, but somehow their sense of the importance of such things managed to survive their experience in the interrogation houses.

. . . I could hear Edoardo screaming above the noise of the football commentator, and then the radios being turned up further. I believe they threw salt into his mouth when he screamed —a common practice there—for I heard him calling for water. The screams eventually stopped. . . .

To this day I offer prayers of thanks for the national team of that year, which went on to win the World Cup. I well remember the prisoners in their cells praying silently during the broadcasts for victory, for we could only imagine what wrath our disappointed jailers would bring down on us if the team had ever lost. . . .

Apparently, the policemen interrogating my brother-in-law went too far; for the next day, a nervous-looking officer came to my cell to inform us that a coroner's inquest had determined that Edoardo had been killed in a shootout with police agents. Unfortunately I could not keep myself from laughing, whereupon the officer knocked me to the floor and began kicking me. . . .

When I was released a few months later, I went to visit my sister. She wanted my advice; she was desperate to recover Edoardo's remains, and her inquiries had led her to an official who offered to tell her where her husband was buried in exchange for her sexual favors. Since there was no way of knowing if the official was telling or even knew the truth, I was able to persuade her, with much difficulty, to decline his offer. . . .

"What do you think will happen to you," I asked Ferdinand, "if you're caught?"

"Caught?" he said irritably. He wanted, increasingly, just to talk and be let alone, and though his manner was still so relaxed as to suggest the reptilian, he would sometimes surprise me with his impatience with my infrequent questions.

"If they're able to prove who you are," I said.

He looked out the window, his fingers over his mouth. It was raining, and the big maple tree, just visible in the night beyond our half-reflections, slouched toward the ground under the water's weight. Countess, looking for a warm spot, walked stiffly to the striped throw rug behind the couch, turned around twice, and lay down, perfectly assuming the rug's oval shape. She sighed. The rain sounded in the gutters.

"It's an interesting idea," he said. "If they are able to prove who I am. But who am I, really? Da Silva or Ferdinand? I'm both. Just as I'm certain most people are both. Most people contain personae they may not be aware of. But can these personae be exorcised? Am I forever the same man who, who—"

"Yes," I said, "but what I meant—"

"You see, when I told you, back in the days of your innocence, that it was not me these allegations referred to, I meant that, I meant precisely that. Da Silva is not me. I am a different person now. I've always considered that an American idea, I would never have entertained it before I got here. I don't know why any American would have trouble understanding it. Have you ever read, by the way, Max Frisch's *I'm Not Stiller?*"

"No, I don't think I've heard of it."

"No? Well, it speaks to this problem directly. Unfortunately, it affects me so deeply that I can't reread it as often as I'd like."

"Yes, but Albert," I said, not wanting to be put off. "What will happen to you if the authorities are able to prove that you, if you like, were formerly da Silva?"

The room, as had become his custom, was in near darkness; two small lamps were switched on, one beside my chair and one against the wall behind him. "Well," he said slowly, "it depends. It depends upon the extent to which I am discovered. I could not be extradited, because the 1985 general amnesty in Brazil means that there can be no charge against me, nothing to extradite me for. Another possibility is that I could be sued, here in America, by some of those I interrogated or by their families. You probably didn't know that was allowed, but yes, absurd as it truly is, a fairly recent law allows it. It might be the prime example of litigious culture run wild, I think—seeking money from one's inquisitor for emotional damages. But I think it's very unlikely that anyone will take that route either. For one thing, I don't have enough money to make such a venture worthwhile. But more than that, I don't think any of these activists are really interested in money. They have more abstract aims, they want to take the high road. They imagine a giant finger pointing right at me, and they further imagine the whole world's attention could be captured by it. Going into a courtroom to try to get my money would make them feel sullied—as it should."

He followed that thought to some conclusion, without talking. To regain his attention, I said, "So then you're in no real danger at all from this?"

He smiled. "No, on the contrary," he said. "If they do enough digging, I'm in a great deal of danger. I told you another half-truth when we spoke on the street that day a month or so ago. I didn't come to the United States until 1970; but I did, as I said, come illegally. Political asylum was out of the question, you see, because the U.S. publicly supported Brazil's government. Of course I came with the extensive and invaluable help of certain people in Washington, but they would never admit to it now; indeed, they told me at the time that if I was ever discovered, I was out in the cold as far as they were concerned. So if these people, the newspaper men or BNF, if they are able to trace my movements back twenty years and discover that I entered the country with falsified documents, that I'm technically an illegal alien, I'll be deported. I think that would prove an ideal solution for all of them, you know? An ideal that waits to be discovered."

"And what will happen to you," I said, "if you are deported back to Brazil?"

"Oh, I will definitely be killed," he said, rolling his eyes at the question.

"Killed?"

"In no time at all. I'm sure you don't understand the depth of feeling about that period back there."

"And that doesn't scare you?"

"Of course it scares me," he said. "It terrifies me. Where do you get these ideas? I am willing to do just about anything to avoid it. One of the things you learn," he said, "from seeing human beings under the duress of torture is that they will do anything, endure anything, in order to cling to life. It's one of the principles upon which our methods were based. Anything to stay alive. This is by no means a noble impulse."

We listened to the loud hiss of a car driving slowly through the standing water on the road beyond the fence.

"You know," I said, feeling myself color, "it occurs to me that it's odd for you to be telling me this. Because so far as I know, I'm the only person who knows all this about you, who could put all this together for whomever. So you've put me in a strange position here, and yourself as well. Why are you telling me all this? How do you know I won't use it against you, turn you in?"

I was angry at him, in truth, for having burdened me with a decision I didn't want to think about making, a decision there was no need to ask me to make; and I wanted to repay him to some degree by frightening him. But he was not at all frightened. "I know you won't," he said. "For one thing, you have already given me your word, as I'm sure you remember. But that's almost beside the point. You are a good man. You wouldn't do anything to endanger the life of a friend."

"I'm not your friend," I said.

"Are you my enemy?"

He looked at me evenly. We both knew the answer to that. In fact, all his answers to my questions were, if not patronizing, then merely polite and indulgent. I was aware, then, that he knew me to an unsettling degree, and that this was not because he was gifted with rare astuteness but because I was myself so fathomable, so easy to know. He knew perfectly well that I was incapable of resolving the questions raised by my relationship with him. To turn him in, he had been careful to mention, was to sentence him to death. Nothing in my life to that point had rendered me capable of judging, of weighing Ferdinand's life against the lives he had scarred, the lives he had ruined. He, of course, could have made such a decision in a moment. I'm sure the irony of this did not escape him; but, ever polite, he did not let on, gazing at me, gazing at my weakness, with an expression of friendly interest.

There was a jingling of tags, and a soft, high, whimpering sound. Both of us looked over to the rug where the dog, eyes closed, paws waving, the muscles in her flanks jumping, mouth curled in a small sneer, was deep in a dream.

When I thought back to 1964, the year Ferdinand was taking part in a military coup d'etat that would refigure even the private lives of most of the citizens of his country, I could remember vividly only two events—though I suppose there's nothing deficient in that. How much stays available to us of any distant year? One is, of course, Jack's birth on February 8, the coldest February 8 in Manhattan's recorded history. We were living in a walk-up apartment on East 66th Street whose bedroom window faced the river, so I remember thinking, weirdly but almost instantly, when Ellie's water broke that at least we would get to spend the day in a building with proper heat. The other—which I may well remember in more detail, because it took up such great, concentrated blocks of my time—was my membership on the AAK creative team charged with revitalizing, through a massive ad campaign, the laggard American tourist industry. Actually, though the campaign itself was launched in 1964 (perhaps even in April), most of the work on it was done the preceding fall and winter. I could have fixed the dates exactly by looking in the personal files I kept out in the garage, had I the desire.

The Travel USA account was the single triumph that put AAK on the Madison Avenue map to stay. While we never grew to the monolithic status of a J. Walter Thompson or a Benton & Bowles, that was predominantly a matter of our own choice. We have turned down, or turned back, a number of merger attempts over the years, preferring to guard our independence. But at that time, AAK was just two years old, and its fortunes rose and fell from week to week in the agonizing fashion of most new business ventures.

I had been there for less than a year myself; I was working desultorily at Ogilvy & Mather, which was vast even then, when Jim Acker himself called to ask me to lunch. Jim could talk anyone into absolutely anything over the course of a lunch—he became famous for it. By the time the check arrived, the two of us were already smoking the cigars he had carried with him, to seal our agreement in a gentlemanly style. Jim could tell, he said, just from looking at my work that I was too creative, too restless, to be happy in the regimented surroundings of O&M; I was readily seduced by his vision of an innovative, cutting-edge agency, where, he told me as if speaking of a gigantic brain, the creative side dominated—even though I knew that AAK had been struggling to stay afloat for most of its two-year run.

Ellie was not enamored of this decision, particularly since we were trying—for the last time, we felt, having endured the heartbreak of two miscarriages—to have a child; I wished more than once during the arguments that ensued that I could have convinced Jim Acker to come over some evening for dinner, because I could never seem to explain to Ellie the glory, the satisfaction, the necessity of making this jump as forcefully, as spiritually as Jim could do it. But his workday, as he struggled to get his agency off the ground for good, extended past the dinner hour on most days; and in any event, I would have been far too embarrassed by the modesty of our three-room apartment to have him over. I looked up to him a great deal. I believed, and still believe, I suppose, that Ellie was scornful of my attempts to cast this career move in terms of imaginative development. I could see in her face that she thought it pretentious of me to look at my work in those terms. As far as she was concerned, it was all just salesmanship, and therefore the only qualitative aspect of it worth weighing was job security. From that point of view, Ogilvy & Mather was a veritable paradise; she thought I was crazy to leave, and thus two months later her pregnancy, which we had so looked forward to, came as a kind of reproach. I remember I could become quite angry with her when she belittled the idea that there was any private, creative satisfaction to be had in what I did for a living; long periods were spent in red-faced silence. Small city apartments are not good places in which to disagree.

I could admit to myself, though never to her, that I too had some solitary doubts those first few months, which nagged me all the more after Ellie left her job at *Life* to follow doctors' precautionary orders about her pregnancy. While I was given a much freer rein than I was used to, the accounts to which I was assigned—the only accounts we had at the time—were local clients, dairies, restaurants, small banks, piddling little places run by stubborn, provincial people, and decidedly not lucrative. Then one afternoon there was a hurried call for a meeting in Tim Kellogg's office; the partners, the creative director, and the business manager were all summoned personally, hurriedly and quietly by Tim's secretary. By the time the last of them had gone into the office and closed the door behind him, everyone at the agency had stopped what they were doing and were staring, from their desks, at the closed white door. Though there was no specific reason to expect bad news, I, at least, hadn't realized until that moment how I was unconsciously geared toward it, ready for doomsday at any time. Mercifully, the suspense didn't last long; just a few seconds after they had assembled, we all heard a giant whoop, which was hard to account for but was surely not the sound of a collective failure. Five minutes later, the door opened and Jim Acker came out. He was smiling broadly and holding a Dixie cup. He took in with pleasure the expectant gazes of his staff. Then, in a loud, politician's voice, he said, "Mr. Waldenmaier, Mr. Trowbridge, Miss Gates, Mr. Smith, Mr. DeLynn, Mr. Finley. Would you come to my office, please?"

He stood holding the door as we filed bewilderedly past him. As I walked by, I caught the smell of what was in the Dixie cup he still held: champagne. He closed the door.

"Lady," he said with a smile, "and gentlemen, a little while ago Tim Kellogg got a phone call from none other than the

United States Secretary of Commerce, awarding AAK the Travel USA account. This one account comes just short of doubling our agency's entire yearly billings. I'm pleased to say that the other partners and I have picked the six of you as the creative team for this account."

Clearly he wanted to watch us feel honored, shocked, and grateful, and it was no trouble to oblige him. He had gone down to Washington two weeks before to pitch the U.S. Travel Service personally, one of more than thirty agencies to do so, and now he was turning over the largest account in the agency's short history—the agency's future, really—to us. For once, Ellie was infected by my own excitement, and that night we had a quiet celebration of our newborn optimism.

I came to the office the next day somewhat surprised to see that for everyone else involved in the project, the euphoria had completely worn off. The fact was, there was an awful lot riding on our performance now, and none of us had ever had to work under that kind of pressure before. I had never seen Acker look so little composed; when I saw him that afternoon near the men's room, he glared at me quickly and then looked away, as if he were fighting back the impulse to ask me why I hadn't come up with anything yet.

The six of us—three copywriters, three artists—split into pairs, agreeing insincerely to share with each other whatever we came up with. Acker paired us all up, I'm sure, just off the top of his head (there were no allegiances or dislikes among us to be considered, so far as I knew), and so I was teamed with Dorothy Gates. One of the few women in the ad business back in those old days, Dorothy was a prodigiously talented illustrator with a marvelous sense of the composition of an ad, of the balance between art and effectiveness. She was also thirty, single, and quite sexy. I felt a stab of pleasure when it was decreed that we work together on the travel campaign, but I was able, as one often is, to stop myself from thinking this feeling through, to restrict it to a kind of childlike pleasure at her nearness.

We began spending long hours together at the office, and I confess her attractiveness—or perhaps it was simply the fact of her womanhood—was at first an impediment to me in terms of producing good work. The kind of double-brainstorming that goes on in these sessions depends in large measure on your willingness to verbalize any idea that speeds through your head, no matter how inane; sometimes your partner will see a seed in some remark of yours that you didn't pick up on, and sometimes the idea in question, once it's floating around, simply isn't as stupid as you believed it to be. But more than that, if you have that kind of internal censor going, then you're never going to tap into the unconscious currents of fear and desire that are the deep level at which most good advertising operates. And I was afraid of sounding like an untalented moron to Dorothy in a way I would never have been afraid working with a man. For whatever unsavory reason.

"Okay," Dorothy said tentatively, a red Magic Marker cap between her teeth. She had black hair drawn back in a long braid, and disproportionately large breasts, which she seemed at pains to conceal. "So who's our target?"

"Our target is mostly the middle class, people who wouldn't normally think of visiting the U.S."

"And why wouldn't they?"

"Because the middle class in Europe, for instance, has less discretionary income than the middle-class clients we're used to."

"Good. And I guess there's a flip side to that, too."

"Which is?" I said.

"Which is they know their American counterparts are richer

than they are. Think of the image they must have of America. The land of wealth. The land of riches. Everything there costs a fortune."

"It's nice if you live there, but on what we make, who can afford to visit?" I said, catching on.

"A potato costs four dollars there, I heard!"

"The cheapest hotel room is eight million zlotys!"

And so it was that two days later, anxious to show something, we turned in a mock-up to Acker. The research wasn't complete, but the numbers weren't important at that point; we were excited about the concept and wanted to get it in front of him. The head was, "America on £8 a Day"; obviously different denominations could be plugged in, depending on what country the ad was running in. We felt this confronted the problem head on; no sense, we told him nervously, in avoiding the real issue for most would-be travelers just for delicacy's sake.

Twenty minutes after we gave this to him to look over, he called us into his office.

"Dreadful," he said. "This is the least sexy ad I've ever seen. When dinosaurs roamed the earth, this is the kind of advertising they saw. Where is your imagination? I've given you the single sexiest product in the entire world, the United States of America, to sell, and this is what you come up with? If people want to save money on a vacation they'll go to their parents' place. Same as any other country. America! America! Get with the drama of it, would you please? I'm going to do you both a favor and pretend you never showed me this."

Ellie was very sympathetic when I came home that night. I sat dejectedly with a martini in front of the television set; she brought my dinner to me there, and sat watchfully beside me, patting my hand from time to time. Those were good days for us, in fact. We were excited by the prospect of a family, and spent hours together half-earnestly theorizing about our child, about our future, homes we would live in, places we would take our son or daughter, things we would permit, things we would forbid. Ellie was happier than I'd ever seen her. Marriage is one thing, but a child (this is news to no one, of course, but it seemed that way to us) is a promise of a very different sort; our futures were newly synchronous, which, in the present, seemed to synchronize our feelings not only toward each other but toward everything.

Dorothy and I quickly figured out the reason why we seemed to do our best work after five P.M.; neither of us had a separate office back then, and it was difficult if not impossible to concentrate well with so much inhibiting activity going on around us. So we began planning to stay late, and putting off the exchange of our ideas until then. Dorothy was the one who suggested it; that fact somehow seemed to remove any sense of impropriety from it, for me, and so I readily agreed. It was necessary, that was all; I didn't even spare enough thought to it to rationalize it. Ellie didn't appear to mind; she knew I was working with a woman, though they had never met. She said she understood, and asked only that I let her know if I'd be having dinner at the office or at home. On several occasions she apologized for not being able to wait up for me when I got home. If I remember right, she was about five or six months along at the time.

Over takeout food in the abandoned office, the only ambient noise the mysterious groans of the elevator as the cleaning crew moved through the building, Dorothy told me that she had been engaged for nearly two years to a man in the Manhattan district attorney's office; finally losing patience, she had forced the issue, and got him to disclose that only cowardice was preventing him from expressing his desire to break it off. I asked her if these late work nights weren't cutting into her dating life. She looked at me as if I had said something risqué, and replied that her dating life was not as prolific as the men in the office no doubt imagined it to be; she said, without much sorrow, that it was difficult to find a man who was willing to accept the simple premise that she had a career which she enjoyed and which made great demands on her time. I said I found that hard to believe, which was not the truth. Her figure, not so much shapely as bountiful, was a continual shock to me, accustomed as I was to Ellie's own vogueish slenderness, before her pregnancy, of course. Dorothy asked me many questions about my unborn child—she suggested a new name nearly every night—and especially about Ellie. She repeatedly said how much she'd love to meet her; I would smile weakly and say how much I'd like that too, all the while conscious of the deliberately vague hope that this would never happen. Our conversations would grow in intimacy, but they were always circumscribed by the amount of time it took to finish our sandwiches or our Chicken Delight. When she was finished, Dorothy would abruptly throw out our garbage, grab the remaining napkins, and wipe off her hands, one finger at a time.

"Well," she'd say, "back to it?"

The next idea we produced was built around America's natural beauty; different ads featured panoramic views of the Grand Canyon or Monument Valley or even, for a change of pace, man-made landmarks like the Lincoln Memorial or the Golden Gate Bridge. The tag for each was "Bring It All Home." The copy itself played not just on the natural desire to see America's wonders, but on the desire to be the *first* to see them, to be the one person in the neighborhood in possession of the snapshots and the air of authority. Stubbornly I embedded in the copy for each ad a reference to the cost of a one-week stay at the location pictured.

Acker, his pale eyebrows working crazily, his hands framing his forehead and twisting through his already wavy, brown hair, was in a near panic by the time he had looked through our designs, Dorothy and I taking turns explaining, in tones of diminishing certainty, our thinking. "I'm worried," he said when he saw we were through. "I confess to you I'm worried. We have ten days before we're due to go down to Washington, and under most circumstances ten days is plenty of time, but you just seem totally off the track here."

"What do you think we should be doing differently?" Dorothy said morosely.

"You know what I think it is?" Acker was less than ten years older than I, but had been in the business much longer, and sometimes adopted a paternal air. "I think you're too hung up on the supposed enormity of what you're doing. You're not god damned goodwill ambassadors, all right? What we have here is a product—I mean that literally—and you have to find some way to make the consumer realize his deeply felt need for this product. It's *exactly* the same as deodorant, or snow tires, or margarine. With this one main difference. It's *easy*. Think of all the days you've sweated blood to come up with some new way to tell people that they need a new car battery or a new mouthwash! Maybe that's the trouble—maybe it's so incredibly easy you can't see it. You're selling the most multifaceted, the most coveted, the dreamiest product ever invented. I don't want a god damn social studies lesson, and neither does anyone else! Not only would most people just as soon see the Lincoln Memorial on a postcard as in real life, I think most of them would *prefer* the postcard!"

207

When we had waited out the rest of this tirade and were turning to go, Acker added, in a softer voice, "Listen. Don't repeat this to anyone, but the other teams are doing even worse than you. I fully expect you'll be the prizewinners here. They're not as good as you are. I'm sure you won't let me down."

Dispirited, Dorothy and I agreed that, in spite of the time pressure, we would take that night off—go home early, clear our heads, and try to make a new start the next day. I called Ellie to let her know I'd be home by six, if not before. She said that the stores were still open then, and so maybe I'd like to come with her to look at some baby furniture. I said I couldn't.

It was the first full evening we had spent together in several weeks. By the time we went to bed—something else we rarely did at the same time anymore—I was in a bitter mood. The apartment suddenly seemed very cramped; it was difficult, for instance, to maneuver around one another in the kitchen, even more so with Ellie's ever-expanding girth, which also appeared larger and more troublesome than I remembered. After dinner she seemed constantly to hover around me, to stare at me; she spoke, to overcome my silence, of inanities shared with fellow mothers in our apartment building. Every good thing she mentioned about the fortunes of someone we knew or had seen seemed like an accusation to me. I held her very happiness at having me home against her; it was oppressive, belittling, inconsiderate of my problems. Most frustrating of all was that my resolute bad temper, which I made no effort to conceal, had no effect on her happiness or on her generous disposition toward me. I heard her singing in the bathroom as she got ready for bed.

At the time, the deepest explanation I was willing to concede for this sudden revulsion toward domestic life was my anxiety over the rejected work I had been doing at the office. The agency's fortunes were riding on the Travel USA account, and my worries might well have extended—though, looking back, this would have been excessively paranoid—to my own job safety. But in reality, of course, as I was able to recognize not long afterward, what was driving my behavior was my desire, however childishly expressed, to extract myself from the moral dilemma of my sexual attraction to Dorothy Gates. I had never been unfaithful to Ellie in the ten years of our marriage, and though it was terrible to think that this was simply because I had never had a true opportunity to have an affair, perhaps that was the case. I felt that indefinable air of receptivity from Dorothy—though my perceptions may have been clouded by certain fantasies about her moral lassitude, fantasies born of the innocent facts that she was single and, by virtue of her having a career, a flouter of convention. (I wasn't alone in holding these notions; Dorothy's nickname among the men in the office was "Pearly.") But if there was another reason besides mere lack of opportunity for my never having had an affair, it was this: there was always a chance Ellie would find out, and I was certain it would devastate her, and I wanted to avoid that at any cost. Was there any shred of nobility in such reasoning? The adultery itself, in other words, would mean nothing to me; I had no fear of doing wrong, but only of having to suffer the possible consequences of it. Married people have affairs, of course, and always have had them. But now that I was close to such an experience, it was plain to me how little the idea of my marriage really meant. To subvert it, I had to overcome not guilt or love or a sense of virtue or moral qualms, but mere, circumstancial cowardice and fear.

Part of the process by which I was declaring it okay to cheat

on my wife, then, was my unconscious determination to interpret her every action, her every attention, as oppressive or stupid or simply incompatible with the way I wanted and needed to
live my life. I was receptive to unhappiness because I thought
my unhappiness would justify anything. Even on the occasions
when I was right to interpret something in this way—Ellie did,
after all, have her low moods, her ungenerous moments—I took
them not at face value but as a kind of life sentence, as a portent
of everything to come. "Should I have to live the rest of my life
like this? Can I?" I would think when she nagged me about
something. I wanted to feel pushed, in short, rather than to
jump.

I underestimated, though, my own inertia; the push would
have to come from two directions. It was one thing to flirt with
Dorothy in the office, quite another to find some way to propose
to her that she sleep with a colleague and a married man. Five
nights before our deadline, as we shared a turkey club sandwich
with the whine of the janitorial vacuum cleaner in the background, I sunk to the level of telling her that I was not completely happy in my marriage. I listed for her, with some exaggeration, the things that bothered me about my wife. I was only
dimly aware of it at the time, but I was operating on the principle that if I could, subtly, remove any moral obstacles *she* might
feel toward sleeping with another woman's husband, it might
make it easier for her to proposition me.

"That's a shame," she said sympathetically. "I had no idea.
And with a baby coming, too. It's too bad, because you're really
a good man, you know? You deserve to be happy."

I sat paralyzed, glad that the dim light would prevent her
from seeing me blush with nervousness, as she finished her half
of the sandwich. A woman in a powder-blue uniform, dragging

the vacuum cleaner, passed slowly by our desks, without looking down at us.

"Well," Dorothy said softly, wiping her hands. "Back to it?"

We were finally wise to the fact that Jim Acker wasn't looking for a literal approach. Most foreigners, we reasoned, already knew of all the main American tourist attractions; if Yosemite or the like was going to draw someone to visit this country, then it would draw him whether we showed him yet another picture of it or not. What was attractive, then, to the rest of the world, on a more abstract level, about America? Opportunity, we thought: principally the opportunity for wealth and the kind of fast social advancement uncommon in most other countries. It was difficult, of course, to reconcile this with the idea of a two-week trip, but we thought we had found a way to do it. Dorothy put together a very clever visual showing a young boy, seen from behind, wearing a kind of oversize cap that made him beautifully reminiscent of old Ellis Island photos, looking out the window of an airplane as it descended toward New York. In the background, rising out of the harbor, was the small but clearly visible Statue of Liberty. The headline was "Sweet Land of Liberty." "Over the centuries," my copy read, "millions of people from all over the world have come to the United States to get a new start in life. Well, America is still the land of opportunity. Come spend two weeks with us. Wherever you go—the beaches of California, the mountains of Colorado, the canyons of New York City—you'll breathe the air of optimism and promise this country was built upon, and you'll go home with exactly what you want from a vacation—a fresh start. Or maybe you won't want to go home at all. In America, after all, anything is possible."

"Well, maybe you don't belong in this business after all,"

Acker said. "Maybe you should both be working for the fucking Smithsonian. Maybe you both should be *in* the Smithsonian. In case you've forgotten, this agency is supposed to be the cutting god damn edge. This is the most stupendously boring ad I've ever seen. Norman Rockwell would be proud of you two."

Dorothy looked as if she might be about to cry; both of us were very tired. "Look," I said sullenly, "instead of just piling insults on us, maybe you could be a little more constructive, and tell us what you're looking for."

He sighed. "See, that's just it. If I was looking for something like this, I'd just tell you to go out and do it. But I'm looking for you to use your subconscious, and I can't do that for you. I'm looking for you to surprise me, that's the whole point." He looked at our mock-up again. "Actually, in some ways this is a positive development, compared to your earlier efforts. It's moving toward the symbolic, but you haven't really gotten there yet."

"The Statue of Liberty isn't a symbol?" I said.

"The Statue of Liberty is a dead thing. Do you hear me? A dead thing. You are working in a new world here. We do not honor old symbols. We create new symbols. What's more, you can never rest in the creation of these symbols, because, A, they're disposable by their very nature, and B, a new one comes every week, superimposed over your old one. I know it's more difficult to apply the principle in some cases than in others. But you're getting hung up here. I'm telling you you have to let it all go. Let go, let go, let go."

"So we're saying," Dorothy said wearily, "people aren't interested in the real America but in the symbolic America."

"I'm saying that your big mistake is in making the distinction. America is the paradise toward which the rest of the world prays. Like heaven, it *is* imaginary, whether in fact it has a real existence or not. That's why it's such an easy sell. When you say here"—he slapped the cardboard—"that America is about opportunity, you're missing your own point. America is about the new, the new, the new. America is the country that invented advertising. Everything is for sale, every belief is up for grabs, every choice is revocable. That's why we do what we do. The only constants are the most basic desires, and I mean the most basic. You are not speaking to those desires with this Emma Lazarus bullshit. Now you have to take the next step. Go on, get out of here."

We worked the next few nights with an air of grimness, as if we were carrying out a task of terrible import. In fact, the more light-hearted and impish our work became, the more weary and somber we were in our execution and discussion of it. Time was running out not only on our deadline for the campaign, but on the special set of circumstances—long nights alone together, working in close proximity, forming an attachment—that had seemed to me to be my best chance to have an affair with near-total passivity. But it was clear by then that the hoped-for advance was not going to come from her. To this day I wonder how she would have responded had I suggested to her the discreet, no-strings affair of my imaginings. I said nothing, because I was too afraid of revealing myself to her and having to see myself in her eyes, from that moment forward, as an unscrupulous husband, a false friend, a lecher. I told myself, though, that I was afraid not of exposure but of the damage that any awkward feeling would inflict on the few crucial working hours we had remaining.

It seemed, if my senses could even be trusted anymore, that our heads, our fingers, rested closer to each other as we bent over her broad desk, quizzing each other on details, politely compromising our few disagreements. We spoke in needlessly quiet tones, considering how alone we were; in fact, we never discussed anything personal anymore precisely because extraprofessional questions had moved from the sometime topic of our conversation into the very body of it, into our nervous eyes and most of all into our voices. Late at night we would stand outside the office building in our winter coats and talk for a few minutes more, postponing our chaste goodbyes. For all their dry-mouthed significance, these sessions had a corresponding unreality that was remarkable to me; for I wouldn't have gotten two blocks from the office before even my most diligent memory of Dorothy's every word and gesture that night would seem hopelessly ambiguous and impossible to interpret, and I would convince myself that I had imagined the whole thing.

Three days later we brought to Acker mock-ups of the first three of what would eventually become a series of eight ads. The kickoff was a photo—staged, of course, but expertly made to look candid—of a group of Japanese tourists on Wall Street. All wore suits and carried cameras. What looked to be a packed lunchtime crowd swarmed all around them; all the American businessmen wore conservative suits, too, and carried briefcases, with one exception. On the far left of the frame, having just walked past the group of Japanese, was a gorgeous young woman, blond hair down to her waist, wearing a micro-miniskirt and boots, and carrying a briefcase. All the Japanese eyes were following her; one man, crouching slightly, was surreptitiously taking her picture. The headline was held over from our last attempt: Sweet Land of Liberty. The copy, too, needed very few changes; with that photo above it, it read as if delivered with a wink and a salacious smile that were just right. The other two we prepared used different visuals; one, a London banker-type in pinstripe pants and bowler riding a huge motorcycle through the desert, and the other a wide-angle shot of the appliance department at Macy's.

When Acker had finished looking through these, he stood up from his chair, came around the desk, and kissed me on the forehead.

Dorothy and I still saw each other every working day, and some extra gentleness in our speech served as a reminder of what we had done together. The opportunity for further intimacy, if indeed it had ever been there, was gone. One might think that, unable to have something I was still near to, I might have retreated into fantasy, might have been tempted to play out a scene for myself in which everything went smoothly, in which our desires were in perfect unison, and I was able to sin with impunity, which would have been, to me, the same as not sinning at all. But, at some point during those weeks, my fantasies had begun to run quite another way.

More and more often, sitting at my desk at AAK or walking the twenty blocks home at night, I would realize with genuine surprise that I was lost in a kind of black daydream that when I arrived at home, policemen would be waiting grimly, almost resentfully at my door, to deliver to me the news that Ellie was dead. It was always an accidental death—hit by a cab or a drunk driver, or shot by a mugger, or just some painless medical fluke. Our unborn child had died along with her as a result of her injuries. Distraught, I would shut myself in the bedroom, unable to speak. Friends, having heard somehow, would rush over, elbowing past the policemen; they would take over the task of calling those other friends and family members who had not yet gotten the terrible word. Grief was not excluded from this fantasy, though of course grief is not really possible to imagine. I would be at the center of everyone's concerns. There was the funeral to be gotten through. But then, when that was over, came a surprising realization. I was still a youngish man, less than forty; and I had been handed my parallel life, the life I had renounced, not without some lingering resentment, when I married, the life in which, as I childishly imagined it, I was once again free to act on any and all of my desires. It was all returned to me, even if against my will.

A scenario in which, say, Ellie and I were divorced, or in which I had an affair that she found out about and thereupon left me, or—for that matter, since this was one's fantasy life, in which, in theory, everything is permitted—killing her, would not have had the same meaning at all. To be perfect, it had to have no stain at all of my involvement. Even in my fantasies, it seems, the important thing is *not to act*—to be blameless, to be safe, to be passive and untroubled, not to have to choose. That one fantasy, the dark, unconscious source of which I seemed helpless, for a period of two or three months, to locate and stop up, was mercifully short-lived—once Jack was born, it became impossible to entertain—but for a long time afterward I was haunted by it. Since I had no great moral investment, apparently, in the matter of my marriage, it followed that I had nothing to show for my decision (or failure to decide) to remain faithful except regret at having no knowledge of a particular area of human passion, a type of regret I feel more often now as I enter old age. I do love Ellie—as I loved her then—but my love is a weightless thing. It may seem unfair to oneself, even pathetic, to be haunted by one's own imaginings, and perhaps it is. But when one's life has passed in unthreatened comfort, in utter safety, what else is there by which one might judge oneself?

The eight advertisements, which collectively came to be known as the Liberty campaign, began appearing in periodicals worldwide in early 1964. Though it is brazen, perhaps, to try to draw an exact parallel between such things, the following year tourism from those countries in which the ad ran increased by an average of eleven percent. The ads won several industry awards, which Dorothy and I accepted together at a dinner at the old Hilton in New York. Twenty-six years later, I still had mine framed on the wall of my office at AAK. Dorothy was wooed away to Leo Burnett in 1965. Just a year or two later, I heard, she got married, started a family, and got out of the business.

We had stopped to rest before turning back, just ten feet or so above the waterline, our shoes sinking into the sand still wet from the receding tide. The air had the telescopic clarity that belongs to autumn. Ferdinand, the veteran of these excursions, had thought to bring some sunglasses; I held one hand over my eyes as we stood there, on the ledge of the continent, staring off across the glittering, vacant surface of the ocean. Behind us, the dog, who always seemed rejuvenated by our trips to the beach —in the car on the way over, she kept trying to climb into my lap to get a better look out the windshield as we got closer to the water, and Ferdinand had had to sternly order her to lie down in the backseat several times—bounced around in the sand in as youthful a manner as her old legs would allow.

Ferdinand, again in a sort of trance in which he barely seemed aware I was beside him, was cataloguing the Communist-led atrocities that were allegedly committed—he wouldn't knowingly lie about it, I felt, but his paranoia was plain—in

Brazil even after the military coup. I found it uninteresting—or, rather, what I found interesting about it was its air of self-justification, even though, if asked, he would insist he was only providing necessary background. This insistence of his, once his process of autobiography had begun, on leaving absolutely nothing out came to me as a poignant yet increasingly irritating surprise.

"In 1969," he said, "shortly before I left the country, a band of criminals who decided to call themselves the Eighth of October Revolutionary Movement kidnapped your ambassador, Charles Elbrich. A real prick, incidentally, but of course there was no question of allowing anything to happen to him. We were forced to free fifteen notorious prisoners in exchange for his release. It was ironic that the very disorganized, anarchic quality of this Communist opposition required us to be that much more vigilant."

"You know," I said, "whenever we talk about the past, it sounds very much to me like you're trying to explain away what you've done. But whenever I've asked you about what actually happened in the interrogation houses, what your specific duties were, you won't talk about it, as if you're ashamed of it."

"I don't talk about it," he said evenly, "because talking about it conveys nothing."

"But are you sorry for what you've done?"

I turned to look at him. The wind scarcely moved his thinning hair; his eyes were invisible behind his dark glasses. "Yes, I am sorry," he said. "I am sorry that there is evil in the world. I am sorry that sometimes we find things simpler than they truly are. I am sorry there is no one to make our choices for us. I am sorry we don't still live in Eden. What do you want me to say?"

I shrugged. "Maybe it's not the right question," I said.

"You never know what you will do in defense of yourself, of the things that make up yourself, until you are called upon to defend them. You never know how you will choose until you have to choose."

There was a certain wisdom in that, self-serving or not. I had, at times, dwelled on the weakness I felt sure I would exhibit under torture; I would confess what I knew, lie if I knew nothing, or perhaps, if such a thing is possible, choose to die rather than to suffer. There seemed little shame in such an admission. But would that same weakness not come into play if I found myself on the other side of the relationship? Would I choose anything if the only other choice available to me was to give up my own life, or even just the things that made up what I knew as normal life? It was hard not to come back to these questions—even though I knew that they, too, were self-serving in their own way, a kind of moral parlor game, a false substitute for experience and truth.

With this in mind, I asked him, "Would you rather not know? Would you rather have lived in ignorance of these things, and never find out how you'd react to that kind of danger?"

He frowned. "You know," he said, "it's not just the fear of being killed that has kept me a fugitive all these years. These issues are deeply personal. No one can understand why I have done what I've done, because no one has lived this life but me. I can question myself, berate myself, punish myself all I want, but the thought of having to endure these things from people who have no idea what they're talking about is unacceptable to me. It is an inviolably private matter."

We were silent for a while, the wind fluttering our trouser cuffs, the small waves breaking and receding like supplicants near our feet.

"You understand," he said, "for instance, why I don't ask you for your forgiveness."

I said I understood.

It's not an athlete's professional career that leads him to grow accustomed to adulation, to special treatment; that comes earlier, in the impossibly dreamlike adolescence in which everyone admires you, those you want to fear you fear you, every girl wants to be with you, adult men instinctively welcome you into their company. Insecurity, normally the benchmark of the teenage years, is banished. No wonder athletes want to extend their emotional dreamtime into their adulthood. Things change somewhat, though, when you hit the big leagues. You no longer have the hometown boy's protection. In your hometown, for example, you never had a total stranger come up to you on the sidewalk and scream expletives in your face the morning after a subpar performance. You never had teammates who took your extraordinary abilities for granted.

It didn't take long for Jack, who had seen more than his share of the down side of being a professional athlete, of being the property of a strange and fanatic citizenry, to discover that his legend was still untarnished in his native town. In fact, he was all the more revered now—not only because he was the most prominent athlete from Belmont in living memory, but, more important, because he had been to the kingdom; he had inside knowledge of the Olympian world of pro baseball and of its denizens. Almost from the day he arrived home, he began spending his evenings out at local bars, restoring his self-image as one of the world's privileged. Old high-school friends and total strangers soaked up his every answer to their questions, which had the banality of gossip—who's a good guy, who's a jerk, who's on drugs, who's a racist, who's gay, who's the most prolific adulterer, who can drink the most, who's the most oppressive believer in God. Any information of this sort, which could not be acquired from the morally sanitized sports pages, made these barflies feel like insiders; I imagine that, just to make themselves feel really transcendent, they would go home afterward and disparage Jack to their wives. Night after night, Jack would get a lift home at closing time, having consumed many beers and paid for none of them, shout his goodbyes, and stumble drunkenly onto his childhood bed, while I listened from my own bed and thanked God that at least somebody had had enough sense not to let my son drive himself home.

He wouldn't be up when I left for work; in fact, I knew from Ellie that he often wouldn't be up until around one in the afternoon. He explained with an unconcerned smile that this was a habit one developed from playing mostly night games. When he had eaten something and felt better, he would call a friend to get a ride back into town to pick up Ellie's car.

Nor was it only men for whom Jack held such fascination. Women—or at least a certain strain of woman—found his impeccably male credentials as a pro ballplayer very attractive. He is, of course, a very handsome (to myself, I would say beautiful) young man; I'm not sure how much that had to do with it, though. In any case, Jack had never had to seek out the company of women. Many of those long, drunken farewells in the driveway, over the sound of an idling engine, which I listened to as I lay awake at two or three in the morning, involved muffled, female voices. One warm afternoon when I came home from the office a couple of hours early, having phoned from the train station and gotten no answer, I stopped dead in the front hall as I was loosening my tie and heard, to my deep mortification, the sounds of a rather theatrical female ecstasy coming from over my head. With no idea what to do, I took a magazine off the pile of mail on the bureau and sat down in the living room to read it, blushing in solitude. The sounds reached a peak of sorts and then ceased, and a very short time afterward a blond woman in a St. John's sweatshirt, younger than Jack by several years, came down the stairs alone. Before she reached the bottom, she turned, saw me, and screamed.

Jack, who had apparently had no intention of leaving the bed where he was surrounded by his teenage memorabilia, came running. "Jesus," he said when he saw me, half embarrassed and half relieved. "What are you doing home so early?"

"I called," I said, expressionless.

"Man," he said. A grin was starting to steal over his face. "I had no idea."

"Aren't you going to introduce me?" said the blond woman.

Jack didn't answer her and after a moment she left. When the door had closed, I said, "Just be glad I wasn't your mother."

"Don't worry," he said. "I had that covered."

He did call his agent in New York a couple of times, and for the first week waited halfheartedly for the agent to call him back with news of an offer from another team. But the chances of this happening, however remote to begin with, were all but nonexistent this late in the season, as Jack knew. Nonetheless, he accepted offers from various friends in bars to work him out on the high-school field, to keep his arm loose and his body in shape and to give him some opportunity to see his skills admired. He would trudge out to these engagements once his hangover had abated, at three or four in the afternoon, keeping his body in peak muscular condition to no real end, simply because the glorification and maintenance of the body was all he knew. Then, home for a shower and some dinner, and out drinking again.

Of course he took the occasional night off from this schedule, and those nights were the only times I saw him. Generally,
after dinner was finished, we would go into the TV room and
watch a baseball game together. He made much of this being a
rare pleasure for him—to see a game as a fan sees it, without
having to worry about warming up or staying mentally prepared
in case he was called upon to pitch—but it didn't seem like fun
for him at all. And while it was edifying to have him there to
explain, unasked, many of the fine strategic points of the game
that I otherwise would have missed, watching these games together was on the whole extremely discomfiting, a bizarre,
freighted parody of a father-son activity. He was unconsciously
bitter, even toward those whom he praised.

We watched the Astros play the Mets. Darryl Strawberry
came up to bat for New York.

"Away, away, away," Jack said, mumbling.

This was shorthand for Jack's recommendation for pitching
to Strawberry; keep the ball on the outside part of home plate.
The Houston pitcher did just that, retiring Strawberry on a pop
fly to third base; Jack grunted with satisfaction.

The next hitter was Howard Johnson. "Dead fastball hitter,"
Jack said. "Get ahead of him, stay off-speed."

The Astro pitcher threw a curveball, close to the plate. The
umpire called it a ball.

"Oh, where was it?" Jack said, louder. "That umpire did me
over all the time. Just be consistent, that's all I ask. Fat pig."

Johnson hit a fastball off the outfield wall for a double. The
TV showed the pitcher walking around behind the mound, trying to settle himself.

"Stupid shit," Jack said mirthlessly.

This sort of malevolence was always painful for me to wit-
ness; three or four times during the course of a game I would

get up and ask Jack if he wouldn't like another beer. It was my only available pretext for a break, and I resorted to it often even though I was frequently met in the kitchen by Ellie and her exasperated stare; she had expressed to me her concern that Jack was doing too much drinking as it was, and she didn't understand why I would do anything to encourage him. Since the idea that the pleasures of spending time with my son might be diluted by anxiety would not have occurred to her, she assumed that I was doing it simply in open defiance of her wishes.

For her part, though she worried about him, she forgave him everything, or rather, she didn't consider that anything was his fault to begin with. She could become quite cross with me, not just for daring to criticize Jack in any way—his seeming lack of interest, for example, in the future—but for allowing any suggestion to show that I was not thrilled, in an uncomplicated way, to have our beloved son returned to our home. It wasn't hard to see what was going on here. She still blamed me, apparently, to some unfair degree, for Jack's kidnapping by the forces of professional sports in the first place—for no better reason than that professional sports was representative of all in the world that was idiotically, incomprehensibly male, and therefore my responsibility. She was determined to keep the family together this time, in spite of the fact that our son was now a grown man. In search of those lost years, she treated him as if he had not aged a minute since he had left home, which suited him, I saw, down to the ground.

"Well, Dad," he said one evening, having finished dinner though Ellie and I still ate, "shall we retire to the TV room? It's about game time."

I looked down. "Actually," I said, "I'm going to have to excuse myself tonight. I have to—there's a friend of mine, a neighbor, who lives down at the end of the street, and I promised I would go by and visit him tonight."

"Oh yeah?" Jack said. "Anyone I know?"

"No, he didn't move in until after you were gone," I said.

"You going too, Mom?"

She was looking at me, tight-lipped, trying to glare without being obvious, furious that I would, in her scheme of things, opt for an evening with a grisly murderer rather than bond with my only child. "No," she said. "This is a friend of your father's."

All of this, especially my own speech, struck me as transparently loaded, and I was scared, as I had been scared before, that Jack would begin asking me awkward questions and I would have to endure more misunderstanding. But, incredibly, he did not seem to have caught on to anything unusual; in fact, his interest in the whole subject had obviously expired. Ellie, though, would not let it go.

"Your father has been busy turning himself into the neighborhood eccentric," she said to him. He looked at me, amused. "Apparently this new neighbor has got some past torturing innocent people in South America. He went on the lam and is living here under a false name. Your father finds all this cruelty absolutely fascinating. He's been spending all his free time for two months at this beast's house."

"Get out of here," Jack said. "A torturer? On Fairly Avenue?"

"He is accused," I said sharply, always grateful for the chance to pretend to know less than I did, "of very serious crimes, yes. He claims it's a case of mistaken identity."

"God knows what they talk about," she said, still not looking at me. "Thumbscrew methods, I suppose, or maybe he lets your father look at his iron maiden. Apparently there's some thrill involved in this which I'm afraid I just don't get."

As long as this disagreement stayed between the two of us, she could say what she liked; but I could not countenance being humiliated like that. "You have no idea," I said angrily, "what you're talking about. You've just made up your mind about it without—"

"Well excuse me if I don't get it," she said, "but I'm not alone. Frannie doesn't exactly get it either, or Don Greaves, or Adele Bond. I'm the one they all ask about it, not you. I'm the one they feel sorry for, as galling as that is. Forgive me if I can't really explain it to them, since you can't explain it to me."

It hadn't escaped my notice that those people, in fact most of the people in Belmont, weren't really talking to me anymore. They still said hello, without anger or curiosity, but I could see, at the train station or in the driveway or in town on an errand, how they avoided me to spare themselves, as you will do when someone you know has suffered such a grave embarrassment that you don't know what to say. We hadn't been invited to anyone's house since Labor Day. But I was not about to give her any satisfaction. "Really," I said, "I could not care less what—"

"Okay, that's it," Jack said calmly. He stood up. "If you two are going to fight, I'm excusing myself." He gave an indulgent shrug of resignation, as if the whole thing were beneath him, and, incurious as ever, took his plate into the kitchen.

When I came back home that night, Ellie was in bed and Jack was still watching TV. Bored but intent, he didn't hear me come in. I stood in the doorway behind him, out of his sight; he was watching a different ballgame now, one that had just begun out on the west coast. But he watched differently, I saw, when he was alone. He sat motionless in a posture of indolence, the right hand holding the remote control resting on the arm of the chair. In the ten or fifteen seconds between each pitch in the game, his thumb would begin working, and he would check in on four or five other channels before bouncing back to the baseball, in time for the next delivery. There was barely time to register the images that would flash onto the screen with every new station; but somehow this was preferable to enduring ten seconds of down time as the batter regained his concentration and the pitcher checked the sign.

At first I had to smile, for this was a statistic come to life, the bane of so much of my industry. If only he knew, I thought, how many millions of dollars, how many thousands of man-hours and hundreds of earnest meetings were devoted to foiling him in this thoughtless activity—him with his remote control and his dazzling flights of attention. And here it was, right in my own living room. Most sons, of course, are bored after a certain age with their fathers' descriptions of what they do all day; but it struck me then how nearly impossible it would be for me to explain my work to Jack, because he was who my work was for. He was a member, as it were, of the target generation.

It was as easy, or, rather, as evocative, to think of him in these terms as it was to think of him as my son. He had been gone so long—longer, I mean, than the eight years since he was drafted into professional ball. Ellie was right, in one sense, about the strange maleness of the game. The sense of my inadequacy that it brought to both Jack and myself very early in his life all but put an end to our relationship, in a practical sense, as father and son. I don't mean that I am uninterested in athletics, or indeed unathletic. Only the father of a prodigy, perhaps, will know what I mean—and even then, to have your child outthink and outgrow you in the arena of chess or the violin is much easier, I submit, than in something as tied to one's masculinity as sports.

I remember with both fondness and pain playing catch with him when he was just six or seven; pitching to him on the empty Little League fields and chasing down the ball when he hit it; chalking a rectangular strike zone against the side of the garage for him to throw against when I was at work, or too tired. But his talents, such a joy to discover at first for both of us, soon ballooned to the point where I was slightly intimidated by them. By age twelve he could throw so hard that I couldn't bear for long the pain it caused me to catch him. He dominated all the boys his own age, so naturally he looked to me for a little competition as well as guidance. But I don't know how to throw a curveball, or to hit one, even though I went so far as to buy books on the subject on my lunch hour and read them on the train home. Baseball is baseball, I know, and so all this may seem silly and oversensitive of me, until you cast it in general terms: the particular things my son needed to learn from me, at the age of thirteen or so, I didn't know.

One of the surprising things one learns as the father of a prodigy is that there is a veritable army of knowledgeable people whose life's work it is to step in precisely at the point where the parent begins to fail. In my case these were people like the Dewey High baseball coach, Cal Hopkins, who worked privately with Jack before he had even left grade school, and the coach's friend, whose name I have forgotten now, a minor-league official who got Jack into an exclusive baseball-skills camp the summer he was fourteen, and the ultimate insiders, the major-league scouts, who would sit alone in the stands at the high-school games writing in a pocket-size notebook and whose hats I would see resting on the front-hall bureau when I walked in my front door after work. It was possible, of course, to be both grateful to these men for Jack's sake and to resent their very existence, their polite assumption of my boy into their mysterious society.

A future in the major leagues was Jack's whole life then, and he saw that I had no authority, really, to teach him what he needed to know about it; such authority, once relinquished, is impossible to recover, and thus I felt I had no right to give him any advice now. It is hard, sometimes, to distinguish what is viscerally, inexplicably true from what is merely stupid or self-fulfilling; but this sense of our estrangement was quite real to me. I was able to see him, in the strobe light created on the white walls of the TV room by his incessant flipping of the channels, as an abstraction. And this abstraction was a curiously circular process. For as he came to seem less and less like the son of my flesh, the son of my blood, I saw him more clearly as my son in another sense entirely, by virtue of his imposing, beautiful, troubling physical presence, by virtue of his evident hunger for the inconsequent image, my legatee, my life's product, outside of my control.

I underwent the punishment known as the Telephone, which consisted of both my ears being unexpectedly and forcefully slapped at the same time. As a result of this punishment, I was deaf for several days. Three days later, while cleaning my ears, I noticed that they had bled. . . .

I underwent the torture known as the Chinese Bath, in which my head was repeatedly submerged, for long periods, in a gasoline drum filled with cold water. . . .

It might have seemed unfair to me that the very volume of citizens who were tortured by the police, the very machinelike, prolific quality of the apparatus of repression, also served to rob the victims whose testimonies I read of any sort of complexity, of uniqueness, with a few especially barbaric exceptions. All the victims, speaking in their plain, dogged voice on the printed page, came to seem one victim; while the one human being, in this long chain of human suffering and cruelty, whom it was given me to watch and to speak with began to seem unfathomable, manifold, individual. But complexity, in this matter, was not something to be prized. It was the enemy, in a way, designed to cloud judgment. Simplicity was the goal, and thus I found a kind of solace in the stark, dull pages of the red binder, a relief from the tearful confusion I sometimes experienced when face to face with Ferdinand.

My interrogators brought me from my cell into what was apparently the living room of a farmhouse. It was rather elegantly furnished, though the furniture itself had been pushed up against the walls by Captain da Silva's men after he had commandeered it. . . . I was put into the Dragon's Chair, and after a while my head was plunged into a large tank filled with water and held there for more than a minute. . . .

A truly good man, perhaps, would have been affected by these repetitive tales in a different way. He would be roused to action on behalf of the powerless, leaving behind his home, his job, his security; or, more likely, he would simply be moved, over and over again, to tears, tears of rage and humiliation and empathic pain, without becoming distracted, without becoming inured. But all that the sheer onslaught of these stories—as they filled the red binder and then, when that was through, as they filled the pages of the newspapers and the television screens and even the fat junk mail left in the box at the foot of my driveway—brought home to me was the realization that, as Americans, we live in a shadow world, insubstantial, illusory, sheltered, fragile, a dead branch of evolution. In Belmont Ferdinand was an oddity, a monster, but in fact the earth was rife with people like him—and like his victims; their familiarity with the equations of danger and belief, word and consequence, life and death, was the common way of the world, an immutable rule among human laws in Syria, South Africa, Cuba, Haiti, Romania, Korea, Nicaragua, Iran, Chile, Argentina, Cambodia, the Soviet Union, China, Ethiopia, Kuwait, Israel, Tibet.

In Curitiba, I was in prison with a man whose name, he told me, was Teodoro Fleury. He was in the cell directly across from me. He was taken to be questioned several times over the course of three or four days. He would come back bloodied, on his ears, mouth and genitals. At the end of the first day, he told me, with a weak smile, that he had escaped further beatings only because the officer who was kicking him had, to his consternation, become exhausted from the effort and had to quit. The next day he had to be carried back to his cell after questioning. The next day he screamed when they came for him; they had to beat him just to get him out of the cell. They carried him back several hours later. . . .

Subsequently he became totally silent; he would not even answer when I called out to him. The guards would carry him without a struggle back and forth to the interrogation rooms. . . . Very late at night, on the eighth or ninth day, I was awakened by a loud banging noise. I went to the door of my cell. Teodoro, like all of us having to make use of what he came across by chance, was trying to drive a nail into his own head, using the heel of his shoe for a hammer. Without thinking what I was doing, I called for the guards to stop him. . . .

With four days to go before my final day of work, I came

back from lunch to find a pink "While You Were Out" memo on my desk, informing me that Sam Boyd had phoned. Caroline had checked the box indicating that he would be expecting me to call him back. I sat down and read this simple message several times over. I stood up, meaning to go outside and ask Caroline if Boyd had said anything else when he called, anything else at all; then I sat down again, patting my thigh to try to calm myself. After a minute of thought I got up again and closed my office door, a time-honored general signal that I did not want to be disturbed. While Caroline might well have wondered what there was to keep me so busy now when I had been all but idle for the last three months or more, it was far more likely, given her lack of connection with her own surroundings, that she wouldn't spare it any thought at all.

Boyd called back shortly before five. Caroline called me on the intercom to say he was on the line.

"I'm busy," I said, trying to sound impatient. "Could you get rid of him?"

He called again the next morning, and Caroline again put him off expertly, with what difficulty I did not ask. When I came back from a late lunch and stopped by her desk to ask about the RSVPs for the upcoming retirement dinner, she said, "Oh, and that Mr. Boyd says that since you're so busy at work, not to bother calling him back. He'll get you at home."

"Ah, good," I said feebly, smiling, and went into my office and closed the door.

Having thrown out Boyd's messages, I called information for the *Newsday* number. The switchboard transferred me to him, and after one ring I heard the familiar, impolite voice.

"Boyd."

"Mr. Boyd, this is Gene Trowbridge returning your call."

"Oh," he said, brightening. "I thought I might hear from you."

"Let me just tell you that I don't respond well to harassment of this kind, and if I have to—"

"Harassment?" he said. "If you think an unwelcome phone message constitutes harassment, Mr. Trowbridge, then you've led a more sheltered life than I thought."

"Yes, well, if you're threatening to start calling my home, that's a different matter."

"It's listed in the phone book," Boyd said. "But look, I don't see any need for us to get into these fine legal points. I'm not trying to damage your reputation in the community or anything like that. I just wanted the chance to ask you a few more easy questions. Any time you want to end this conversation, you obviously have the means to do so. All right?"

"Off the record, of course," I said.

"As you wish."

"All right, then."

"So," he said. "Did you get that material I sent you?"

"I got it."

"And did you have a chance to read any of it?"

"I read pretty nearly every word," I said.

"Really?" There was a pause. "And?"

"What do you mean, and?"

"And what did you think about it?"

"I thought it was tragic, absolutely shocking. It moved me very deeply."

Both of us waited stubbornly.

"Let me guess," Boyd said sarcastically, "what your next sentence is going to be."

"But of course there's nothing in there that might confirm,

or deny for that matter, any of the accusations that you've made."

"I thought so," Boyd said. "Now, I've told you already what I believe about you and Mr. a.k.a. Ferdinand. I've told you that I think you're protecting him, helping him to conceal himself, for some reason. I'm sure, actually, that whatever reasons you have for this are well-meaning ones, because he's a nice guy, because it was a long time ago, because you gave your word, whatever. I mean, I know you're not a bad man. I know this doesn't involve money or anything of that nature. So my purpose in sending you that BNF file was to show you that whatever your reasons are, they can't possibly stack up against the kind of suffering this man has caused in his lifetime. I figured that once you understood the scope of what he'd really done—I don't know what he tells you—you'd see what you had to do."

"What makes you think I have all this power?" I said. "What makes you think it's up to me? You know so much about him, why drag me into it at all? I'm just a neighbor."

"All right," Boyd said, sighing. "You know, I haven't just been sitting here at my desk these last few weeks, waiting for your call. Not everyone approaches knowledge as passively as you do. I've been keeping an eye on you. I know how much time you've been spending over there. I know when you go, and I know how long you stay."

I closed my eyes and leaned forward in my chair. When I opened them again, I saw, through my office window, the corner offices stacked like blocks in the building across the street, and everyone diligently, imperviously working.

"And I'm not the only one who's watching," Boyd went on. "You think your life takes place in a vacuum, and maybe it used to, for that matter, but not anymore. I have those visits documented, and I'd certainly be willing to publish that information if that's what it took to get you off the moral fence that you seem to be hung on."

"You can't tell me," I said, trying to be contemptuous, "that you'd even attempt to run a story about a man being visited frequently by his neighbor."

"It could make its way into a more general follow-up story."

"I'll sue you for every nickel you and your newspaper have," I said.

"The last refuge of scoundrels," Boyd said. "The song of the truly desperate."

"Listen, son," I said, entering a dangerous place as I lost my temper, "don't you dare lecture me about what to do. Things are a lot more complicated than you're old enough to imagine. And don't try to pass yourself off as the white knight here, either. We both know what your own interest here is. A, to sell newspapers, B, to get a big scoop to advance your career ahead of the others there."

I heard the infuriating click of his cigarette lighter. "What a petty world you live in," he said. "In point of fact, the da Silva story will do neither of those things, because readers, and therefore editors, are only really grabbed by stories of evil that are so excessive or so bizarre that they come off as completely individual, completely unique. If I gave them the Klaus Barbie of Brazil, the Idi Amin of Brazil, they'd be all over it; instead, the very fact that there were, conservatively, dozens of sadists on a par with da Silva in Brazil somehow makes his case less rather than more interesting. But you can think whatever you like about my own character. It doesn't change your moral dilemma here."

"I have no moral dilemma. By the way, what did you mean earlier, when you said that you weren't the only one watching?"

"What kind of man are you, Mr. Trowbridge?" he said. "That's not a rhetorical question."

"This conversation is over," I said. He was saying something else as I hung up the phone, but I didn't catch it.

I sat there for a few minutes, facing the windows, seeing nothing, collecting myself. I tried briefly to think as Boyd might think, to determine whether he would have anything to gain by calling my home, or leaving incriminating messages; but I couldn't reach any conclusion. For all he knew, I had kept my wife apprised all along. Maybe his know-it-all exterior was just some pose he had picked up from popular mythology, or maybe I was as easy to denounce as all that.

I felt the redness in my face, and in replaying the conversation to myself it occurred to me that I had perhaps become a little carried away in talking to Boyd, that I was probably speaking quite loudly. But when I opened the door to my office and looked out, everyone was absorbed in their work and no one, not even Caroline, glanced my way. No one had heard anything. My reputation was as solid as a cliché, the secrets of my self protected, in this place I had done my part to build.

"Do you believe," Ferdinand said, "that there are sins for which it is impossible to repent?"

I tried to give this question the thought it deserved. As we walked, we passed Countess, who, in pursuit of some unfamiliar smell, slowly dug a hole in the dune above us. I was walking a half step behind Ferdinand in the hope that he would not notice my continually turning around to see if there was anyone behind us.

"Yes, I do," I said solemnly.

He nodded quickly, as if this was the answer he had expected. "And when I say the word 'repent,'" he said, "what do you understand me to mean?"

Again I thought hard and, to my distress, nothing came immediately to mind. "Well," I said, mostly to avoid the embarrassment of silence, "I've never been a really religious man."

"Oh, I'm certain," Ferdinand said. "But I'm not talking about that. Everyone, I think—or all but the very crudest people—has some innate sense of sin, and thus of expiation. Surely you haven't gone through your whole life without feeling some guilt, large or small. It doesn't have to be a matter of religion."

He waited for me to respond. "Well, that's not a simple question," I said. "I suppose that the way to abolish guilt is to indulge in enough good works that on balance your life would be a good one, if you know what I mean."

"Ah, well, I disagree," he said, seeming pleased with my answer. "And I don't mean to dismiss that idea idly, because I thought in just that way when I left home twenty years ago. But all that does, really, is whitewash one's character. The aim of it is not to atone for one's sins but to erase those sins from the record, as if it were a math problem where equal values could be struck from both sides of the equation. No, too simple, dangerously simple, and too selfish—it doesn't even acknowledge those who were sinned against. American thinking. Everything you do is a lesson in your true nature, and nothing is gained by simply forgetting it, or pretending it never happened."

"So what's your solution?" I said sullenly, feeling slightly patronized.

"Rather than turn away from the things you regret doing, you must dwell on them. You must relive what you've done, redo it in a sense, every day. Each day brings a little more self-knowledge—which in turn makes the next day's reliving of events a little more painful. You have to work toward an understanding of yourself."

"And of those you have made to suffer?" I said.

He frowned. "Yes, of course," he said. "But then it's not really possible to understand them as completely as you understand yourself. It's a slow process. In fact, it's a never-ending process, or it ends only with death." He sighed. "This is what I have been doing. Not repenting, really, so much as moving toward the moment of my repentance. I want to be accepted by God."

"So you do believe," I said, "that you've sinned?"

He cocked his head. "How can I say this," he said. "I believe that I was on the right side of a conflict that was too large and too complicated for individual human understanding—mine or anyone else's—at the time. Yes, I believe that I did wrong. But that doesn't mean that I accept the judgments of others. Though it all had to do with the public good, it's all, in the end, strictly, inviolably, between me and my God. And that is why I stay hidden. I resent anyone else's presumption to intrude. I cannot let the process be interrupted. Otherwise, it's all been for nothing."

"Don't you ever wish," I said, "that none of this had ever happened to you?"

"Wishing for things like that is a sin in itself," he said. "It accomplishes nothing."

"Why did you leave Brazil?"

He walked in silence for fifty yards or so before answering. "It will sound simpler than it was," he said. "In 1969, a police station in Rio was destroyed in a bomb attack by a Communist organization. A very good friend of mine, named Souza, someone whom I had known since my first days in the army, was killed. I quite lost my reserve when I heard this news, and I gave the word to my subordinates that they should make the discovery and capture of the bomber their first priority. Three days later, a lieutenant came into my office, smiling proudly, and holding a signed confession from the man who had planted the bomb. The lieutenant and I shared a drink to celebrate his good police work, and I even hinted rather broadly that there might be a promotion in it for him."

Ferdinand paused for a minute, then shook his head once violently as if there were a fly buzzing around him.

"The next morning, a different lieutenant burst into my office. He, too, had in his possession a document in which a different person confessed to bombing the police station and murdering my friend Souza. The details of the confession were completely different from the one which had been brought to me the day before. Two days later, I received another admission of guilt. In all, four different people wound up confessing to the attack, under duress I could well imagine. Clearly, my junior officers had gotten the impression that the capture of the murderer of the captain's old friend was a method of personal advancement for them. This is hard to explain, but what shocked me about this episode was not so much the fate of the four unfortunate prisoners, whom I ordered released, but the sudden realization that the state intelligence network of which I was a part had simply become so vast, so refined, so *good,* that its own effects could no longer be trusted. The truth had no weight anymore; we held more power than the truth did. I wanted out, I suddenly felt very exhausted. In that atmosphere, though, my resignation could have been reason enough to arrest me. So I contacted the American embassy, where some people owed me some favors, and they agreed to help me."

By now we had walked quite far, and I was slightly short of breath.

"Can we turn back?" I said.

"Yes, let's," he said, though he didn't seem tired himself. The beach was still empty in both directions. He whistled for the dog, who had gotten about a hundred feet ahead of us; she ran back, moving down near the waterline where the footing was better, and slowed to a walk beside me, panting happily. She and I, who had never owned a dog, had recently become quite close. Over the past few weeks, without quite seeing it, I had taken nearly all my affection—that which I couldn't show Ferdinand, that which I couldn't figure out how to show Jack, that which it would have been fruitless, under the circumstances, to show my wife—and transferred it to the old Countess, who now looked on me almost as a second master, lovable, easily manipulated, generous with food. She lifted her noble forehead up against my hand.

"Come to the house this evening, Gene, if you can," Ferdinand said. "I've got something to ask you."

The ocean billowed toward us quietly, patiently, like the endless snapping of a bedsheet.

On the day of my retirement dinner I found myself suddenly unsure of my role. I had no hand in organizing it, and so there was no need for me to be there early; on the contrary, I was sure I would have been in the way as the young people from the agency and from the catering service set out place cards and counted chairs. At the same time, I thought that since I was the ostensible center of attraction, it would be seen as bad form, even as outright rudeness, not to be there as the guests arrived. No one at work had given me any instruction at all other than the time and address, and I was too proud to call and ask. Consequently I spent most of the afternoon pacing around the house, or flipping without interest through magazines, or, when I could steal a moment alone, going over my speech, which I had typed out myself rather than let even Caroline see it.

Caroline was not invited to the dinner, nor, I'm sure, had she expected to be; she would have been thoroughly bored, I could well imagine, by the other guests there and by the slow barrage of incomprehensible inside jokes about advertising from men old and dull enough to be her father. Still, I had developed a real fondness for her, born of the guilt I somehow felt for her conspicuous lack of enjoyment of working for me. She would be staying on at AAK with a new boss. Nonetheless, I wanted to mark in some way the end of our association. I couldn't have taken her to lunch, which would have been the obvious gesture; the two of us hadn't exchanged sixty minutes' worth of nonprofessional conversation in the four years she had been my secretary, and I didn't see how that was going to change now. So, instead, on my last day I gave her a present—a rather lavish one, for some reason, as if only excess could reach her. When she opened the box and saw the earrings, she gasped and put them on immediately, to my relief. Even though she remembered to thank me, I was struck by her seeming lack of understanding that these earrings were a representation of something, that I had gone out myself and selected them from among other earrings especially for her. She was quite obviously happy with these elegant new possessions, but happy in the way she would have been if she had won them in a contest, or if she had found them on the street. I'm not sure what it was that I expected from her.

The same could be said in a more general sense of that whole day, the last of my working life. At around four-thirty a group of about twenty co-workers burst into my office laden with booze and gag gifts—a cane, an inflatable seat cushion for all the sitting around I was going to do, a gift bottle of the Glencairn scotch that they knew I loathed—and there was considerable, genuine, unsentimental merriment for the short time

241

it took us all to have a drink or two. But goodbyes, in my experience, particularly group goodbyes, invariably go on just a little too long. Not wanting to neglect anyone, I uttered variations on the same banalities to almost everyone, the exceptions being those to whom I could say, to our mutual relief, that I would see them at the retirement dinner and thus could postpone our farewells until then. Waving and smiling, I inched toward the elevator. As I descended, wearing my thin overcoat and clutching the one genuine (though still humorous) gift I had been given—a very cleverly done, framed collage put together by the art department in which I myself appeared, in retouched photos, as the Hathaway shirt man, the Indian in the famous anti-litter PSA, the Marlboro man, Clara Peller, Bo Jackson, and a few other icons from the different phases of my long career—I felt embarrassed and sad, and wished that I had the whole leavetaking scene to do over again.

We were going to drive into Manhattan for the dinner rather than take the train, since we were all wearing evening clothes. Jack, I had been happy to learn, was anxious to go, having little else to do anyway. When he came downstairs at about four o'clock in his tuxedo, I thought I knew part of the reason for his acceptance; he looked stunningly handsome, more at home, if anything, in formal dress than in a doubleknit baseball uniform. He strode around the living room amid our redundant compliments, striking exaggerated model poses, trying unsuccessfully to make a joke out of his own youthful beauty.

Driving relaxed me, or at least gave me something to do, so I took the wheel as we headed west toward New York, against the dominant flow of traffic, squinting into the low sun. There was little conversation in the car. I wondered what was going through their minds, particularly Ellie's, as they headed toward a ceremony in which their husband and father would be paid tribute for his life's accomplishments.

We parked in a garage on West 57th Street and walked to the hotel. The three or four homeless men and women we passed, I noticed, cut off their droning appeal and stared at us as we went by, as if we weren't worth the effort, as if there were some law of nature whereby we had gotten to wear these tuxedos precisely by ignoring the pleas of people seated or lying on the sidewalk.

The three of us walked abreast into the lobby, the door suddenly choking off all the ambient street sound as it swung shut behind us. Music played as we walked toward the desk, our shoes plunging into the deep carpet; but before I could ask the concierge anything, I was surprised to see my own name spelled out in white plastic letters, with an arrow beside it, on the hotel's Events of the Day message board.

"This way," I said needlessly to Ellie and Jack, who had seen the sign just as I had and were already heading toward the ballroom. As I walked behind them, I touched my chest for the twentieth time to be sure the speech was still in my inside pocket.

There were only five people in the capacious ballroom when we walked in, all of them huddled around the table that bore the carefully arrayed, full bottles of wine and liquor. The bar was attended by a handsome young man, a struggling actor in all likelihood, probably Jack's age or younger, who wore a white jacket, held his hands behind his back, and when he wasn't mixing a drink had the patiently expectant look of a butler. His hair was perfectly groomed, his politeness impenetrable; he leaned forward slightly from the waist when addressed. He alone among the nine of us looked as if he had been to these functions before and knew what to expect, knew what was expected of him. After I had introduced my family to my former employees, we immediately began competing with the others for the attention of the young bartender, all three of us, apparently, feeling keenly the need for a drink. Over the next hour, as all the guests arrived, I noticed that the bar was the first stop for every single one of them, as if it was the young man who had to be consulted, who held some behavioral guide to this awkward, increasingly morbid-seeming rite of passage.

I had, indeed, gone to Ferdinand's house as he had asked, past the downcast eyes of my wife, the evening after what would be our last trip to the beach. He welcomed me with his usual, relaxed air, betraying nothing of his purpose, which had fixed me in a state of fear all that day.

"Thank you for coming," he said. "I know it's late."

"Well, don't worry," I said. "Tomorrow is actually my last day of work. If I'm a little tired, people will probably just think that I'm lost in introspection or something."

"Ah!" he said excitedly. "I'd forgotten, yes, of course!" He went into the kitchen and returned with an unopened bottle of brandy and two large snifters. He poured us each a small serving, and then, as I sat down, he lit a candle on the long table between our chairs. I watched him as he solemnly warmed the bottom of the snifter over the candle flame, then I stood and did the same. When I straightened, I noticed that he was still standing, and looking at me with what appeared to be great respect.

"To the end of a brilliant career," he said. "To a peaceful retirement, and an enduring name." We drank, the fumes seeming to fill my skull as I inhaled.

He sighed loudly, as we sat down. He smiled at me. We sat that way, in silence, for half a minute.

"You mentioned," I said, trying to keep any tremor out of my voice, "that you wanted to ask me something."

He nodded. "Remember today," he said, "we were discussing the issue of repentance?"

"Of course."

"I have no job now, Gene, and haven't for years. I don't socialize, I don't spend much time away from home. I wasn't always like this. I have come to realize that these past twenty years or so, these years of my exile, have in fact been a process of asceticizing my life, of whittling it down to just one task, and one task only. That task is to prepare myself to be accepted by God. Do you follow me so far?"

I nodded.

"Of course I am sorry for what I have done. But being sorry is only the first step. I have to be sure I understand fully what it *means* to be sorry. I have to be sure that, when I die, I am not repentant simply out of fear of what might await me. My life now consists of my preparation for death. And I tell you, that preparation is not over yet. I am not ready. I know that we are old men now—but in fact, that's what scares me; the men involved in this, the men who are pursuing me, they are all younger than we are, they would consider my attachment to life rather foolish, they wouldn't understand, as we understand, the unique preciousness of one's last years. My greatest fear, greater even than the fear of death itself, is the fear of dying unprepared. Such a moment, such a transaction, is sacred, and it would be the height of barbarism to deny me that, to hurry me off the planet, which is in essence what my accusers want to do."

He was, to my horror, growing quite emotional, losing his trademark calm, though perhaps even this was just an effect intended to impress me. We stared at each other above the motionless candle flame.

"I have a plan," he said. I felt my heart pound. "I'm going to try to escape from this town. I need you to help me."

Terrified, my first reaction was to look for a loophole, a way out of my obligation—not my obligation to help him, but the obligation to choose.

"You're not under any kind of arrest," I said. "You're as free a man as I am. What's to stop you from simply driving off, just like anyone else?"

"Nothing, in a legal sense. But of course, if they see me go, they'll follow me, and wherever I stop, they will resume their efforts to punish me there. That's no escape at all. I need complete secrecy—a new location, a new name. A new car. I need solitude."

I leaned forward and poured myself some more brandy.

"I can't drive out of town in my own car," he said, "since I'm too old for chase scenes, and even if I managed not to be followed, cars are too easily traced. So are planes—even easier, in fact. The moment they noticed I was gone, they'd check Kennedy and LaGuardia. The train is good—no names, no identification, just a cash sale—but the problem with it is, even if I manage somehow to reach the railroad station ahead of them, it's a simple matter to have someone waiting for me at virtually every stop. Trains can only travel their one route, after all. As enormous as this country is, you see, it's extremely difficult to move anonymously within it, if there's anyone who doesn't want you to."

"What does this have to do with me?" I said.

"I need you to do one simple thing. On a day which we'll

determine, I will call the taxi company at the train station and have them send a cab here to take me to Kennedy Airport. I could as easily drive myself, of course, but this way anyone listening in on my line will be tipped off ahead of time. I'll also call the airport and buy a plane ticket, one-way, to somewhere evocative—I thought Miami would be good. I'll go to the airport, but I won't get on the plane—instead, I'll have a rental car reserved. I'll wait at the gate for a while, then go to the counter, pick up the keys, and go. Of course, once they catch on, they'll have the make and license number of the car I'm driving, but by then I'll be completely out of their sight, and if everything goes well they'll never catch up to me in time. I'll drive only as far as the nearest subway stop, ride into the city, and then I'm free. It's easy to disappear there. Or from there."

"Why not just take the cab all the way to the subway stop?" I asked, stalling.

"Because it's a simple matter to tail a cab—they may tail it anyway—but they'll have to have some new man pick up the tail once I'm inside the airport, and that man will be on foot. Even if he sees me getting into the rental car, he won't be able to do anything except try to run after me."

He swallowed the rest of his brandy. He was a prideful man, certainly, and I don't think he relished spelling out for me the small, irritatingly crucial details of his flight. Nevertheless, he offered me a reassuring smile before continuing.

"Here is where you come in," he said. "Since it's safe to say my own phone is no longer secure, and since they'll know something's up if they see me drive into town to use a pay phone, I can't make the call myself to reserve the rental car. I need you to do it for me. I'll give you my Visa number, the flight information, et cetera."

He looked at me and added in a playful, almost mocking

tone, "You can see that this plan poses absolutely no risk to you whatever. I knew that would be an important factor. Just a simple phone call. There's no reason at all why you should be implicated. You don't even have to leave your home."

I closed my eyes.

"Of course," he said, "if it would make you feel safer, perhaps you should use a pay phone yourself to call the rental company, just so there's no record."

"Let me ask you something," I said, feeling rising anger. "The very first day you met me, did you have this moment in mind? Were you able to tell right away that I was particularly weak, or easily manipulated? I'm not sure anymore why I became involved in this relationship, but for your part, have the last few months just been laying the groundwork for this request?"

He looked confused. "No, I don't think so," he said. "I began talking with you in part because I thought you were an intelligent man, well above the level of your neighbors here, and in part because, as much as I'm alone by choice, it's hard not to miss the company of men, it's hard to resist the urge to talk. But only after I'd gotten to know you very well did I decide to ask this of you, only after I was sure that you were a good man and would understand."

"A good man?" I said. "Let me ask you this: wouldn't a good man feel an obligation to all the people you terrorized as well, all the people who want redress for all the harm you've caused them? Wouldn't a good man feel at least an equal, if not a greater, obligation to help them if in a position to do so, and not fail to do so simply because he had never known any of them, and found their suffering impossible to share?"

"So you are on the side of vengeance, then?" Ferdinand said. "You believe my pain would make up for their pain?"

"I'm not on any side. None of this should have come to rest on me. It's a million miles from my life. It's not for me to decide these things. Jesus, how I wish I'd never come over here."

Countess, made curious by my raised voice, left her position behind the couch, walked stiffly over and sat beside my chair, placing the top of her head beneath my fingers. I took my hand away; she looked up at me, surprised.

"What I hear you saying," Ferdinand said, "is exactly right. It's not for you to decide. Nor is it for any man. Only God may judge. And only by this one act of mercy on your part can you insure that, in fact, God will be the one to judge us all. Because I tell you frankly, though perhaps you've already figured it out, that as the one person capable of helping me to escape deportation, if you withhold that help, then you are in effect sentencing me to death."

I rested my forehead in my hand. I felt close to tears of resentment; all I wanted was silence.

"Since you haven't said yes right away," Ferdinand said, "I can see that you need to think about it. Perfectly understandable. It's a serious matter. So you will find a way to let me know? I wish I could tell you to take your time, but that is one of the most unsettling things about this whole situation—not knowing how much time there is. They could be hopelessly off the trail of my past. Or they could be at the door right now."

Though Ellie had considerately promised to drive back out to Belmont after the dinner, I tried to restrict myself to one drink every forty-five minutes or so, wanting to sharpen my sensations of this evening. It was the kind of event you find yourself remembering even as it is still going on. After an hour or so of drinking and milling about, the tuxedoed crowd was herded by the polite hotel staff to their tables, so that the serving of the dinner could begin. To my relief, there was no dais on which to be displayed while eating, only a raised podium and microphone in front of a large video screen; we were seated, along with Tim Kellogg and his wife, the head of the Ad Council of New York and his wife, and Tony Hobson, at an arbitrarily designated head table. Courses came and went with professional stealth; the main course, as is inevitable at any dinner for twenty or more, was chicken, that most blameless of entrees.

The men at the table all wanted to talk to Jack, and he responded easily, while drinking the pleasant table wine with gusto. When I wasn't drawn into conversation I looked surreptitiously around the grand room, at the heavy white drapes hung over the towering windows, at the decorative white columns, the other glittering tables, the other guests. There were many ancillaries, of course—new wives, important clients, people I worked with every day, people I just didn't recognize—but luminous among them were people deeply associated with my past, old friends and working partners, people I still cared for greatly though I had not seen them in years. Someone, I thought with amazement, must have actually researched my life in some way, in order to come up with these names, these people. It's one thing to run into an old friend on the street, or even to call and arrange a reunion for old times' sake; but to be confronted, all at once, with as many as twenty-five or thirty such people is quite overwhelming, like a vision of one's own funeral. Full of feeling, I stared undetected for as long as I could at the faces of these old associates, but when they turned in my direction, I would smile, raise my glass, and then avert my eyes.

Dessert was cleared, champagne poured, and Tim Kellogg,

who had volunteered to be the master of ceremonies, stood and walked to the podium, to vigorous applause. Ellie took my hand underneath the table. After a joke or two, a request for applause for the Park Lane staff, and a mention of my name that prompted still more whistling and clapping, he pointed behind him to the white screen and said, "And now, a tribute to Gene, prepared by the staff of AAK with love and gratitude and without a single request for overtime."

There was a brief loop of TV spots I had helped create—many of them so horribly dated now, by the restless aesthetics of advertising, that no one, not even I, tried to suppress laughter. Next came a handful of taped tributes from colleagues and clients who, for whatever reason, couldn't attend in person that night. Two of these were particularly touching: one from Gordon Anderson, irremediably ill now and in a wheelchair, who talked quite wittily and lucidly about the early years at AAK, though the editing of the tape suggested that he had forgotten the purpose for which he was reminiscing and was unable to stop; and the other from Dorothy Gates, my old Travel USA partner, who had been tracked down all the way out in California, and whose face was now so poignantly aged that I barely heard a word she said.

The lights came up, and a few live remembrances were delivered, all in a light vein. Tony spoke, and my old partner Dana Bradley from the boot-camp days at Ogilvy & Mather, and Phil Reynolds, from Glencairn scotch, who may have had too much to drink, for he became rather maudlin as he spoke about his brand's rise to prominence. Finally, Tim introduced me; and as I rose, the room rose along with me, huzzahing and clapping as if we were at a political convention while I took my place behind the microphone, waved my modest thanks, and unfolded my speech.

———

When I came home from Ferdinand's house that evening, Ellie was asleep and Jack was home, half drunk, in front of the television. I was sharply distressed to see that he wasn't out at a bar somewhere. The house seemed too small for us all; I had the illogical need one sometimes experiences for room to think. I wanted urgently to be left alone, to be alone; I wanted, at least within my own home, consciousness all to myself.

Jack saw my shadow on the wall and jerked around in his chair. "Whoa! You scared me," he said. "Come on in. Grab a chair, grab a beer."

"No, thank you, I'm just going to," I said, and trailed off, not wanting to say I was going to bed but equally loath to say I was going to go sit in the living room in the dark to get away from him.

"No? Okay," he said—far more attuned to the television than to the less vivid life surrounding it.

"Been over visiting your friend?" he said.

But before I could answer, his head jerked again. "Oh, almost forgot," he said. "Some guy named Mr. Boyd called. He didn't give his first name, but he sounded like he knew you. He left his number—it's by the phone. I told him to just try again tomorrow."

I nodded, and looked at the TV blankly for a minute.

"Did he say where he was calling from?" I asked.

"Nope. You don't know him?"

I shook my head.

"Huh. Pretty rude of him to call so late, then. It was just like an hour ago. Oh, wait, I love this."

He restored the sound with the remote control, and we

watched one of Weiden & Kennedy's Nike spots featuring Spike Lee and Michael Jordan. Both men had entered that firmament of celebrity, that higher stage, wherein their very image was enough to command brand loyalty. It used to be that an athlete pitched a product by awkwardly reading simple ad copy, sitting or standing, either addressing the camera directly or speaking to a wide-eyed child actor. Now that bridge between fame and commerce has been rendered unnecessary, and the handful of Jordans in the world have gone from spokesmen to metaphors; all that they need to do to sell is that which they do most beautifully, in this case, play basketball. Loud rock music blared over the closing logo.

"That's so great," Jack said admiringly, muting the TV again. "That's not one of yours, is it?"

"Afraid not," I said.

I stood up to leave. On an impulse, though, I stopped and said, "Jack, can I ask you something?"

He looked up, surprised by my serious tone. "Sure thing."

"What ever happened to all the money you were making playing with the Braves?"

"I still have a little left," he said, surprised but not offended. "Why, are you thinking of charging me rent?"

"No, of course not, don't be silly. I just wondered, that's all. It's a lot of money. I wanted to be sure you weren't in any kind of trouble."

He shook his head. "No, not really. I mean, I guess I didn't manage it very well. Part of that is because I rented probably too nice an apartment in Atlanta, and then when I left I got into this thing with my landlord where he wouldn't give me back my security deposit. And part of it is that I never expected to get cut. I thought I'd be getting those paychecks at least for the rest of the year. But I wasn't doing any drugs or anything, I know that's what you're worried about."

I smiled. "Well, that's good," I said. "So. What are your plans now?"

He looked thoughtfully into the corner of the room. "You know," he said, "I think it may work out to be a good thing, getting cut. My arm feels better already. I think the thing to do is just stay in shape over the off-season, rest the arm completely until January or so, then get my agent in gear and see what comes up."

"See what comes up? You mean, what offers come from other teams?"

"Yeah, of course," he said. "What else? Show those front-office scumbags in Atlanta how badly they fucked up."

"Yes," I said, distressed, "but, well, I don't mean to be pessi-mistic but I think you owe it to yourself to be prepared, at any rate, for the worst-case scenario. I mean, let's be coldly honest for a second here. You're not coming off your best season ever. I think we have to consider the possibility that you won't get any contract offers. Have you thought about what you might do then?"

He stared at me with a look in his eyes of concern border-ing on fright; I saw that, as delicate and as commonsensical as I had tried to be, I had said something that hurt him very badly.

"Don't you believe in me?" he asked.

My first instinct, naturally, was to correct him, to point out that it wasn't a matter of belief but of laying out, in his leisure, some practical contingency plans. But he understood the ques-tion more perfectly than I did. Jack's quintessentially American profession was based on a vast architecture of belief: in the enduring character of a few archetypal dreams, in the buried power of its mythical constructs, in the primacy and eternal regeneration of physical gracefulness and beauty, in the stoppage of time, in the idea that spirit is rewarded and ambivalence punished, in the axiom that held together millions in cities all over the country, that loyalty breeds winners and winning is purpose.

I reached out and put my hand on his shoulder.

"Of course I do," I said. "Of course I do. I'm sorry, it was a stupid question. I believe in you. You're my son. What else should I believe in?"

On my way through the kitchen I grabbed the piece of paper with Boyd's number on it, tore it into quarters, and stuffed it into my pocket. I sat on the couch at the far end of the living room, confident that I was outside Jack's attention though I could still hear the drone of the TV, and watched the window and the empty street beyond.

The affair that had commenced two months ago with my barging into Ferdinand's home and naively demanding that he communicate to me what he knew of life's brutal verities seemed destined now to end in the same ignorance in which it had begun. I would never learn that which I had set out to learn; characteristically, I suppose, I had expected to learn it too easily. In any case, it was too late now. I had gained nothing, except, perhaps, a discouraging new perspective on the morally undeveloped life accidents of birth and circumstance had made it possible for me to live. And now the gates were beginning to close. It was chilling to think that, there at the age of wisdom, the choice that Ferdinand was trying to force upon me was too difficult for me to make.

The pressure I felt that night, and for the next few days, was extraordinary. It came to me with some force that the only thing I really cared about in this life was my personal security in all its detail, because that was the only thing I had ever been asked to care about. That security wasn't really threatened now—both Ferdinand and Boyd seemed to be respecting it, even if only for purposes of cultivating me—yet I still felt a persistent fear, vague yet powerful, with no real focal point even in imagination, and for that reason all the more debilitating.

Then it struck me what position I was in: I was afraid that, at any hour of the day or night, someone, in some mysterious official capacity, was going to come to my home, was going to pound on my door, was going to ask me to come with him, ask me to tell him what I knew. Even in my terror, of course, I was laughable, a weak echo, indistinct, ignorant, a pale replica of what another life might have made of me.

"Thank you very much," I said. "Thank you. And thank you for coming here, to escort me, as it were, to the gate of the next world, the world of catching up on one's reading, tennis in the middle of the day, and driving my wife crazy. Thank you, too, to the marvelously helpful and almost supernaturally efficient Park Lane staff. I have this vision of the nightly dinner for all the new arrivals in heaven, where, to ease our fears and instill in us the sense that this is just the final earthly ceremony, they serve us chicken. . . . And thank you most especially to the handful of people at AAK who spent so much of their time over the last month or three organizing this little bash. I can assure you that their unfeeling bosses did not see fit to lighten their workloads accordingly, though if it were still in my power, I'd give them all next week off.

"Well, the thank-yous are the easy part. I must confess that, aside from the fact that it gives me the opportunity to express my gratitude, this is the portion of this wonderful night that I looked forward to the least. Perhaps some of you from AAK can say the same thing. . . . No, but I see here nearly all of my dear friends, people whose creative and administrative talents I have lived in awe of for nearly forty years. And you all expect me to deliver a summation of those forty years. It should be a reasonable expectation, really. But you don't see how unreasonable it is until you get up here where I am, as the honoree or roastee or what have you. How do you sum up a life?

"Part of the answer is this: the total of any life, the meaning of any life, is in the people one meets, the friends one makes. In that sense, my work has been done for me. Within these four walls right now I see not just reminders but embodiments of my entire professional and much of my personal life, from Nagle Associates and Ogilvy & Mather and the railroad flat on 66th Street, to AAK and threatened eviction from the railroad flat . . . to, of course, AAK's glory years. So if you all just take a moment to look around you, you'll certainly have a fuller, more comprehensive, more articulate biography of a life in advertising than anything that I could provide.

"In fact, for the big finale tonight, I've arranged to have the waiters lock all the doors from the outside, thus to create a kind of Pompeii for future ages to discover, with myself as king. . . ."

The next day, desperate to be away from the telephone, I more or less intentionally missed my train, and even walked circuitously through the shadowed, autumn-cooled midtown streets, looking, in my suit, like a man waiting for the bars to open, finally arriving at the office around ten-thirty. I didn't dare look at the two phone messages Caroline had taken for me, for fear one of them was from Boyd. Tim and a mutual friend from

Adweek were taking me out to lunch, so after just ninety uneasy minutes behind my desk, I was able to escape again. I told Caroline on the way out that I might be late returning.

"Don't forget you have a two-thirty," she said without looking up.

"I do? With whom?"

She looked over at the open appointment book. "Thomas Freilicher, second interview," she read.

Young Freilicher was indeed waiting in reception when I came back, martini-warmed, from lunch at about two-thirty-five. He shook my hand firmly—young men nearly always seem to think a firm handshake is considered crucial by men of their father's generation, as if we were all as shallow as hillbillies — and waited for me to be seated before sitting himself.

"How is your girlfriend?" I said.

Somewhat surprised, as was I, that this had been my first question, he said, "Oh, she's great, thanks. She's just gotten a job at Condé Nast, actually. She's very excited. Nice of you to ask."

I nodded. "And have you done," I said in paternal tones, "what I asked you to do?"

He unzipped the black portfolio bag beside his chair and, leaning forward, passed me two large boards. I lay one down on my desk and tipped back in my chair holding the other one, to get a good look.

It was a TV spot for AIDS awareness. The visuals were cleverly sundered from the voice-over; the latter called for the sounds—as in a radio play—of a woman bringing a man home to her apartment. There was tipsy laughter, which grew louder with the sound of a door being unlocked and opened. The image was a slow pan of a cemetery. "So here it is," the woman's voice says. "This is where I live." "Nice," the man says. Slow fade to black, with no break in the sound. Fade back in on a shot of the AIDS quilt unfolded at the base of the Washington Monument. "I'm sorry it's such a mess," she says. "Don't worry," he says. "And in here's the, uh, yeah," she says. Fade out, and in again on a shot of the minute of silence that's a part of the Gay Pride parade in New York and I suppose elsewhere, too, people with their faces lowered and their fists in the air, standing in the middle of the street, some embracing, some crying. Sounds of kissing, and of pleasure and surprise. "So," the woman says in a voice charged with desire. "You know, I don't have any, I mean, I always felt it was kind of weird to just keep a box of rubbers around. Kind of promiscuous-seeming, you know?" They laugh. "Well," he says, "it's a myth about guys carrying them around in their wallets." They laugh some more. Fade out, and in on a shot of a man in the late stages of AIDS, in a hospital bed, staring at the camera. "Oh, what the hell," the woman says. "You seem like a nice guy." Fade out, and into the tag, white letters on a black background: "Love Life."

The second, the perfume ad, was simply one photo, with no type at all save for the words "Scandal for Men" in the lower-right corner. It was a family snapshot, in black and white, of four people sitting in a docked motorboat, facing into the camera, off the stern. The people's hairstyles, makeup, and especially the bathing suits suggest the late fifties or early sixties, as does the quality of the Polaroid-like photo, which in places is browned with age. In the seat to the right is the mother—wearing makeup even on a boat ride, thin, pretty in a parched sort of way, her hair permed, her face strained by a smile she has obviously been asked to hold too long, staring doggedly at the camera. To her left—as far to her left as she can get and still be in the boat—is an impossibly luscious, Bardot-like young woman, eighteen or twenty, with long blond hair and a relatively modest bikini. She looks foreign, nothing like the rest of this family; she is evidently some kind of au pair girl, an impression strengthened by the fact that she has pinned within her arms and legs a young boy of ten or twelve. They are wrestling— perhaps she is trying to get him to sit still for the picture—and his head is up against her large breasts. They are both laughing. His eyes are closed. Finally, kneeling on the seat behind the mother is the father, a thin, nondescript sort of man. Unlike his wife, he has been caught unaware by the moment of the snap- shot; though his head is aligned with hers, his eyes have strayed onto the spotless flesh of the au pair, in her playful struggle with his young son. But it is the boy with whom we are clearly meant to identify. In fact, the picture is now in his possession, as we are led to believe not only by its apparent age but by the fact that it has been folded as if it were kept in a wallet or some other private place. The photo spoke volumes about innocence and darkness, about the sexually forbidden—and thus had both nothing and everything to do with the quality of the advertised perfume.

I looked over the top of the board. Freilicher was sitting with his fingers interlaced, watching me intently; a small smile played on his face, as if he were struggling not to show how pleased he was with what he had made. It was hard to believe these images of sex and death had ever been buried deep within him.

I stood up and held out my hand. His face lit up. "You're hired," I said.

"But it's the other part of this answer that troubles me, or at least confuses me. My own professional life spans, in a way, the era of advertising's rise to power. When I began, we were frontiersmen, though not always willing ones, and there was something faintly disreputable about having gone into this line of work. People didn't really distinguish it from being a door-to-door salesman; having a job in advertising was kind of like not getting into the right college. And now, in 1990, advertising has become a global phenomenon, a cultural imperative, its development as a science paralleling its development as an art. Politics—and I don't mean just political campaigns—is greatly dependent upon us. Nations rely on us to an increasing degree for the conscription of their armed forces. We are truly at the point where we can say of advertising what for years has been said of war—that it is the continuation of politics by other means.

"But at the same time, it's important, as everyone in this room knows, to be aware that what we do for a living—as crazy as we get about it, as much as we live and breathe it, as much money as it generates—is essentially frivolous. It's far more ephemeral than, say, making buttons or lamps or even pure art. Nothing that we do is even designed to last—it all vanishes almost instantly. And beyond even that, we all know—we have to know—that it's not good for us to take our work too seriously. Because even if we could get worked up about, say, a particular snow tire, there's a good chance that somewhere down the road we'll be asked to sell just as wholeheartedly a *different* snow tire. All our allegiances are always for sale—just as we take it for granted that those of our audiences are always for sale, allegiances to products or to political candidates or to our very behavior, public and private.

"The question is, then, how are we supposed to know how seriously we should take what it is we do?"

261

Minute to minute I wavered between asking myself how I could have gotten in this far and trying to convince myself that I wasn't in it at all, that people were only interested in using me and thus that I had no responsibility. Paralyzed by an inability to choose what was right, I nonetheless told myself that my constant near-panic was a reaction to the injustice of having been falsely implicated, of having to choose at all. If only I could be left completely alone, I told myself, I would be able to figure all this out.

And I would not be hurried. When I drove home from the dry cleaner's with my tuxedo two weeks after my last conversation with Ferdinand, I saw that the blue van had returned to the corner opposite his house, accompanied this time by a brown, boxy-looking American car of the sort that had to be government issue. I drove past them and into my own garage, fighting down the bilious relief I felt at the thought that the matter might after all be resolved without me. When I walked inside, Ellie said, "Some man from *Newsday* called here. Any idea what that's about?"

Without an instant's hesitation I said, "Oh, Sam Boyd? He's one of their business writers. He's just doing a short piece on my retirement. Just needs a quote, I think. I'll go upstairs and give him a call right now."

"How nice," Ellie was saying as I vanished up the stairs. "I'll have to remember to look for it."

I closed the door to our bedroom, yanked off my tie, and dialed Boyd's number with shaking fingers.

"Boyd."

"Can't you leave me alone, for God's sake? How dare you talk to my wife! You have no right to pressure me like this, no right to tell me what I have to do!"

"Mr. Trowbridge, would you just relax? I didn't tell your

wife why I was calling. I could be selling subscriptions for all she knows. I'm not out to ruin you. In fact, I'm out to save you. I have a proposition for you that may help you to see your own silence in a whole different light."

"What's that?"

"Did you go past Mr. So-called Ferdinand's place tonight?"

"Yes. So?"

"See any police vehicles?"

My heart jumped. "I saw some cars," I said. "I'm not sure who they belong to."

"They belong to the Immigration and Naturalization Service. Apparently your friend entered the country illegally, sometime after he was believed to have been killed in Brazil in 1969. He's been very smart about the documentation he's used, but they've been on his trail the last month or so and apparently they're poised to arrest him."

"You keep saying 'apparently.' Aren't you—"

"See, the INS has been pretty good about keeping me up to date, informally, of course. But they have their own agenda, they want the glory of the capture, too, and so they make sure the information they give me is always one step behind them, if you see what I mean."

I heard Jack stomping around in a pair of cleats in the hallway outside the door.

"Which brings me to my point about what all this has to do with you, Gene. Listen. If I know you've been spending a lot of time over there, chances are good they must know it too, correct?"

He waited for an acknowledgment; I said nothing.

"They know as well as I do that you might be a valuable source of information that would be helpful to the case. Here's the thing. If they come knock on your door and ask you about it, and you lie to them, as you've been lying to me, then you'll have committed a felony. Whereas if you tell me, and I publish it, as my source your identity is legally protected. Not that they'd really go after it, I'm sure. They're not interested in punishing anybody. They just want to know where to look."

The relevant sentences began forming themselves in my mind. It would be so simple, I thought. Just that handful of words and I'd be out of it. So simple to send a criminal to death.

"Mr. Trowbridge? Makes sense, doesn't it?"

"You're lying," I said.

"What?"

"You're lying to me," I said, and quickly hung up the phone.

As if of its own accord, an image of Boyd—his small features, his preppie wardrobe, even the wife and child, probably imaginary, he had mentioned when we first met—popped into my head. It came as a shock, in fact, to remember that I had seen him before, that I knew what he looked like, because his existence had been so firmly and so truthfully reduced to a voice in my ear.

Only then did I recall that I had forgotten to utter the words "off the record," that magic invocation, at any point during our conversation. I went into the bathroom, closed the toilet lid and sat down, trying to recall every word I'd said to him, one hand on my heart. After five minutes, I stood, looked in the mirror to see if I was presentable to my family, and went back downstairs.

For the next two days I avoided the telephone, I avoided the street, I avoided the windows, like a wanted man. I occupied my time imagining the local disgrace it might already have been too late to avoid bringing down on myself and my family. On Sunday afternoon, when, mercifully, Ellie and Jack were both out of the house, I noticed a man in a suit ringing Fran Phister's doorbell across the street; he spoke to her for a few minutes, then bowed slightly and went on to the next house. When, half an hour later, he knocked on my front door, I was standing in the upstairs hallway, motionless, wracked with shame. He knocked a second time, then went away.

When I was alone in the house, I let the phone ring unanswered. When I was not, I fairly dove for it on the first ring. These were my first days in retirement. Though in a practical sense I wanted to intercept any call from Boyd, or from the police, my deepest fear was that the caller would be Ferdinand himself, who must, I felt, with each passing hour have been more and more aware that I was not going to return to his home, that I had abandoned him, that in fact I was longing for his arrest.

But, respectful of my wishes no matter how cowardly they must have appeared to him, he never called me at home. There was an undeniable, if bizarre, honor in it. He went about his usual, modest business, walking the Countess, going into town to the pharmacy or the market or the post office, always under surveillance now that made no attempt to conceal itself, feeling the circle closing around him.

Four days before the dinner at the Park Lane, a letter arrived for me with a local postmark and no return address. An unsigned card was inside, with one line of handsome, unfamiliar black script.

It read, "Will you take the dog?"

"Fortunately, as of eleven days ago, my obligation to answer difficult questions has ceased. . . . No, but seriously. What troubles me, as I ride off into the sunset, is the thought that advertising, understandably unsatisfied with restricting its awesome powers to the supermarket, has brought to American life an era in which every belief, no matter how strongly held, is negotiable. People are eager to be persuaded. It's a self-fulfilling prophecy. We live in a culture in which every product—and, in this sense, even our very attitudes are products—has equal weight, since it's all a matter of how attractively that product is represented to us.

"I worry, sometimes, to put it another way, that we've simply gotten too good. That we have refined what we can do to such a degree that the truth is no match for us anymore. One can easily see how this knowledge could be, and indeed is, dangerous in the wrong hands."

I put the card from Ferdinand in my pocket. Thirty-six hours later, at about ten-thirty at night, police cars began to gather silently, their lights flashing, at the foot of Fairly Avenue. Several press photographers were there as well. The revolving red lights cast sudden shadows on the lawns and lit the trees in a ghostly manner; neighbors began walking out to the edge of their property, as they had done on a similar night two and a half months before, when Ferdinand's exile was first violated.

I didn't see him arrested. Ellie and I stood on our porch, from which all we could see was the gathering of cars, the end of Ferdinand's hedge, and an occasional silhouette leaning lazily across a hood.

Ellie, at the end, was surprisingly sympathetic toward me. Perhaps she saw how shaken I looked, or perhaps she was just relieved at the thought that the whole affair had been gotten through without any serious damage, public or private, to us. "I noticed you stopped going over there the last few weeks," she said softly. "I kind of guessed that he had finally confessed to you."

I looked at her, but said nothing.

"Oh, honey," she said. "I know you liked him. I know it's much more complicated for you than it seemed to me, because I never actually talked to him. But if he did what they say he did, then he couldn't get through this life without paying for it in some way. There was nothing you could have done about it."

She stepped behind me and put her hands on my shoulders. "I do love you," she said. "I'm willing to just forget the whole thing."

A few minutes later, Jack came striding up the dark lawn, hands in pockets, the lights sweeping over him. Not as reticent as his elders, he had immediately run down to the corner when the police started to arrive, to catch all the action. He told us that Ferdinand had walked out of his house, his hands cuffed behind his back, between two men in suits, who led him slowly toward one of the police cars. One of them put a hand on the back of Ferdinand's head to help him in. Other than a loud shout bringing the relaxing officers to attention when the front door to the house opened, Jack said, the entire operation had transpired in complete, eerie silence. He said that Ferdinand looked resigned. Of course, he couldn't have told that with much accuracy; it might just as easily have been some cliché he had adopted from some television show that seemed suitable to the situation, since that was the first time Jack had ever seen Ferdinand in his life.

"Advertising changes so quickly that it's very difficult, especially for an old codger like myself, to pretend to give advice. In fact, I think I've been considered something of a dinosaur by the younger set for the last few years, and there's nothing wrong with that. So I don't pretend to know what you should do;

maybe if you followed my brand of logic to its conclusion, you'd all quit your jobs and go to work as cabinetmakers or something. But it's too late for that, in any case—advertising is an institution, a world institution, not just a force but a virtual law. There's someone waiting to take my place; there's someone waiting to take all your places.

"But that's not what I'm after in any case. Because I know that the people in this room—who wield a tremendous, perhaps inordinate amount of power in the world—are good people. What concerns me is to think who you will eventually be replaced by. I know that I don't need to tell you to use your power wisely. All I'll leave you with is the reminder never to forget that you have that power, regardless of the sometimes silly ways in which you are called on to exercise it. Capricious power is the most dangerous of all. And it can corrupt you. Living as we do atop the culture of shallow-rooted beliefs can corrupt you. I know you won't let it.

"Well, this has come out perhaps a bit darker than I, and probably you, had expected. So let me end on a happier note, by thanking all of you from the bottom of my heart, and especially my wife, Elizabeth, and my son, Jack, of whom I'm very proud. It's been a great run.

"Thank you, and goodbye."

Who sent you here?

I am sorry there is no one to make our choices for us.

Can these personae be exorcised?

You're as free a man as I am.

Can we turn back?

My greatest fear, greater even than the fear of death itself, is the fear of dying unprepared.

What will happen to you if you are discovered?
Maybe it's not the right question.

Ferdinand's deportation proceedings were quick and to the point, so unglamorous that they received scarcely any media coverage at all. I learned of the official recommendation that he be repatriated only by coming across a small, photoless story, under Sam Boyd's byline, buried deep within *Newsday*. Of course I could have called him at any time to find out what was happening, but I did not, nor did he ever try to contact me.

Ferdinand was returned to Brazil the first week of December. I didn't know how it was possible to learn what happened to him after his arrival. I had only his word to go by, and perhaps I had no real desire to risk having it confirmed.

His house became government property, and was quickly resold, at a low price for the area, to a young, childless couple who moved out here from Manhattan. The husband works for the U.S. Attorney's office and had gotten a tip on the place. I didn't go over to welcome them to the neighborhood, though Ellie did; she reported that they were very charming, and almost giddy with pleasure over owning their first home, though they were going to do some substantial remodeling, and were having the big spreading maple cut down to improve their view. They couldn't understand, Ellie said, how anyone could have let it get so overgrown.

Jack had said, when I thought to ask him later, that he neither heard nor saw any dog on the night of the arrest. There was no one I could have asked about what had become of her—not that I would have anyway; it would have seemed an exceedingly odd question. Of course I could never have taken her. Everyone in town would recognize her as Ferdinand's dog, and to stroll around with her would seem pointlessly bold, absurdly incriminating. It was so impossible that I wondered briefly if Ferdinand had meant his request as some kind of subtle rebuke to me. But that kind of thing, I'm sure, would never have occurred to him. A dog is a dog, and deserves our love, that's all. He felt her loyalty to him, and wanted her provided for.

Old and ownerless as she was, I imagine she was simply put down in some humane fashion. But I try hard not to think about the dog, because I am ashamed of the incongruous emotional effect the subject has on me.

In February, days after his twenty-seventh birthday, Jack's agent called; he had been offered a contract in the Class AA Eastern League, with an affiliate of the Cleveland Indians. He hung up the phone with a wordless shout, gave his bewildered father a high five, and began dancing with Ellie in the living room. Two days later, he packed and left for the Cleveland organization's spring-training complex in Arizona. He is a very long way from the major leagues, and I will be surprised if he ever makes it back again; but of course he has no such doubts. By now I am nearly as unwilling as he is to see the day when he will have to learn to do something with his life besides play some form of baseball.

It's just Ellie and I again now, for the foreseeable future. I can see that she misses having him around, though of course not nearly as much as she did after he first left home at nineteen. Things are as good as they ever were between us. It's a kind of revelation to me just to see her going about her everyday pleasures and errands, just as she has done more or less out of my sight for the last eight years and longer, according to a loose routine that she seems, touchingly, not to have adjusted to my new, watchful presence. She is gone two or three hours a day with her camera; apart from that, she works in the garden when the weather permits, and visits friends, and idly shops, and reads voraciously books I never guessed she would be interested in. At night, we sometimes see a movie or try a restaurant outside of Belmont itself, with a spontaneity we could very rarely indulge when I was still commuting. The novelty of such evenings, after nearly thirty-eight years of married life, has yet to wear off. When we return home, we watch the late evening news, or at least the first few minutes of it, before climbing up the stairs to bed; we change, and get under the covers, and give each other a brief, chaste, understanding kiss, one of which, I sometimes realize, will be the last, before the room goes into darkness.

We are having an early spring this year; and I find I have begun going again to the still-abandoned beach, sometimes for a long walk, but most often just to sit. In another two months, once Memorial Day has passed, it won't be possible, or at least not enjoyable, anymore. If Ellie is home, I don't tell her where I'm headed, for fear she will want to come and walk with me; I say I'm going to run some errands, or play tennis at the indoor court a few miles away in Eastport, or just for a drive. "Have fun," she says, and smiles, glad I am finding things to do.

I park in the small lot behind the dunes, the tires crunching on the sand blown over the road by the March winds. Though no one is ever there, I try to walk far enough down the waterline that anyone else who might happen to step through the gap in the dunes to watch the light surf, or to see who belongs to the one car in the lot, won't be able to spot me. Then I sit down in

271

the sand, gingerly, as an old man sits, and wait. If it's in the middle of the day, when the sun is overhead and not close to either horizon, the empty sea and the empty beach gradually bring down on me the drowsy sensation I come for, the sensation of a kind of caesura in time, in which I am safely suspended. The only thing that moves in my vision is, of course, the tide; but even the tide, when I am in the right frame of mind, is suggestive to me of immortality somehow, its timeless quality, the earth's endless respiration. Every sound repeats itself. The day opens up, to reveal the day within it. Alone in the landscape, seated in that niche in the wall of time, it's possible, I find, to truly believe that these silver afternoons will never end; that I shall not die before I know myself.

About the Author

Jonathan Dee is the author of *The Lover of History*. His work has also appeared in *The Village Voice, Newsday, Mirabella,* and *The Paris Review,* where he was formerly senior editor. He lives in New York City.